here & there

Dawn Locklear

Brian Moseley - Cover Design and Book Construction

Stefanie Wright & Dani Segelbaum - Editors

here & there

Copyright © 2022 Dawn Locklear

All rights reserved.

ISBN: 9798413242988
Printed in the United States of America
San Luis Obispo, CA

www.sparklespins.com

6 5 4 3 2 1

IN MEMORIAM

Thanking all the women and men that helped me grow…to be alive, authentic, loving and being loved.
Mommy, Daddy-O, Cordie, Pammy, Princie, Nagymama, Aunt Toots, Uncle Duane, Grandpa, Uncle Gordie, Mommy K, Uncles Vaughn and Johnny, Aunt Barbara, June-Mom, PopPop, Liz, Louise Hay

ACKNOWLEDGMENTS

Thank you Suzanne for the first typing, The Long's & Milt for the time, Fams: Robyn, Elek, Kalligan, Locklear, Pecaut. Michelle RW, Sheree C, Nancy J, Chris W and Mary P for encouragement. Jeff C, Joanna K, Ali AR, Marian W, Crystal and Wilson H for the kickstarts, as Jim and Brian brought it through to the finish.

To my Families, Friends and Angels that have come along here & there…been here for me, cared and supported me through the years.
Thank you.

DEDICATION

This book is dedicated to My Wonderful Man, Jim. You have given me the courage and love to be me.
I love and thank you.

And to my Readers, allow your passions and purposes to be abundantly fulfilled…

"To that brave band of thinkers, who dared to become subscribers to 'Art Magic'...the battle of free thought and liberty of conscious against the forces of ignorance, prejudice, bigotry and superstition."

-<u>Ghost Land</u>, 1876

"Everything can be taken from a man but one thing:
the last of the human freedoms — to choose one's attitude in any given set of circumstances. To choose one's own way."

-Victor Frankl

Prologue

Dead on Impact

These three words explain her shattered dreams. Like a storm, torrential devastation grips her. Grief is a set of shackles that clutch every part of her body. Her life has been stripped away.

With the exception of that horrid headline, her father, Stefen, assures her that the TV news stories and tabloids all over the country reported his death with great sadness as he was a popular icon: "Michael Desport, Super Star killed in an airplane accident." The public doesn't know that overwhelming numbness guides her and so what people say or do has no real bearing anymore. Friends and family are trying to comfort her and it is falling on deaf ears because panic is consuming her.

Even so, do the articles speak of her life off-handily as if it were just any other day? Riding in the back of the limo, she glances out the window at the throngs of people waiting outside St Monica Catholic Church for his service. "Oh God, Dad, how am I going to get through this?"

"Hold on Lauren, I am here for you," Stefen attempts to calm her when she turns to him in anguish at the site. He

whispers soothingly to her tear stained face and bloodshot eyes, barely hidden by a black veil. When the long, black limousine stops, he helps her out. Her beautiful black heels are immediately soaked through as she looks up to see the beautiful old mission church.

There aren't a lot of steps yet it seems to take forever to get through the swarms of umbrellaed people.

"...too bad he was cut down in his prime..." someone whispers.

"...such a well loved man..." another calls out to her.

Then a woman forces her way into Lauren's path, shouting "...he was mine, not yours..." before she is hauled off screaming by security.

Finally reaching the doors, inside the antechamber, she is helped off with her overcoat, just as other's umbrellas fling water, spraying her. Stefen apologizes to her for this and guides her away from the area. He leads her on the long walk into the expansive sanctuary as murmurings of the congregation echo.

Stefen stops where her mother is in the front pew. Her strident, hushed tone claws through Lauren's delicate state. She demands, "You *must* sit here, after all you and Michael were going to be married." Not that she cared or paid a great deal of attention to Joseanne, as she isn't a loving mother, but in this case as always being the master of etiquette, Lauren obeys. She notices Joseanne's glare is for her, as Stefen balances her panic of unsteadiness and

steers her to sit in the front pew as Joseanne designates and moves over to make room for them.

It's as if Lauren is in a tunnel, every face is a blur and when her name is called out, she has difficulty identifying where the sound comes from.

People's utterings of ''…he is with God now…", are more than she can bear. Her desperate attempt to maintain a silent composure collapses as she loses control and cries out. "NO. God can't have him yet because he promised he would never leave me."

Shaking and sobbing onto Stefen's shoulder, he holds her protectively close. There is a hum of consolation at this outburst; the shaking of heads and wiping tears in understanding. Even gasps as people cover their mouths in appall. As a consequence, she shivers as if it were a blustery January morning instead of the rare hot and muggy March downpour in Santa Monica.

Faint hauntings of bagpipes begin to sound, distracting her to a time when she could see his twinkling leprechaun eyes and mischievous smile. When she could hear his contagious laugh and be pulled out of her despair for a brief moment.

Chapter 1

Lauren Ashlynn was instructed to remain in the 'orange room', the designated lounge for show guests before their appearance. Her breaths came short and in shallow pants as she waited anxiously. It was a time of firsts. She was a first time author, her book sales were skyrocketing, and now she was on set for the first time to be on TV. To be interviewed on a famous Los Angeles morning talk show with a live audience, no less.

She glanced at the monitor. The pretty blonde broadcaster, Bambi, was saying as a lead-in to her first guest, "...I'm really excited to see the 29th Super Bowl in Miami Gardens. The 49rs and Chargers at Joe Robbie Stadium in just less than a few weeks!"

Pastries and drinks were laid out in the room on a buffet table at a side bar, but the sugary smells were making Lauren feel queasy and she was far too nervous to sit, so she stepped out to escape the odors. She wanted to be inconspicuous at the edge of backstage, so she stood pressed with her back to the wall next to the ajar orange room door. She was mesmerized at how deftly the personnel moved around all the wires, lights and equipment. The mastery they displayed as they quickly and expertly operated the show.

Her attention was diverted to the bustle around the tall, lean man standing against another doorway near her. The corners of her mouth turned up in amusement as the fawning program director rushed to him and shook his hand exorbitantly.

In an elated loud whisper, as if he was announcing him to the world, "BT O'Reilly, famous private detective and author of a new best seller. It is really good to meet you. I am such a fan and I just *luved* your book! I will have you before the cameras inside five minutes."

The program director rushed off, to attend to Bambi who was waving at him. Lauren caught snatches of their conversations: Bambi was complaining about having the other author thrust at her, as he made noises of agreement and assured her they didn't have a choice for the decision had come from upstairs.

All the while he barked orders to his minions through his headset in hushed inflections.

Lauren's eyes were glued to the handsome Mr. O'Reilly, who was much more attractive than the photo on his book cover revealed. She had read one of his books and liked the adventure mystery. He seemed quite at ease, despite the fast-paced surroundings and she enjoyed watching him.

All at once, she realized he was watching her too. Disconcerted, she turned to get back to the orange room just as this most significant guest moved quickly towards her.

"Is this your first time on TV?" BT asked.

"Does it show that much?" She laughed nervously.

"Just concentrate on what you have to offer, remember who you are, and most of all don't forget to breathe!" He grinned with brilliant white teeth and his big brown eyes crinkled at the edges.

She started to thank him, mouth agape to speak when the program director returned. Lauren thought she caught him giving her a snarky look because she was talking to the famous guest. Not wanting to cause any friction and afraid of being caught outside the designated orange room, she turned and went back inside. As she closed the door, she saw BT being whisked away to the wings for his entrance.

Restless, ruffled, and feeling more apprehensive, she reminded herself to take deep breaths and rolled her shoulders to calm down. About to sit, she was startled at the knock, as an assistant popped her head in the doorway, "Miss Ashlynn, we will be ready for you in about 21 minutes. Oh, you look a bit nervous. Please remember to breathe and maybe drink some water. You'll be fine!" It was a cheery assurance, even if it felt like something she said to any nervous guest. Then she was gone and closed the door just as fast.

Lauren poured herself a glass from the pitcher of iced water, as her attention went to the monitor. The TV host boldly flirted and announced when BT strode on stage. "And here he is! BT O'Reilly in the flesh! Mr. O'Reilly, I am thrilled to meet you as I know my audience is!" She gushed and shook his hand.

The audience stood and roared with enthusiasm. She continued to shake his hand, which encouraged the audience even more. When she let go and gestured for him to sit in the opposite chair, she brazenly sat at the edge of her chair brushed his knees with hers.

Lauren found herself embarrassed for Bambi as she flirted outrageously with BT O'Reilly. After all, Lauren had watched her for many days prior to this on the show and she'd proven to be a professional reporter. But as Lauren watched, she became fascinated as it became clear what Bambi was actually doing. She was prompting the all woman audience, riling them up, as their cheers for him became more rowdy.

He was gracious through Bambi's antics, and played along with the audience while he beamed his gratitude. After a few moments, she scooted back in her chair and the audience stilled. Bambi's polished style was back in place as she started asking her questions.

There was another sharp knock at the door to the orange room as the program director marched in. His introduction was terse, he quickly escorted her to backstage for her interview and left her standing there. His demeanor to her was completely opposite of his to BT O'Reilly, so she tried not to let his dismissive attitude demoralize her. The realization did dawn upon her that she was only filler on the show.

Despite the blow, she clung to what the star had told her and took a few deep breaths. Lauren worked through her emotions quickly; she was here to follow someone famous that everyone was happy to see, and to dive into depression

was not going to help her now. Especially when her whole premise was to offer suggestions on how one could overcome the most dire of circumstances!

She heard Bambi say. "Next up is Lauren Ashlynn. We have another author in the house, ladies! Stay tuned, her book is very different from Mr. O'Reilly's. Thank you BT for being on our show!" Then a man called out. "Cut! Four minutes people."

As Lauren figured this was the commercial break, BT left the stage and walked straight toward her. Again he gave her his dazzling smile and held out his hand in greeting. She took it, and heard him say. "Remember to breathe Miss Ashlynn, I feel you trembling."

"Yes, thanks. I am breathing and nervously trembling. Yes." She stammered.

"You'll be fine, because your book says so! I look forward to finishing it!" He remarked just as he was escorted away by an assistant. Another one was at Lauren's elbow to lead her to the same chair BT warmed for her. She sat up straight and felt the lights beating down on her. Bambi acknowledged her with a slight nod of greeting from her chair, then went back to her notes.

Once the cameras came on, there was no time to think because Bambi was introducing her to the audience, albeit with much less enthusiasm than when she introduced BT. "Lauren Ashlynn," drawing out her name with a dramatic flair. "What makes your one and only book better than BT O'Reilly's many?"

5

"As you know, Bambi, I am not BT O'Reilly. Nor do I try to be." She said in an attempt to soften the sting. "I am a woman of substance that expresses an alchemy of joy to people who are hurting in their lives. I love the way Wayne Dyer interprets The Law of Attraction, in that people need to know they can believe and trust in themselves by honoring their lives and selves. Then attract and manifest their desires."

Bambi must have liked that answer because not only did the audience applaud, she continued as a journalist, "I must admit I am somewhat skeptical of what sounds like a lot of positive thinking. I don't think that is enough to fix one's life. Do you?"

"There is vast power in positive thinking, but only when it's used in tandem with facing one's truths about themselves first. Being honest with our shortcomings and bad habits reveal what we have created in our lives. Addressing these allow us to move through any pain that has occurred so we may heal and learn to trust ourselves. Ultimately, we learn to depend on ourselves and choose to be happy. And walk in your own woman-hood or man-hood."

"Thank you Lauren. That's about all the time we have here today. I appreciate your candor and your presence here to reveal a different approach to life!" Bambi turned to the audience who started to stand, holding up Lauren's book. "The book is called, I've Got This. Thanks to our viewers and to you all in our studio audience, you helped make it a fun time!" The gallery began to clap loudly.

"Cut." Seemed to come from nowhere. The end of the segment was announced.

Where Lauren's bravado had come from she did not know. Maybe it was a miracle that blossomed like what she wrote about in her book. At any rate, it worked. Because the audience had given her a standing ovation, which thrilled her. Bambi responded to the audience's approval of Lauren, shook her hand and humbly said, "Thank you for being on our show."

"Wow!" Lauren declared to the empty orange room, where she returned to pick up her purse and coat. She had just introduced a large audience to her book. She beamed with pride at her accomplishment, because it was what she set out to do. And she did despite the fact that she had to muster up reserves of courage against the dismal treatment of some of the studio people and her own nerves.

Lauren felt proud she did it with grace, even ease, despite all the tension she fought. Answering the questions with fortitude seemed to have given the audience hope. Now it was time to treat herself to a needed and well deserved holiday. With a renewed posture of confidence, she strode to the big studio doors and pushed them open.

The cold January winter air hit her immediately as she stepped out to her awaiting limousine. While riding, her thoughts returned to the day, musing, *as frosty as the weather is, I feel warm inside. I am grateful for this financial success and all being well with the world. And frankly, I can't even believe I befuddled that woman! Under the circumstances I was so scared and intimidated. Wow...*

7

To stop thinking of work would be difficult. Resting was not one of her strong suits, because she was driven and loved to work. To be casual and lay out by the pool just to read for the fun of it, was not something she ever did. *And besides, it is too cold to seriously consider anyway.* Yet the thought left her invigorated nevertheless.

Her limo pulled up to the exterior of the beautiful Beverly Hills Hotel. She was thrilled to be in the famous pink hotel, and made her way to the elevator. After she checked in last night, she had quickly arranged her belongings for the early wake up call and tried to get to sleep early. It wasn't easy, but she managed despite nerves and adrenaline.

As she rode in the elevator, she continued to toy with the idea. And finally reconsidered, what the hell? *Just do it! Just like the Nike ad says!*

As she did last night, she marveled at the luxurious suite. The decor, fully appointed and in keeping with some of the 1912 history was a delight. She walked over to the closet, changed into her sweats, picked up a book and went to the pool.

Lauren found her way poolside, and the chill seemed to energize her, freeing her somehow. She observed the peaceful and expansive courtyard that was combined with the pool's spaciousness. The area was completely deserted, which made for an odd sense of unexplored gaiety. This was unusual for her because she rarely explored for the sake of joy. For a treasured moment, she allowed herself to wonder about letting go enough, just for the sure pleasure of her new unknown.

8

"Pick a chair, any chair will do!" Lauren said recalling an old saying under her breath. Smiling at the fact she was unaccustomed to such simple pleasures of sitting by a pool, she found herself beaming at her surroundings. Upon settling onto a lounge chair, she immediately felt relaxed.

Startled by a splash of water, she looked up from her book to see someone doing laps in the unheated pool. She was baffled that she hadn't noticed him before, so she considered that he must have been under the water when she approached.

A waiter appeared with a steaming cup of cappuccino and a blanket. Quietly he introduced himself. "Mademoiselle, my name is Pierre, if you need anything at all, just wave. I will be looking out for you. Are you warm enough?" He inquired with a slight and attractive French accent.

"Quite fine, thank you." She smiled up at his kind face and took the blanket from him as he set the coffee on the table beside her. She snuggled into her blanket and sipped the hot liquid, while the warm cup soothed her chilled fingers.

Lauren blew into her cup, when she felt a presence. She looked up to meet the most incredible, emerald eyes she had ever seen. She felt her face flush as he stared into her own violet eyes. She first noticed he had only a towel around his neck. Her eyes traveled the length of his body, and it was as if he had just gone for a midsummer swim in his dripping green trunks because his skin was free of goose bumps and he wasn't shaking from the cold.

9

Before she could speak, Pierre quickly emerged with a luxurious robe and several towels. He efficiently placed the garment over the wet man's shoulders and disappeared into the hotel.

The handsome man broke their glance, to ask, "Do you mind if I join you?"

Lauren motioned and he pulled another lounge closer to her. His voice was resonant, thrilling somehow. "My name is Michael Desport."

She quickly looked down to divert the intensity of his gaze. Despite herself, she couldn't help but smile and looked back up at him to ask, "To swim in such freezing conditions, are you doing what they call a 'Polar Bear Plunge'? You must be chilled to the bone."

"I was, until I saw you!" His eyes twinkled.

She was embarrassed and sputtered a slight laugh. Again Pierre appeared, interrupting them. "Excuse me sir, you have a phone call. Shall I bring you the phone?"

"No thanks Pierre, I will take it inside."

"Very well, sir." The waiter left.

Michael stood in farewell as Lauren smiled up at him, she said, "it was nice meeting you."

His expressive eyes showed delight. He was overtly flirting with her when he announced. "We will see each other again!" He turned and strolled to the hotel.

Lauren opened her book and tried to read but was lost in thoughts of him, and excited by the distinct connection. To her pleasure, he was sleek and wore the dripping water quite well. To see him again would certainly be easy on the eyes. But pangs of insecurity quickly intervened to disrupt her wellbeing. Returning to herself, she decided it was simply a nice encounter and that was all it was or could be.

Pierre walked swiftly toward her with another cup of cappuccino. She took it as she thanked him for his thoughtfulness. He then handed her a small monogrammed note: MCD.

Please have dinner with me tonight.
-Your PolarBear Friend

She was pleasantly surprised, but recalled her last thought and briskly told Pierre. "Please tell him thank you, but I cannot accept his invitation." Pierre nodded and walked away.

Lauren put the second cup down and struggled to concentrate on the book, but she was hopelessly distracted. She couldn't quite place him and was giddy as he was interested in her.

She found herself considering his features, they were chiseled to perfection. The black hair outlined his flawless skin, while the darkened shadow of his beard brightened his

white teeth. She did want to spend time with him. She certainly had stepped out of her comfort zone earlier at the studio and now with this encounter to be sure.

Curiously, he seemed too good to be true and that scared her. Falling for charm had been her problem in the past. Although he appeared different, could he be the one? Arguing back and forth with herself, she created that old mountain of doom and gloom in her mind. She saw herself screaming while falling to the bottom of a pit. *Just why did you write that book if you're jumping to conclusions, and already hoping for the one, jeez, you got it bad! Manifest my love!*

In frustration, she argued with herself some more, then decided, *I am here for me. I need rest and relaxation and I am going to get it. No one is going to stop me.* Despite her emphatic stance, the familiar wave of despair began to swallow her confidence. It drew attention to her lonely life and disheartened soul. It dissipated the pleasure she fought so hard for, and nagged at her with a longing to have the chance to share her life with someone worthy. *And that's why I wrote the book!*

As she continued her interior battle she also struggled to remember where she thought she had seen him or perhaps heard of him. "Michael Desport". She repeated his name over again. Then it hit her, he was an 'actor'. In fact she had seen a few of his movies. Feeling foolish for thinking he could be 'the one', she muttered aloud. "Boy, am I nutty. The cold must be freezing my brain cells."

The wind picked up and the day turned biting cold. She gathered her blanket and book, as Pierre came to her assistance. She returned to her suite and was welcomed by an unbelievably large basket of flowers. Closing the door, she marveled at the arrangement. The flowers were loosely placed, dramatic in color, creating a lush and irreverent array.

Lauren recognized the monogram on the card. She read inside:

Please reconsider.
-Your PolarBear Friend

As hard as she tried, she could not control the giggles and warm fuzzies that started to break down her barriers.

A hot bath was in order. She poured the scented bath crystals under the running water. Stepped into the tub, as the bubbles surrounded her entire being, she felt the relaxed state wash over her and continued to contemplate *him*. His broad shoulders and strong body, made him appear taller than his frame allowed. Oh, she had it bad for him alright and dozed off.

Finally alert to the cooled water, she was finished with the bath. Lauren stepped out and wrapped herself into a long, warm robe. Then advanced onto the balcony to watch the sun dip into the horizon, and noticed that her suite overlooked the swimming pool. Their lounge chairs were still side by side, and a smile danced at the edge of her mouth with fondness at the memory.

She was cognizant of the wind change and how it made the temperature shift and feel warm, when it should have been cold. As the clouds moved across the sky quickly, she announced aloud, "there's such a disturbance brewing like the proverbial 'calm before the storm.'" This observation verified her reflections, that the weather often mirrored her life.

Her reverie was interrupted by a knock at the door. Lauren padded across the floor and when she opened the door, her eyes grew large and her jaw dropped. He was deliciously attractive in his charming attire: tweed trousers, suspenders and an opened sea foam colored shirt. She met his eyes, flushed and felt beautiful in his sight. This was one of the few times her hair had the perfect look of whispy-tendrils outlining her face and neck.

"I hope you don't mind, it's just that I had hoped you would be a wee bit hungry!" Michael's voice stirred her soul with his slight Irish brogue.

Behind him, stood several waiters with carts of luscious food. She invited them in. He had brought High Tea, which included a bottle of peach champagne, two chilled flute glasses, and many plates of fine delicacies.

As she marveled at the feast, he stood very close to her. Lauren immediately felt the warmth of his body and it made her realize all that stood between Michael's seducing eyes was her robe. He whispered in her ear, "Now it is my turn to be dressed!" They both chuckled at their secret, as the waiters finished setting up.

"Thank you for this amazing surprise. Let me excuse myself for a moment."

"Sure." Is all he said, but his eyes held desire for her.

As she dressed, she heard the "pop" of the bottle and giggled in delight for the second time that day. The Tea was exceptional; there were cucumber and watercress finger sandwiches, delicious peppered toast lathered with a relish-cheese, and exotic jams for the scones.

Michael kept the conversation moving with his sparkling wit and fun stories. Then he mentioned the weather changing and he was glad for a storm. He explained, "I especially enjoy the depth of color that the gray skies produce in the surrounding areas. Trees are greener and the hills show hues that appear mystical."

"I enjoy storm-weather too although raging storms can be quite eerie. Michael, thank you for the flowers and coffees today. You are very generous and I am especially enjoying this High Tea, as well as the company." She smiled wide.

He spoke gently, "I know this great little place for dinner. Shall I pick you up at eight? What do you say?"

Their eyes devoured each other, as they continued to enjoy the pastries. Then she whispered, "That would be nice."

His expressive eyes lit up with delight at her acceptance. He stood ceremoniously, bent over her, took her hand in his, and turning it over kissed her palm. Then he gently righted it to kiss her knuckles with a formal bow. He let her go,

15

walked over to the door and did a bit of an Irish jig. At that, he left her to her dropped jaw for the second time and her now undeniably tingling heart.

Chapter 2

Michael was prompt. At eight, he was standing at her door. She opened it to see him dapper in a handsome, tailor-cut, pinstripe suit. He greeted her with his magnetic smile and reached for her hands. "You look amazing!"

Lauren left her hair up with the strands of wisps that adorned her beautiful neck line. The bright plum suit accentuated her petite body and accented her eyes. She was glad she chose the more conservative suit for the studio interview earlier, because this one made her feel feminine. She loved the pencil skirt that reached below her knees, with its high slit at the back. The short waisted jacket was made to be worn open, so that a soft cream chemise was displayed.

"Thank you. You look great yourself." She said as she released his hands to close the door behind her.

They walked to the elevator together, he wouldn't stop looking at her. As he pushed the down arrow-key, she asked "What? Do I have something on my face?" She felt his gaze so acutely on her.

"Yes you do!" He cupped her cheeks and exclaimed. "A look of stunning beauty!"

He let her go as the conveyor doors opened. She was stunned speechless, and her lower lip trembled as she bit it to steady herself. He led her out through the lobby and down the colonnade toward the restaurant. She kept her hands clasped together, and clutched within them her small beaded bag, because he made her so nervous. His incredible eyes continued to beam at her.

When they reached the restaurant, they were immediately greeted and whisked to a small corner table that overlooked the lovely tropical gardens outside. The expansive bay window showcased the softly lit waving palm trees, numerous ferns and flowering hibiscus plants.

Champagne awaited them in an elaborate bucket. He asked her if she liked crab legs, she nodded as the server poured their glasses. Michael made casual conversation and she gradually became more comfortable as it turned out it was easy to be with him.

When the crab came, she grinned broadly in delight. He looked at her questioningly. "It's beautifully arranged and I don't have to break the legs apart!" She exclaimed. Arrayed on the plates several legs had been cut open so the meat popped out easily and there was no messy cracking needed or struggle to eat them.

He chuckled in agreement. They continued to converse and enjoy the delicacy, as a simple beet-walnut salad was put aside their charger sized plates. He entertained her with funny stories from his work that made her laugh and enjoy his company all the more. She liked hearing him talk, and although an actor he seemed real with her.

At one point he softly asked of her plans, and not wanting to discuss them, she changed the subject smoothly. After dinner they enjoyed a Drambuie liqueur and watched the bright flames from the fireplace across the now empty room.

The evening passed quickly, it was after midnight when they left the restaurant. He asked, "do you mind if we walk a bit?" She nodded and he guided her out into the hotel gardens, a light drizzle touched their faces as the cool air made for a nice stroll. But when they turned a corner, they saw lightning and heard the roar of thunder just as a sudden downpour pelted them with large, fat raindrops.

They looked at each other in astonishment, laughed and were forced to run. Michael grabbed her hand, led her through the back of the hotel, and they entered a small alcove of the kitchen. Lauren could not remember when she had laughed so hard and felt such joy. "This is wild, sneaking in like this!" She giggled.

"I want ice cream!" Michael declared. He helped her up onto a stainless steel work table. She sat and allowed her legs to swing in a carefree way. He tossed her a towel to dry off her wet heels.

But her mood darkened as she watched him scurry about. Although he appeared to look curious, she could not help but notice a studied kind of pretext in his search. It led her to wonder if he had done this same thing in this same place with other women before. A suspicious feeling crept in and it was unpleasant. "Damn it, I'm having too much fun to question his motives," she said under her breath and tried to push aside the rising cynicism inside her.

He strode up to her, dipping a large serving spoon into the icy five gallon carton. "What was that you said?" He inquired as he laid a drop of chocolate coldness on her nose.

"I said 'what motivation you have!'" She replied with a smile, pleased with her fast comeback.

Softly he kissed the ice cream off her pert, little nose. He moved to her lips and opened his to find hers, just as a loud noise from somewhere inside the huge kitchen interrupted them. They scrambled, he took her hand and they were off.

Once clear of the kitchen area, they stopped running and laughed on their way to the elevator. When the doors opened, they nearly fell inside in their rush, but felt safe that the coast was clear and both burst out in a bout of relief and hilarity. Almost immediately however (and with great difficulty to contain their guffaws) they tried to avoid eye contact with each other on account of the distinguished elderly couple that followed them into the elevator. It was obvious from their palpable displeasure they were definitely not amused by Lauren and Michael's private joke, disheveled appearance and uncontrolled mirth.

When the crabby couple got off on their floor, Michael pushed the button to close the elevator doors, and they finally looked at each other which prompted another outburst from them both. They held their stomachs from the near agony of hysterics. By the time they reached her room, they were wiping tears from their faces and continued to hold their stomachs, from the intensity of the experience and from sheer enjoyment.

They both leaned against her closed door to collect themselves. Panting hard, they slowed their laughter. Minutes passed, and soon he reached down and kissed her forehead, whispered into her mouth, "breakfast will be at 9". He bowed his head, bid her goodnight and left.

She walked into her room, totally oblivious to the raging storm outside. She did feel that an equally charged disturbance was erupting within her. Lauren glanced at her bed and noticed it had been turned down. Truffles and forget-me-nots had been placed carefully on the down pillows.

She crawled up onto the large, soft bed, grabbed a pillow and hugged herself tightly. Released a cry of joy and murmured, "hold on girl, 'this is going to be a bumpy ride'", in her best Betty Davis imitation.

"Who is this man, and how can *he* be happening to me? This only happens in the movies!" She demanded answers from the empty room. Getting none, she went to the bathroom to change for bed.

The night was alive with thunder. Multiple booms made the doors and windows rattle. Lauren found sleep impossible. She felt anxious from excitement and fear, causing her to toss and turn. She was delighted with him and was enjoying how life felt fun and new in his presence. But her nemesis - the old typical fear - reared its head that the evening scared her.

She walked over to the windows, looked out over the lightening filled sky, and questioned herself out loud: "but

why can't I just enjoy myself and not get so overboard with emotion? He seems interested in me, and I certainly am in him.   So what is the problem, LAUREN?"   The window steamed up with her words.

She reflected upon the strategy she always observed in business: directness and honesty.   Being a practical woman, she considered the same could apply to her personal life. She dared herself to have fun, and reasoned Michael could show her how.

"And if it is goodbye tomorrow, then so be it. Life will go on and hopefully I will at minimum have had an experience I will remember fondly."   With this final statement, she wandered back to bed and fell into an uneasy sleep.

The sun rose, although it only illuminated the sky to a dark gray.   Her restless night had left her with dark circles underneath her eyes and a bad hair day.   Lauren's complexion was wan and so was her mood.   "The mirror doesn't lie. It is as if yesterday was magic and today's reality has smacked me in the face," she sighed to her reflection.

To revive herself, she stepped over to the French doors, phone in hand. She called room service for coffee as she watched the wind and rain thrash the beautiful courtyard below.

Finally the waiter brought the hot stimulant. She swallowed the first sip, and it helped to raise her mood. She showered and dressed quickly. She dashed to the elevator, but as she approached the doors closed, and she tried not to succumb

to superstition. Lauren found the stairwell which she hurried down and worked up a slight sudor.

Exiting the stairs, she paused to look at herself in a hallway mirror, and fumbled in her pocket for a Kleenex to dab her forehead. She turned and found the extravagant atrium. The decor was impeccable, in addition to being bright and cheery. As though by design, it lightened her mood in spite of the blustery storm outside.

Her eyes found Michael, sipping his coffee, looking relaxed and quite casually elegant in his worn-faded jeans, white Nikes and T-shirt. His blazer was of exceptional wool tweed that complimented his eyes, and the sleeves were rolled up as though he could take on anything the world threw at him and be pleased about it. He stood as she walked up to him. "Good morning!" He announced as he smiled at her.

"Top o'thee morn' to ye!" Surprising herself with a spunkiness she didn't know she possessed.

"Are you Irish?" He tilted his head quizzically and asked.

"No, but I have always wanted to be!" She exclaimed and beamed.

Michael laughed, deep and robust. She couldn't help but laugh with him. His enthusiasm for life was contagious.

Breakfast was a delectable selection of her favorites; fluffy eggs, crisp hash browns and bacon. The enthusiastic conversation flowed easily and sparkled with fun and gaiety. She even regaled him with some of her funny stories.

They talked for an hour, and with no forewarning, the sun peeked through the clouds. And so did Lauren's underlying anxiety. It was though the sun reminded her of reality, and shined a light on the struggle of her life. Trying to hide her panic, she rose and said. "Please excuse me Michael, I have to pack my things. Thank you for a lovely time."

He tried to shift her sudden change in attitude, with his most charming grin and pursued, "take a walk with me. We have a nice reprieve from the weather." Then with eyes gleaming, he bent his head closer to her and whispered conspiratorially, "I had fun last night with you. And in case you were wondering, I do spend a lot of time here at this hotel. They actually allow me to visit the kitchen after hours and always keep ice cream for me!"

After signing the bill, he led her to the gardens. They wandered without a set destination, silently moving through the courtyard. The wind died down and clouds paraded across the sky in a fantastically massive array of shapes and colors. The painted sky helped Lauren quiet her feelings of dread.

However, it was Michael's turn to become serious. So much so that in contrast to his bright and tan complexion, his nature took on a dark, even purple dim. He wanted to know her better and yet somehow he felt he already did. He grasped at that moment that he wanted her with him always. But it seemed she wanted to leave him. He had no idea where she was going or to whom. He had many dalliances with many women, and last night was very typical for him. He was mystified. *"Why is this woman so*

different?" He asked himself. And how could he make her understand when he didn't himself?

Slowly, he spoke, "Lauren, I want to spend more time with you. There is so much we need to do together." He remembered when his father was serious, he had taken on his same formal style.

Caught off-guard, Lauren lowered her eyes to escape his serious gaze. He did not let her turn away. They came to a spot in the garden where he guided her upon a large, multi-colored rock. As she stood on it she was absolutely eye level with him. He cupped her chin in his hand and met her eyes, and he waited for her to respond.

His other hand held her with a deliberate intention at her waist, silently willing her to trust in him. For the first time in her life, she felt free to express her innermost thoughts and had no reason to lie about her feelings. Lauren explained she didn't want the life her parents had had. Her response had been to work too much, and ultimately her priorities had become solely focused on her career.

She divulged even more and truly opened herself up to him. "And I'm tired of being afraid of life. I want to know what it means to live and have no regrets. To have a relationship with no game playing. I want to trust that a man and a woman can love each other with a passion that lasts. To have mutual respect and communicate with an open-mind that will allow growth and enjoyment to be shared, and doubled between them. I can't believe I'm saying all this, I don't know you. I know this is too much too soon, but...", she trailed off, moved her head back to see his whole face.

25

Lauren waited to see his reaction. This felt deeply important to her, even a little momentous. She was committed now after she spouted her feelings. In the split decision, she felt liberated, like nothing she had ever felt toward a man. She also knew she had nothing to lose, if he didn't understand then it truly was not meant to be and nothing had been lost because there was no point in a relationship without this radical honesty.

She forgot she stood on a rock, so when she stepped back and started to lose her balance, he caught her. What Lauren saw was much more than she expected; complete acceptance and warmth. His glistening eyes said it all. Michael embraced her and kissed her with a force she never felt before. He held her fast, then pulled back and his hands cupped her face again. She returned his kiss with a full throated passion using her entire mouth and he knew he would never let her go.

Chapter 3

Lauren turns to the tiny window and sees billowing clouds moving fast, momentarily disorientated but also alarmed, she is shivering in distress with a languid perspiration. Goosebumps from the shakes break out on her skin while the low groaning sounds of the 747 engines bring her back to her surroundings and she realizes she was having yet another dream, remembrance of Michael.

Damn you Michael Desport, why did you leave me? You promised you would never leave me. You did, you left me. Her face crumbling, she buries it into the little airplane pillow, and sobs. Whispering to herself in anger and frustration, *I know Baby, there should be comfort knowing you died doing what you loved. But it doesn't help me. Nothing does.*

Exhaustion mercilessly takes its toll. She rises from her seat and makes her way to the lavatory. In this moment, Lauren realizes the oddity that there's no-one around in the first-class section. The worn out stranger looking back at her from the mirror surprises her. Her drawn cheeks, etched lines around her mouth, tired and red eyes all give her a hint of what she'll look like thirty years from now, the visible evidence of her grief unnerves her.

Then the claustrophobia sets in again. It doesn't even require a small space like the lavatory anymore. It happens anywhere or anytime without warning nowadays. Her clammy skin, severe panic and anxiety dog her. Attempting some self-control, she soaks a washcloth in cold water. Applying it to her face, dapping at her throat and neck, she considers this moment in the mirror. *Why did I let Dad talk me into this? There is no way getting away could possibly help.*

Lauren feels the familiar resentment toward him rise up again and her impatience with herself, *I want peace and relief. And will I ever feel fully alive again?*

Nausea creeps into her throat, her thoughts are soundtracked by the roar of the airplane engines. Counseling and drugs helped a little for a while after his death. But ultimately throwing herself in to her work felt like her only salvation. She had deemed it earlier in her life, as a young person, it helped keep her mind off the traumas and disappointments suffered by her folks. Her mother was especially conflicted and troubled.

Now this so-called vacation dreamed up by her father was supposed to change the pace and setting of her life. As if the trauma of losing Michael hadn't upended her entire existence already. And this trip, coming only some twelve weeks or so after the funeral, will make for far too much time to reminisce about Michael. Surely the emotional cost is high because despite the escape she finds in the dreams filled with sweet memories, there are cracks in her consciousness. His sudden demise cankering throughout

28

her reality, and she is struggling to discern facts from illusions.

She applies far too much coverup under her eyes, and adds some bright spots of blush and a cheery shade of lipstick to help fortify herself. Who knows if the face she's painted that feels like a mask will fool anyone? Lauren decides she's done enough thinking for now, and a glass of sherry will do nicely to assuage her aggravation. If nothing more, it will at least steady her nerves. Stepping out of the lavatory, again she is struck by how this section of the plane is like a ghost town. Making her way to the spiral staircase in the double decker plane, she ascends to the piano bar.

The retrofitted circular bar is smart with chrome details and remains impressive even for people used to the luxuries of first class travel. The piano man has the lightest hand with a mere tinkling of keys for background ambiance. She muses how the atmosphere would have felt when the plane was new, and how the lounge with the instrument and musician was certainly the center of attention fancying the essence of a good time.

Lauren turns to take in the 70s styled area, and catches sight of *her*. Deirdre Kennsington. Feelings of jealousy sucker-punch her and the thought of sharing the remainder of the flight with her is more than Lauren can bear.

Per usual, Deirdre has all the men surrounding her at the little bar, clearly enthralled by her, and the audience includes her father. Deirdre is laughing with Stefen Ashlynn, when he catches sight of his daughter, he says. "Darling, come join us. This is the extraordinary actress, Deirdre Kennsington!"

He signals the barkeep for another round as the two women exchange a loaded glance.

After Lauren places her order, Deirdre's dazzling expression changes to one of seemingly sincere sorrow and says, "Lauren, I was deeply sorry to hear of Michael's death. I know he had a great love for you. He was a fine man and a dear friend." Shifting her tone and the topic she chirps, "It turns out you two are staying at the same place on Lanai as I am! Your father has agreed you both will accompany me on the plane I have scheduled to take us there. I insist, it's the least I can do for you."

Lauren wants to oppose this plan but obediently nods instead as Stefen puts his arm around her to agree. She is taken aback how quickly her father and Deirdre's rapt audience return their attention to the bewitching star.

Uncomfortable in Deirdre's presence because of their history, she moves away from the group to a lone empty chair near a window. Lauren chides herself that Deirdre would ever be uncomfortable in her presence, since after all she is an *actress extraordinaire.*

The sherry disappears quickly and Lauren notes with only a passing interest that her gloom and doom emotions have turned to a more apathetic attitude. Lauren can't help but be mildly fascinated as she observes this woman with her seemingly boundless knowledge and energy, glide from topic to topic with the greatest of ease and wit. Lauren has to watch the entire scene unfold. It's clear by the way she enchants her fans that Deirdre understands the art of

30

flirtation because Stefen and the other men are being expertly *managed*. Lauren orders another sherry.

Lauren always thought of this woman as controlling, cunning, and a seductive siren. And maybe she was all these things, but Lauren had to admit, there is a craft to her. Lauren muses as most men are held captive by her, she had assumed Michael had been too. Even though he had assured her otherwise, she was beginning to wonder and second guess herself. Had she misunderstood what kind of person Deirdre was?

Deirdre's voice recedes into the background as Lauren mulls over the irony of them meeting like this and wonders what the whole truth is about the relationship between Michael and *her*.

Chapter 4

Michael Desport loved to run; especially without the encumbrance of his large and clunky cell phone. So when it rang, Lauren hesitated to answer. But when it rang the third time, she picked it up to hear: "Michael, this is your Deirdre!"

Jealousy flared inside her hot and quick and Lauren spat, "he's out."

"Oh I see, please tell him Deirdre Kennsington called. It's important," she said emphatically. "He must call me back immediately. Thank you." Lauren pushed the 'end button' hard and threw the phone onto the sofa. This was the actress that Michael was linked with in all the tabloids after they had done a blockbuster film together. Her physical beauty was greater than Lauren could aspire to have. She stood and stared at the phone, anger and jealousy undid the lovely feelings she had but a few minutes ago. Her self-confidence cracked.

Michael strode in with that leprechaun twinkle in his eyes. Swayed by the joy he exuded, she couldn't help but smile and ventured a calm resolve, to state "Deirdre Kennsington just called and asked you to call her back right away." Lauren turned and walked quickly into the kitchen, dodging him to hide her struggle with insecurity.

He followed and gently asked, "I take it, you know who she is?"

Waved her hand with an attempt at indifference. "Sure, who doesn't?"

He could read right through her and his expression changed to concern, "are you worried about her?" Michael waited and stood very still, looked at her back intently.

Lauren went directly to and held onto the marbled rim of the inset stainless steel farmhouse kitchen sink. Words caught in her throat and her eyes stung from holding back the complicated emotions. The burden of her comparison to a beautiful woman, despite her valiant attempt to be self-assured simultaneously forced her tears to leak.

He put his arms around her and held her tight. *What could he tell her? He had spent lots of time with Deirdre and many others. But what was fun with them could never compare with the completeness he felt with Lauren almost immediately upon meeting her.*

What was it about this woman that turned him so? He could only hold her, trying to explain would trivialize his feelings for her. And then to figure love, it just hit him. And in that moment he finally accepted the fact he was in love with her. It finds you, and never lets go. He always *knew* this, he held her even tighter.

As firmly as he held her, she felt fear, not the security she hoped his strong arms would provide. Lauren knew he had affairs and had spent much time with Deirdre. He wasn't

denying anything, nor would he disclose it. "I don't know what to do and if I did, I don't think I could do a thing anyway," she whispered to herself. Then muttered, "but I'll be damned if I admit it to him."

He heard parts of what she murmured and looked confused as she squirmed away from him. "I said, 'I'll be damned if I'm going to get close to that sticky-slimy body!'" While she tried to force a smile. It was a rather warm February day, he was drenched in sweat more than usual. She had been staying at his house more and more frequently and she had became quite comfortable.

"Oh yeah?" He tried to grab her and missed as she grabbed a wet sponge and threw it at him.

It hit his massive, naked chest, and his surprised expression made her roar with laughter. She lost her footing, slipped and fell on her bum. At that, he stepped aside and seized the faucet by the retractable hose and sprayed her down as well as most of his kitchen.

With a throaty yell, she crawled behind the pantry door and grabbed towels, to throw at him. Lauren got to her feet, ducked below the spray, and was able to maneuver close enough to grasp onto his sides and tickle him. They both slipped onto the cool tiled floor, their bodies entwined with wetness and laughter.

Problems and interferences fled as he caught her mouth with his full lips, his inflamed passion pulsed against her. She returned the burning sensation with her tongue,

discovered the wholeness of him and transported her back to that hungry place they enjoyed together.

In his fervor, he reached for her succulent breasts and tore at her T-shirt, oh how he needed to feel her enveloping him. Next he grappled at the buttons on her shorts as he kicked off his shoes.

She seized his running pants and forced them down over his protrusion.   She felt him pulse in her wet hands which caused sensations of electricity to course through both of them, it made for a complete carnal circuit.   Energized by passion and the rush for satisfaction, they were one within seconds while shockwaves coursed through them.

They found themselves wet, naked and entwined with each other on the variegated gray stoned tile that chilled them as they aroused from slumber.   Michael helped Lauren to her feet, embraced her, looked into her violet shimmering eyes and slathered tender succulent kisses all over her face.

She quivered, from the kisses and chill.   He said with his naughty smile.   "You're cold, let's get you covered up!"   His eyes sparkled with glee.

They made their way towards the back stairs off the kitchen pantry that led to the elaborate master bedroom.   The entire house was luxurious, yet welcoming, spacious and delicious as he.   She was so taken by him, and loved the nuances, graciousness and playfulness of him.

He led her to the magnificent, cherry wood, four-poster bed. Michael threw back the covers with a flourish and wink that

invited her in. She crawled in, he followed and pulled up the sheet as they positioned themselves so he could spoon her. He whispered in her ear. "May I take you to lunch tomorrow?"

She sighed, "hmmm," and fell fast asleep as the sky darkened into a warm and lovely sunset that they missed. It never occurred to Michael to return Deirdre's cryptic message.

Because of Lauren's hectic work day, they decided to meet at the restaurant. When he arrived he saw her standing at a table of ladies looking at what appeared to be a celebrity magazine. Lauren caught his eye and went to him. As they were seated he inquired, "who was in the photo you ladies were so excited about?"

She replied with delight, "BT O'Reilly! Gosh, what they all wouldn't give to meet him! Actually did you know, I did meet him the day I met you! He was very nice, tried to bolster me with confidence before my segment of the TV interview."

Michael sat back in his chair as he hid his feelings of concern behind his dark Aviator Ray Bans. He knew BT well and was surprised at his own pain and/or could this be jealousy? He found himself quite uncomfortable with this new feeling, as Lauren continued to chat about the girl's comments.

Michael worked hard to divert his worry, but if Lauren wanted to meet this man, then he would make it happen. He realized he'd do anything for her. He decided to have a party, and would make sure BT O'Reilly would be there.

Michael stated. "Then I'll have a cocktail party! I'd like it if you'd come to meet him. Or should I say, re-meet him."

"What? You know him, you'd do that? Wow!" She exclaimed with surprise.

"Sure. We've known each other for years. He's an author, I did a movie of his. Great guy." He said flatly.

She couldn't help notice how his facial expression had become sullen, even though he tried to hide it with a forced smile. His eyes, she knew them well and if she could see them, she knew they were dark, as if opaque black contact lenses were suddenly applied to them. He wasn't a sarcastic man, but his tone seemed so. Something was wrong, and she felt dread as the shift in his demeanor left her questioning the shift in mood. At that moment, the waiter came to them. Soon Michael was back to his joyful self and BT was forgotten as they enjoyed their meal together.

The party was fun and entertaining. Many industry people gathered, Lauren knew of only a few of the several stars there. All laughed and mingled with drinks in hand. They circulated amongst the tables flowing with heavy appetizers of shrimp, meatballs in crockpots, wooden Charcuterie boards laden with fruits, nuts, jams, and a variety of crackers and breads.

When Lauren couldn't see Michael in the crush of the guests, she rounded one of the corners and found him leaning at the kitchen sink. It was set deep into the marbled gray counters that glistened from the skylights and walled picture windows. She loved this space and knew the

counters and coordinating tile floors sparkled because they were clean, but more so because of the thousands of tiny imbedded glints in them reflected the incoming light from the skylights.

The palatial, without being ostentatious, kitchen was versatile and functional while being an epicurean's delight. A large island ran parallel to the bright ivory creamed wall of cabinets and pantries. Accenting silver pulls and deluxe appointed stainless appliances complimented the convenient lengthy countertops.

One would immediately feel welcomed to help with the cooking and prep of meals behind the island. As the other side of it was designed to be an open space to accommodate the gathering of people in the kitchen, it was space clearly designed by and for someone who enjoyed entertaining

Although his back was turned toward her, she could tell he was deep in thought. "Michael?" She asked quietly.

When he didn't turn to her, she walked to him, and reached for his hand. He withdrew slightly from her which caused Lauren to steel herself, "Michael, are you alright?"

No answer. He just stood there, his posture declined. Then she *knew*. *The party, BT, all was for her. He planned this party to show her off and give her a chance to meet her 'crush'. Am I being too egotistical to 'know' this to be true? What are you thinking Michael? Why are you in such pain? Or, damn it, is he trying to let me go? Perhaps set me up with this other man? Am I losing him or does he think he's*

losing me? The battery of silent questions made for confusion, then fear.

Ordering her voice to be steady as she addressed his back. "Michael, I want to thank you for inviting me to this party. The people are very nice, even comfortable to converse with. And it was fun meeting BT again. Yet," she began to stutter, "I...I can't help but feel something is wrong between us...you and me I mean. I don't know what it is, but I sure do feel uneasy. Can we talk?" She felt timid, but she had to know. And it had to be now. Too much time had been spent with this man with too many feelings that swirled around to not know the truth. The time had come to cut to the chase.

She leaned over to look into his eyes. She was shocked to see them brimmed with tears. *Oh geez, this can go either way. I know he's a caring person, so this could be his way of letting me down easy?*

Michael concentrated on her voice and her words, he was afraid of what he was going to hear next. He figured the results were in, he took the chance that would allow her to go, and now it was time. He turned to look at her, he was caught off guard by her frightened face and sorrowful eyes.

She immediately looked down and concentrated on her shoes so she wouldn't fall down. An eternity went by. Then Lauren hoarsely whispered aloud, "I love you, Michael. Please forgive me, but I love you."

Overwhelmed with emotion he picked her up and placed her on the counter. Her eyes were wet and she was confused. His were red and excited. He beamed at her and cupped

her chin with his hands. Then he kissed her square on her mouth. It wasn't passionate, it was more like the kind a little boy would give his puppy. He was filled with love, pride and joy. He put her down and gently squeezed her to him until she became still. Content.

Suddenly, people began to swarm into the kitchen. There were two entries, and both sets of bar doors were swinging in and out. The conversations were at a high pitch, speckled with laughter and happiness. Some asked where they had been. Another said, "oh, that's it. You two want privacy. Well, forget it, it's a party!"

Michael turned them both around so that they faced his guests, looked over her head, and announced: "OK kids, it's time for ice cream! I don't care that it's cold outside, it's always a good time for ICE CREAM!"

Chapter 5

"Lauren. Lauren..." Stefen's husky voice interrupts her memory with his apology to Deirdre for her lack of conversation. Although Lauren had prided herself on her self-reliance and independence, she's aware she's allowing her father to continue to control situations for her. Lauren explains meekly to Deirdre, "I am sorry, I haven't felt quite myself these days."

At that, Deirdre's face lights up as she exclaims. "Well, then a party is in order! Both of you will be my guests of honor. I will not take no for an answer."

Lauren's eyebrows furrow as Stefen chimes in. "Yes, this is just what we need." He talks with Deirdre excitedly about party plans and Lauren forces a smile. Sipping her wine, she flushes at her memory and strives to calm her mood swings.

Before Michael, she merely existed. She worked hard at making herself a successful business woman. Emotions were not part of her life and therefore that part of being female wasn't either. Sure, she dated. Those outings were sometimes fun, often not. There just wasn't a man she truly wanted to spend time with or be with for any length of time. Let alone the fact she found most men were threatened by her success and prosperity.

Thereon being with Michael, Lauren learned how to truly live. She found, and understood real joy and a freedom she never knew. Embracing her existence as a feminine woman suddenly became a reality that she enjoyed. She learned to express herself and emotions; therefore, found she could trust herself and love him as well as herself. She grew and had fun. He was real. And for the first time in her life, she felt stable, complete and able to count on someone other than herself.

Now however she finds living worse than before him. Because now she does know better and so there is no going back to her old ways. She didn't really understand she was in survival mode then. That keynote of having no real life was pretending at life. Wrestling with memories of him, she wonders if they are a part of her grieving process?

She understands and even writes that with life comes tremendous pain, as well as accepting loss. It all goes with being a complete human, which can be devastating and also wonderful. Can she give herself permission to respond to these feelings of deep emotion, will she find salvation to thrive again? Is this even an option for her?

She is a desperate woman. Exhausted and feeling like she has reached rock-bottom, her life is emptier than before Michael. Lauren reasons through her overtaxed mind that she can no longer continue the way she is going. Somehow, someway these anxieties have to stop, she needs to let go.

Just great, she relents as her attention is drawn to the boisterous Deirdre and her following. Lauren's old dreaded jealousy comes up, along with feelings of insecurity, making

her question the stability she had with Michael, yet again. As her mind traverses from letting go of anxiety to formulating more of it, she broods over the time Deirdre introduced herself when Lauren answered his cellphone that day.

It was an overwhelming experience. Despite the fact Michael assured her that they were only friends, she desperately wanted to know where she stood in his life. And more precisely, where did Deirdre stand with him? Lauren recalls that Michael didn't oversell "their strictly friendship" relationship, which led her to question if and what he was hiding. After all, he was matter of fact in wanting her to know that she, Lauren, was the One for him after the kitchen water-antics and lovemaking. This lovely reminiscence gives her some relief. A flickering smile of hope darts ever so briefly across her face.

Turning toward the window, she is struck by the raw beauty of the islands. At that, the captain asks all to return to their seats. Waiting for her turn to go down the stairs, she gets to her seat and belts herself in. She hears the plane's landing gear rumble down and realizes how relieved she is that the long trip is finally at an end.

Looking out the window she is in awe of the brilliant visions of the red dirt and black lava formations. They are in a dramatic contrast to the incredible blue-green waters of the sea. Flying in closer to the islands, she has no adjectives that can explain the splendor she observes. As the white coastline borders the lavish greenery, for a brief moment, she forgets her pain.

Yet nothing can prepare her for the welcome she is about to receive. She braces herself for the landing.

Chapter 6

Stefen Ashlynn awaits the second landing that day. This is his favorite place, having been many times for golf and business conferences. He remembers outwardly how the island invites all that see it from the air to rest and relax. He recalls that he has always enjoyed the time spent on Lanai and hopes that the awe inspiring island will give his daughter all it had given him.

After landing on Oahu in Honolulu, they transfer to a small turbo-propped airplane. Deirdre had prearranged this to take them to Lanai. Other than the inevitable transition to the leisurely pace of "island time", it is obvious that she is a stickler for details, as the transfer of luggage and her guests is done with perfection and in a timely manner.

He anticipates the tropical breezes and intoxicating flowery scents in the air. And trusts that his daughter, who is in so much need for this break, will allow herself to let the island fare relax her. Stefen always believed the tropics' beauty offers life and this time he hopes love will come again for her. He knows this is a tall order, tough even, because Michael had shown her more of herself than he, as her father, was ever able to.

He's been disappointed in himself for not being the hero dad. Stefen adores Lauren but would have to restrict his

45

time and hide his feelings toward her when his wife was around as Lauren grew up. This trip however, was actually Joseanne's idea which confounded him. Until he realized she wanted them away because of the headlines. Lauren's life with Michael was continuing to be quite the stir.

He fell madly in love with Joseanne back in the day. There seemed to be tenderness and she had shown affection in the beginning of their relationship. The beautiful socialite that had the world by its tail. She was adored by all, but he won her heart. Or so he thought.

He was brought up to work smart and hard all his life. Although not terribly close to his folks, it was a sheer cry different from what Jos had. Even though she said little about growing up, he knew enough of Milicent to know that Jos did not have it easy as a child. So he resolved that his love and making a loving home for her would make for a loving woman. But alas, no.

For Joseanne had turned icy cold when she carried Lauren. After the nurse handed their newly born child to her, Joseanne waited for the nurse to leave the room. She then immediately thrust the baby into his arms, demanding. "You will be in charge of *This*." And that was the way it was throughout Lauren's life as a child and young adult.

Joseanne became a strange and distant creature, especially toward her daughter. This extended toward him, and they soon took to separate bedrooms. She could show many faces of the caring wife while with others in their social circles. But instantly would turn on him once alone.

Stefen had sneaked chances, made opportunities to help raise, direct the nannies and be with Lauren, yet he was constantly monitored by his wife in how much time he spent with the child. Joseanne kept their social life active, forcing him to be apart from Lauren. He knew his wife was jealous of the baby and growing child, but he couldn't help that.

As a matter of fact, he couldn't help his lot in life. He had always been his own man, vibrant, handsome and attractive to the ladies. He enjoys people and is charming. But when it came to Jos he was and still is at a loss. Even after all he has been through in the loveless marriage, to this day he still carries the crazy notion that she will find love inside herself to share with him and their daughter.

Turning from the window, he glances over at Deirdre conversing seductively with another guest. Stefen smiles to himself at her expert personality of flaunting and flirting. He has seen her movies and meeting her has been quite thrilling as he too is considered quite the flirt. Still he has never betrayed his wife or ever will. Yet he can't help but wonder about the gorgeous star, there's something familiar about her he cannot put his finger on.

Departing the plane, they are greeted single file at the bottom of the short stairway by a sweet smiling elderly Hawaiian woman. She places a beautiful plumeria lei over each of their heads by wordlessly forcing them all to bend so she may kiss their cheek.

When it's Lauren's turn, she gives her the honi, a traditional Hawaiian greeting. She pulls Lauren down to her eye level, puts her forehead and nose to hers, cradles her arms and

softly whispers. "Surrender, my dear. This place is good for that and you. Remember, you are safe." Lauren is left puzzling over this message as the others are already in the hotel limo waiting for her.

Their handsome young Hawaiian driver peaks his head in the vehicle and greets them with a welcoming: "Aloha, my name is Makini. It means wind, as in that's how I drive!" Yet moving slow and deliberate he stows the baggage, takes his time getting around to the driver's seat, and carefully begins driving off the tarmac. They're on "island time" alright.

The country-side is quaint with a rustic charm. The unusual beauty apparent in its contrast, from vividly colorful and lush to forbiddingly stark due to the old lava flows. The drive is informative, as Makini shares the rich history. The land had been developed by the Hawaiian Pineapple company, later becoming more well known as Dole. Tourism and land development is very controlled, he says in a kindly voice but not so subtle warning.

He asks, "Do you know what *lanai* means? All shaking their heads negatively. "Day of Conquest" he retorts. Striking a chord with Stefen, he considers how he can conquer his daughter's pain. And could he help her recover her life?

Manele Bay Hotel is the most exquisite accommodation on the island. Set high on a bluff above the spectacular beaches of Hulopoe Bay on the southern coast. It is dotted with waterfalls and surrounded by luscious lawns. Numerous astounding gardens are filled with unusual trees and flowers.

The Great Hall is stunning with a style and grace of a country mansion that reveals Hawaii's history. The decorators had covered the walls and furnished the decor with artifacts. Fragrant blossoms are everywhere in fabulous arrays of multiple species. A tremendous amount of plumerias overflow in arrangements with ginger stalks, hibiscus, birds of paradise and anthurium showcasing colors abound. The scent is intoxicating.

The people working at the hotel offer warm and friendly greetings emphasized by their contagious smiles. It appears that check-in was prearranged because bellhops appear out of seemingly nowhere to greet them, taking their luggage and escorting them to their rooms.

"Aloha! My name is Kapena," a young man says introducing himself to Stefen and Lauren Ashlynn. As they part ways with Deirdre, he explains his name means "Captain" and assures them, "I take great pride in offering my guests an 'Aloha Welcome'!"

He leads them to an elevator and then to their spacious suite which provides a panoramic view of the Pacific Ocean. Kapena gestures for them to walk over to the French doors which are opened onto the balcony and points out to the sea.

"I would like to introduce you to our island, Kaho'olawe. It has a long and beautiful history except in World War II where unfortunately it was used as a practice bombing site by the US Navy. Recently, with help from protective organizations, it's been saved from that and the Navy has been required to return the land to 'suitable habitation'. To our left is Maui

and further out you can see the Big Island of Hawaii. Please enjoy your stay and let me know if there is anything I may do for you."

Stefen walks him to the door and says. "Thank you so very much Kapano, this is a wonderful introduction and you have already made this moment memorable for us. Aloha!" Shaking hands, Stefen presses a nice tip into Kapano's palm.

He turns to his daughter and suggests. "Why don't you take a nap? I'll wake you in time to get ready for the party."

"Okay." She acquiesces with relief. Kisses him on his cheek and makes a bee line for her chosen room. After collapsing onto the inviting bed, Lauren immediately falls into a dreaming sleep.

After a few moments Stefen peeks into her room, quietly pulls the tropical flowered throw over her, and kisses her forehead. He silently prays, *God, please help her.*

Chapter 7

Michael Desport held tickets to a charity golf tournament which he wanted to play. He flapped them many times onto his other hand, deciding what to do. He wanted to surprise Lauren and take her with him. Ever spontaneous and adventurous, he   arranged with Julie, her assistant, to reschedule her appointments and organize a few other details of the trip. It even included packing a few of her personal things, while Lauren had been out with errands so she was truly unaware of the impending surprise. He picked her up for what she thought was dinner, but to her amazement, he drove to the airport.

"We're going on an adventure!" He exclaimed. "I have a charity tourney in Jamaica, but there will be lots of time for us to play together. And play *is* the name of the game! I have collected some of your things, but mostly I want you to buy new clothes. Dressings that will help play out your fantasies. Listen Lauren", he lowered his voice to a husky whisper, "I want to have a lusty affair with you. Come away with me, My Love, and let's live a dream of mine. One that only you can satisfy, due to this insatiable craving I have for you."

A smile only lovers share was her answer. He beamed and held her hand. They both felt completely alive, excited and fully absorbed in each other.

"Nothing like this has ever happened to me before. No one has ever given me such a surprise! Michael, thank you."

As they checked in, she discovered the resort was designed for intimate experiences. Each bungalow was distinctive in that privacy was of the utmost importance. Private terraces were a common characteristic. Tropical plants and flowers were seen everywhere. Inside, mosquito netting draped the lavish bed making it look romantic. The walls and surrounding opened windows were of white and pastel colors which created a cool, inviting and welcoming atmosphere.

She should have been tired as a result of the long redeye flight, but instead she was invigorated by the mysteriousness of the beautiful hotel and her budding romantic rendezvous. Excitement pulsed through her while she made her way to the resort shops as Michael went off to check with his agenda.

She was curious and found herself attracted to different types of clothing than she would normally be drawn toward. Outside of her proverbial box, she bought items she had only previously fantasized about wearing. Michael had helped her come alive, causing her guarded and quiet demeanor to dissipate. She began to experience a surprising fervor that was bubbling up, she never thought she could unlock the passions she now felt.

She returned to the bungalow with her packages, and found his note:

Your Lover wants you for dinner at 8pm

She stared at it, her lips parted for the very taste of him. Her body stirred for the warmth of him and her flesh ached for the feel of him.

Lauren decided on the fine blue dress that would accent her luscious breasts and small waist. The thought caused a mischievous smile to play about her lips as her inflamed desire smoldered. She stepped into a long, cool shower.

The late February day developed into a hot and sultry night. When she stepped into the sleek, shimmering long garment, her body was already warm to the touch. She sprinkled 'fairy dust' on her braless chest and about her spaghetti strapped shoulders. The saleslady had assured her it was an island potion for true love. Her hair was pinned up with curled tendrils barely kissing her long exquisite neck. She wore towering glass heeled slippers which would allow her to meet his burning eyes.

He watched her as she walked into the entrance of the outdoor restaurant. He looked delighted in how she commanded everyone's attention. Michael took in her beautiful body and had begun to undress her with his eyes as she glided toward him. He could sense that she was naked under the sapphire dress and was intrigued at the sight of her, she seemed otherworldly as if she were alighted of blue phosphorus.

Not one to be taken off guard, he regained his composure and reached for her hand. He removed his white Panama hat with his other hand, bowed, and said, "Good evening M'Lady".

Then he kissed her hand, as their audience watched in awe. The kiss was unlike anything she had ever felt, it melted her completely. She felt utterly hot to the touch, inflamed by the slightest sensation of his tongue. She stood still and admired this man of her desires. He was impeccably dressed in complete white. From his striking hat to his white shoes. He wore a double breasted, linen suit, white shirt and tie. His tanned skin and coal black hair made his eyes glimmer as though they were composed of emeralds.

Michael escorted her to the dance floor and they came together as one. Closer than she thought possible, he began to gently press her body to adjoin his. He held her waist, and moved his other hand ever slowly down to surreptitiously caress her voluptuous derriere. As they moved to the low rhythm of the conga drums, she felt his leg between hers. It allowed the slit of her dress to creep even higher up her hip.

They floated across the floor in their own silent reverie. Lust and pure love pumped through their blood streams. She held her own by devouring him with her eyes, and every so often kissed his freshly shaven, manly face with her tongue. Her hands caressed his hair and neck as her body whispered her intended wishes to him.

The other guests watched them, but the couple were totally unaware. He effortlessly maneuvered her across the floor

that gave her the feeling of flight. She only noticed the twinkling lights above them and slow rotating fans as he dipped her under the enchanting palm thatched roof. They could feel a subtle breeze that emphasized the moisture on their hot bodies.

The music stopped for a moment. Michael used the break to lead her to the beach. She followed pausing for only a moment to slide her sandals off. The night was deeply dark except for the spectacular array of stars. A full moon just started to peer out from the horizon and create mysterious shadows along the waters of the sea. When they reached the privacy of their secluded area off their terrace, he began to undress her.

This time it was for real, unlike earlier with his eyes. He peeled the dress down, and started an endless discovery of amatory pleasures. He became aware of the scents floating on her luscious skin and how her entire being sparkled under the rising moon's seductive lighting.

Michael continued to explore her with his exploratory tongued kisses. His lips found hers eventually, and she set in to remove his tie. Then she undid each button of his shirt gently. Slowly, she taunted him with the slowness of undoing them one by one.

The night was steamy, the moon rose higher and his raw sexuality made him struggle with the anticipation aroused from her caress. He clawed at his jacket to remove it and then ripped off his shirt, while kicking off his shoes. After he tore at and finally removed his trousers, he was led back to

Lauren's fevered smile and vibrant eyes that seduced him with magic.

This man that was usually a gentleman transformed into a lusty rogue. He pushed her down onto the cool grass. She grasped for his protruding manhood. His long starved passion seized control of his body. He found her open and eager to comply with his every move. Her mouth was hot to the touch as he jammed his tongue into hers. His eyes flared with hunger. The soft, pale peaks of her breasts brushed his strong chest, tormenting him with the sweet ecstasy of it.

She was consumed and controlled by the weight of his body. His tongue was like a flame that filled her hungry mouth. Her whole being throbbed with every wet, hurried search of her. The heat took her breath away and set her heart on a wild race within the cavity of her chest. Her hands pressed upon his muscular back then urgently groped and pushed down on his tight buttock muscles to get more of him.

His breath sucked in through clenched teeth as he plunged into her readied wetness with the bold thrust that forged them together as one. The insatiable lust made them both greedy for more. It became a daring and frenzied search for fulfillment. They twisted and devoured each other with a rapacious longing. Lifted ever higher on the crest of their passion rhythmically, they rode the waves of desire.

Ever so slowly they descended to the sweetness of their love. Michael propped his arms at her side to cup her cheeks, peered into her lazy eyes, "I love you," he breathed.

Gazing at each other, they shared a contentment that blended them in a balmy after-glow. Michael slowly slid out of her to unwind their bodies that sparked heady vapors of their love making. Sensations nearly overwhelmed their senses as the cascading moonlight languidly sparkled their sweaty shimmering naked bodies.

Michael moved to gently kiss her glistening lips, eventually moving up to trace the lines of her brow with his tongue, while she sighed a dreamy sigh. In response, she threaded her fingers through his thick hair and pulled his handsome face nearer to her own. She pressed her lips to his, and demanded. "Feed me".

He enveloped her mouth with his, held her close and felt the sensual waves again, shaken from their intimacy. "You want more?" He questioned in a raspy voice.

"Yes. No. I really want food! And you later!" She felt his heat, but was determined to be fed real food. She entwined their fingers, and pulled him up from his knees to navigate him toward their suite.

Yet Lauren caught a glimpse and fell enraptured by the moon-shone sea. She turned him toward it and together they were awestruck as they faced the sea. It felt like a ceremonial encounter of their combined love and lust. They stood side by side, pressed unreservedly to each other in the glowing orb's light.

They walked to the water's edge, dipped into the moonlit sea. The whole world shone just for them. Michael looked into her eyes and announced. "You have given me the

moon Lauren, now let me give you Heaven.   I love you completely. Will you marry me, Lauren Ashlynn, my love, My True Love?"

As if The Universe heard, the silvery lit river from the bright orb shimmered the water in a firework display.   They splashed in the sparkles of moonbeams and submerged their hot bodies in the soft waves. They then stood still once again in reverence, held hands in their commitment of love and gratitude in their here and now of time.

Lauren whispered and squeezed his hand. "Yes, a thousand times yes!" Struck by the magic of their adoration of each other, the shining water and moonbeams, she turned to kiss him. It was a kiss of deliberation, sealing their love. "I love you Michael Desport, my True Love!"

She enjoyed the freedom in the water and she loved the sparkles of the moonlight. She loved being naked with him and so in her glee, splashed him. Then when she turned to face the shore, it occurred to her, "Michael, what if we're seen?"

"No worries, it's completely private here!" He played with her sopping wet hair.

"How?" She pressed him.

"Shush, it's all taken care of.   Now let's feed that other appetite of yours!" He took her hand and playfully led her to their room. Fresh towels and robes were on their veranda to dry off.

She felt completely relaxed, content and happy. They wrapped the cool linens around themselves and walked into the suite to find that he had pre-ordered a late supper for them. It was a succulent presentation of Jamaican favorites and champagne chilled on ice. A sensual, romantic atmosphere was created with hundreds of candles lit throughout the patio and suite.

The lovers ate heartily, laughing and with a continued playfulness with one another. They fed each other from the array of ackee and salt fish, shredded beef, jerk chicken, rice and plantains. They sipped their champagne and relished in each other's company.

Finally satiated, Lauren stood up, took his hand and led him into the candle lit bathroom. She let her robe fall to her feet and tantalized him with her mysterious smile. There was a feistiness that bubbled up in her as she beckoned him into the shower.

Michael was enthralled with the entirety of her beauty. Under the refreshing water, she created suds of slippery pleasures, smoothly scrubbing all over his brown body. They shared in the delight of the clean fun, as it was a cool respite from the hot summer night. As they slathered each other with the suds they were led to become enraptured with passion once again.

Spent for the second time, they toweled each other off and climbed through the gossamer lace that enclosed the bed and collapsed.

The morning light peeked through and awakened Lauren from a restful sleep. She looked upon her spectacular man, and murmured her love of him. Michael wore his sensitivity as well as his sensuality, that made him ever so easy to look at.

She slipped out of bed so as not to awaken him. After she readied herself for the beach, she wrote him a note:

Meet me at the beach...I'm starved!

She walked through their private area off the suite's terrace and sure enough, as he had assured her, it was a completely secluded beach. In the daylight, she collected her bearings, and saw it was unusual in that a small cove was surrounded by a tropical marsh. Lauren noticed the soft sounds of a waterfall and the warm, joyful warbling of the birds.

She hadn't remembered ever seeing an ocean look as beautiful. It was an opalescent green that sparkled as if fairies danced on the surface. Crystals of spray gleamed on the crests of the short waves that invoked arrangements of rainbows. She was struck with reminisces of last night's encounter in the moonlight that danced and alighted her wetness.

Lauren found her perfect spot. She laid her towel upon the warm, soft sand, and removed her brightly colored sarong to reveal her new, stunning white bikini. Thonged in its cut, complimented her small round derriere and sleek, softly golden-skinned body. As she applied an oiled sunscreen it enhanced her sense of sensuality.

She soaked in the rays of light, it didn't take long to doze. At some point she was startled when she felt something tingle on her warmed body. Looking into the sun, she could barely make him out. He cupped sand along her stomach, he outlined the shape of her suit. She laughed as it tickled her and enjoyed his playful nature. His sprinkle of a leprechaun spirit warmed her soul.

Quickly, however, his look changed into one of raw desire, which so often did with the mere thought of her. He scooped her into his strong arms, held her close to him and carried her away into the marsh. Gently, he laid her upon the cool surface of the waterfall pool. The slight ripples kissed her steamy skin and he began to softly wash her.

Lauren's body was immediately responsive to his every touch. Their shared sultriness was an incredible match for one another. It was as though their intuitions were the only needed communication. Just the thought of him induced her wetness. Nothing or no one could compare. She felt complete, alive, sexual and filled with utter joy.

He leaned over her to kiss her. She parted her lips in anticipation. His salty, strong tongue took her through the waves of pleasure and passion once again. Michael gathered her to him again, this time laying her down on the soft moss beside the pool. With such delicate love did he remove her bathing suit. His eyes glistened as her bare breasts were revealed. He nibbled at her hardened, pink stones as his hands roamed her cooled skin.

Their bodies became interlocked. They felt the waves of love and joy melt their souls into one. Their hearts full of

total committed intimacy, they created unconditional love. Their search finally over...

Chapter 8

"Lauren. Lauren wake up. Honey, it's time to get up. The party is in an hour." Stefen carefully wields her from a deep sleep. "You were really dreaming deep. And you had the most beautiful look about you. You were smiling, Lauren. Actually smiling!"

"Yes, Dad. I was dreaming of Michael. It was a time when there was magic in the air. So beautiful, so alive, oh..." Realizing her waking reality, begins to sob into her hands.

Stefen sits next to her, pulling her hands into his own, making space for her to continue. She goes on amid hiccups and convulsive crying. "Everything I touched was a wonder. And if there was a problem, I just took care of it. With him, I had such hope for life. I was never a romantic before him, and then once I met him I believed. I found such a complete comfort within myself."

She went on, "I found beauty and passion there too because he helped me see things differently, me differently. Oh Dad, how am I going to live without him? How can I even function anymore? There was so much more to life than surviving. It was an acceptance of reality, even my biggest fears began to disappear. I discovered what it was to be alive and live and trust. I mean really living to the hilt. Just like he'd say. I

know I was good for him too, we were going to be married, Dad." She covered her face again, sobbing.

Stefen holds his daughter tight, patting and rocking her, "I know Honey, I know."

Finally a bit calmer, she lifts her head to kiss him on the cheek. "Thanks Dad. I love you. I'll get ready now."

"Oh Darling Girl, I love you. Take your time, we can be fashionably late!" Smiling, he tries to lighten the mood for both of them.

Lauren makes her way to her fully appointed and impressive bathroom. Tropical wallpaper and sparkling fixtures anoint a massive room. Looking into the walled mirror, she addresses the reddened face staring back at her. It dawns on her, she has a lot to do to make herself presentable. She had awakened too fast, causing the continued jittery feeling. It makes sense figuring the emotional stress of late, and *that* dream, if you want to call it that. At least Dad is a comfort. Lauren knows he's trying to get her out and about to get her mind off...but why this party and *her?* "Pray tell, why does this woman keep coming into my life?" She asks her reflection.

Lauren takes a quick shower and applies makeup to cover her blotchy face. There isn't much she can do about the dark circles under her eyes, so she adds a dark eyeshadow, nice rouge and coral lipstick to make for an island easy look and hopes she can pull it off. Readying fairly quickly to accompany her father, they make their way downstairs to find the party.

. . . .

"That kid sure has it bad. Michael was a great guy, I cared for him, had a lot of fun with him. I even understood that confounded airplane of his, because he enjoyed it so much. But that poor Lauren. It's really a shame." This is all Deirdre Kennsington would say on the matter if anyone were to ask her.

Anything more means she is getting soft. Mainly because she is everything Lauren is not. Deirdre has never had a need for women friends in her life, they are only competition. Lauren would be no different, despite the feeling of strange familiarity Deirdre feels about her.

Deirdre isn't one for love either. Fun is another thing entirely, and she cherishes that. But to love someone, anyone, would be death for her. She knows this for a fact, and keeps it that way, with emotional isolation being her whole life story. Besides, even if she did slide into a committed relationship, she knows she would be hurt and have to leave him first. Relationships with men are temporary. Use the fun up, then get out. Her stepfather did that and it worked well for him. It was working just fine for her too.

Despite fears, denials and the scare tactics used on her years ago, it's tedious how those old patterns resurface from time to time. Then they break down and fall apart. If she'd allow the soft side of her to open up, it would cause a desperate search for kindness, love and respect in all the wrong places.

"Damn, I've worked too hard to get here. Nothing is going to break down that wall again. No bubbles coming to the surface, no onion layers being pulled off. All that psychological horseshit. I'm not going for that mental warfare again. Forget it. DO YOU HEAR ME?" She realizes she's yelling at her beautiful reflection in the mirror.

Continuing the cycle seems most compelling, and certainly safest for her firmly established emotional walls. Although BT O'Reilly could be considered breaking the rules for, it just isn't worth it. Besides, she owes Michael. She muses. "Damn, he never returned my call that day. He wasn't supposed to fly."

Calming herself, taking deep breaths, her mind begins calculating. *Sure BT is a great guy. And that Lauren definitely needs her mind elsewhere. So let me see what I can do for those kids. I know Michael would approve. Yes, I do believe this new plan will work nicely! Well then, let me get ready for my little social experiment!*

Chapter 9

A flock of birds were startled as he pulled up sharply to miss them, and ultimately had to turn to bypass them completely. The descent was faster than usual now. But he was good. Go around.....NO, I'm right here, it's OK, his thoughts echoed in the cockpit. "TOO SLOW...TOO SHARP...What's wrong? NO CONTROL, shouting out loud. DAMN IT. I've stalled it. Pull up. PULL UP", screaming at the airplane. Suddenly the nose pitched downward, too low to recover, memories flashed through his mind...Lauren, Lauren, I will never leave you. He knew, he knew this to be true.

BT O'Reilly awakens with a start, his flesh cold and clammy. It's always the same. The same damn nightmare, over and over again. It all started with his 'close call'. After he almost met his maker, he decided he would make life precious. During the last investigation he conducted, he had come so close to that SOB, only to lose him in the ambush.

These nightmares, he muses out loud. "They're damned incomprehensible. Being a pilot, I'm not a PILOT. And who the hell is Lauren?" Looking in the mirror, muttering to his disheveled and raw stress of a face, "I do believe mister, you're half a quart low."

The dreams are taking their toll on a man that always has had a strong sense of himself. Questioning his sanity and

sense of self constantly, just isn't his way. And to wonder if he is even in his own body, feeling distant and lost most of the time is nearly existential.

He stomps into the shower, hoping to clear the cobwebs from his mind. But it is difficult to shake the eerie feeling of being outside himself. He is gradually beginning to accept that the accident may have done more damage than he thought, dislodging his firm grip on reality and weakening his resilience. Maybe he needs to get out and have some fun in his life.

Deirdre had always provided that excitement in the past. Being with her would help him forget the insanity. *It will be good to see her again.* Remembering her sexy voice and voluptuous body is enough distraction for any man to forget his troubles. He needs a beautiful commotion in his world right about now.

He recalls with pleasure a time she created a disturbance, and his police buddies were beside themselves lusting after her. It had been a hot day out on the golf course and with all the betting and competing, he had one of his best rounds ever due to her.

Everyone knew immediately who she was, the famous actress who had a reputation for crazy stunts. She was looking for her ball in the shared rough, between the paralleled fairways. Her attire, skimpy as it was, caused a bawdy reaction from the men. She wore a white tank-top that stopped at her midriff. The shirt strained to cover her breasts, while the shorts clung closely to her voluptuous

derriere. The material was paper thin and soaked with the day's heat, showed off her extreme naked sexuality.

She beckoned the boys over to help her, and couldn't help notice the distinctive man that didn't follow them.

"O'Reilly, why the hell didn't you go over? Man, that babe is one hot tooo-maato!" Whistled his pal, Aaron.

The others chimed in with their bird calls and bragging. They got autographs and embroidered new stories to tell to the others at the precinct. Their attention for the game was lost after that, only their mounting tales and beer mattered.

BT could only shake his head and chuckle at them. He finished his excellent game, but it wasn't the same beating them like he did. Although he was awed by her, it was a game to him, just like golf. He just brushed it all aside. And so after the '19th hole', they all parted.

As he climbed into his car, she suddenly appeared at the driver's side window, startling him. And he wasn't a man to be startled easily. She spoke into his large whiskey hued eyes, and said very closely. "I hope your game went well."

"The best. Yours?" He recovered quickly.

Deirdre Kennsington had changed into a conservative but still flattering suit made of   crisp linen, it was sleeveless and short. She was incredible alright, sexy and charming, but almost too beautiful. The voice though, that's what got him, deeply husky. Her demeanor made it obvious that she was used to getting what she wants.

"Oh my, I am only just learning. I don't know much about it!" She explained.

"Well, I have to tell you, I won a lot of money because of you!" BT settled into his seat, adjusted the rear view mirror to distract himself from her.

"That's great. Then you wouldn't mind buying me dinner to celebrate your winnings." Without asking she crossed in front of the hood slow and deliberate, not taking her eyes off him and climbed into his car. With her coyest smile, she added. "Would you?"

Feeling feisty, he shot back with his deep-dimpled smile and decided to drive to his favorite hamburger stand. He hoped he could catch her off guard and have some fun with her. But the joke was on him. She only laughed and took it in stride. They took their bag of food to a nearby park, told stories and enjoyed each other's company. She was down to earth and funny. The star status persona he assumed she possessed was nowhere to be found.

He drove her home and walked her to her door. She smiled up at him and said, "You are a very attractive man. Confident and a definitely take charge person. I do like all that in a man."

"Thank you very much." He found himself a bit chagrined, she had so many different facets that fascinated him. He asked if they could sit together for a moment on her porch swing.

They sat and swung and she confessed to him that she had seen him before. She told him her tale. "I happened to be at a stop light behind a car of ogling gals swooning over you! You gave them quite the flirty smile! Then you peeled away when the light changed, leaving them awestruck. They went nutty! Whistling and carrying on. It was so funny, even after I honked at them, I realized what intrigued me the most, was the way you wore your sunglasses. They were stylishly propped ever lightly at the end of your adorable nose."

Slightly embarrassed by the flattery, he smiled his toothy grin.

Deirdre asked if he wanted coffee, and he didn't want the impromptu date to end so they went inside. She busied herself preparing the coffee while he slid on his sunnies. He realized already that he liked making her laugh, so when she chided him about wearing them inside and at night, he casually replied, "hey when you're cool, the sun always shines!"

They drank their coffee and BT reluctantly bid her good night. She walked him to the door and took his large hand into hers. At that, he bent down to kiss her on the cheek.

"I sure do like you. Good night." She spoke the words furtively, like someone would find out even though they were alone.

. . . .

O'Reilly looks deeply into his own image in the mirror, struggling with his tie. Remembering that he did at one time feel confident and in charge. Lately, however, he isn't sure of much anymore. Unfortunately now, it's only a performance, this confident attitude and appearance.

"I need stability now, and I want to lower the odds of my death. Damn this tie. Damn." He sputters to the BT in the mirror.

As a man that appears to have it altogether, he is finding himself working very hard to maintain it. No one knows how hard he had worked to uphold the appearance of late. What with the book interviews, parties and his friends at the precinct. He is very much alone in the world, except for his few chosen friends and family. He's a man alone in search for peace. He needs to find contentment within.

Anticipation to see Deirdre is an exciting reprieve. He knows she wanted him, but to settle down with her, just doesn't quite feel right. Maybe things are different now, it had been awhile since they last were together. Visions of the beautiful face and exquisitely tight, yet soft body fills his mind that reminds his body of the sensations when they were together. His blood quickens and he feels rustlings of his flesh.

Quickly he forces her out of his mind, so he can at least get on his way to the party. Anyway, there will be plenty of time for that! He makes one last check of himself in the mirror, throws off the tie and heads for the door. What he doesn't know is that the commotion she started that first day he met her, will change his life, forever.

Chapter 10

Maintaining her bold resolve, Deirdre saunters into the ball room. Her arrogant, controlling bite and trigger pulse drives loud complaints to the staff around her because everything is wrong. She shouts out the orders to rearrange her soiree. As they comply, *he* walks in.

Seduction takes over for Deirdre, she is back in her element when she sees BT. Her instinctive behavior of flirting, shows him what he's used to. In a heady laugh, "Oh you, it's incredible to see you. Let me suck you all over, DahLing!"

"Yes, well. Maybe we should wait for that, at least a bit!" BT laughs and bear hugs her. Then earnestly adds, "You look incredible yourself. It's been too long Deirdre."

"Yes my darling, I know. We have to do something about that!" She wants to entice him with her tongue, and nibble at his lips like she's done in the past. Yet, she keeps with her decision and instead just holds onto his neck a little longer. When she notices over his shoulder that Lauren and Stefen arrive, an immediate pang of envy clouds her vision.

Deirdre reluctantly releases him and side-steps him to wave them over. Although vulnerability creeps in, when she sees O'Reilly's eyes on *her,* control is Deirdre's power. Her

discipline is paramount over the situation and so she stays the course. Soon, she is rewarded with the distraction of the arrival of the men's beach volleyball team.

"BT, please will you introduce yourself to my new friends that have just arrived, as I will be back after I get these boys settled!" She says while waving to the strapping young lads.

The out-of-sorts feeling from her encounter with Michael lingers longer than usual. Taking a walk along the beach would be her druthers to shake the cobwebs and attempt to stabilize herself. Yet conforming seems easier than questioning Stefen's motive about the party that he wants to use to distract her.

So, here she is, the room isn't overly large, but probably 30 people already laughing and schmoozing with each other fills the space. Looking about, Lauren and Stefen find their way in. An amazing food display with open bar shows Deidre's generous style.

"Lauren, that man. Do you know him?" Stefen motions to the tall, good looking man across the room that was very chummy with their new friend.

"Dad, why does that man look so familiar?" Lauren says taking her father's arm in defense.

"Do you know him? Because he sure seems to know you. Look at the way he's looking at you!"

"I'm not sure. What do you mean? He isn't...," her hushed tone trails off as the man approaches.

"Excuse me for using such a stupid line, but haven't we met before?" BT asks Lauren.

"That's funny. My daughter just said that about you!"

Embarrassed, Lauren elbows her dad in the ribs. "Jeez Dad." Then recognition hits, she puts the pieces together, "Dad this is BT O'Reilly, BT, my father Stefen." The two men shake hands.

Since Michael, her attitude toward men has become tolerant at best. Recovering quickly, "I believe we met some time ago at the TV studios in LA. You were being interviewed about your latest book. Are you happy with its success?"

"Thanks, it's been holding its own," he says. He snaps his fingers and declares, "You were concerned with your interview, I remember now! It went well!"

Lauren groans, "Complete stage fright was more like it. Yet, it did. Thank you for your encouraging words that day."

"Then we met at Michael's party, I'm sorry for your loss. He was a fine man." BT can't help but stare at her. He knew she was embarrassed already, and with this last comment, he wasn't helping her resolve. Although maintaining her stature is evident and this appeals to him. He wonders what other qualities of her will accumulate.

There is some kind of curious connection, a bond rather than an attraction. Not that he isn't attracted to her, he just doesn't like whatever is happening to make him so uncomfortable. As soon as he saw her standing in the

doorway just now, a peculiar familiarity began to gnaw at him. He is not sure a preservation instinct is taking hold or trepidation, either way he needs to leave.

Deirdre advances them, dripping in sarcasm, "I am sorry I left you to fend for yourselves. Are you getting along alright my darlings? I see you all have met."

"I have to go, Deirdre." BT O'Reilly pipes up. Seeing her disappointment, he says, "I'm sorry. Something has come up, regarding a case. I'll see you tomorrow?"

"No, you can't. You just got here," Deirdre pouts. She knows he means it. Something is definitely wrong, she can see it in his eyes. Although perplexed, she recovers and asks them all to join her for a round of golf tomorrow. Stefen answers in excitement, the affirmative for the both of them.

"It was nice meeting you, again, Lauren and you sir," BT says shaking Stefen's hand.

"Stefen, please. You too. I guess we'll see you tomorrow?"

"Yeah, I'll be there. Good night." He flees.

Stefen, beaming, escorts the two women to the bar. Lauren orders a tonic water with extra lime and is getting irritated with him by being so taken by Deirdre. She can't help but notice the more her Dad showers complements, the more Deirdre becomes relaxed and radiant. Proving again, this woman definitely thrives on attention.

Feeling uncomfortable and left alone as they seemingly become more captivated with each other, Lauren realizes she regrets BT leaving. He was genuine regarding Michael, which really stunned her at his mention and further is made curious why he ducks out so fast.

Lauren finds herself bewildered that she is oddly attracted to him. Actually, it's more like a weird *attached* feeling toward him. Struggling with these confusing thoughts, *What the hell is wrong with you? It's way too soon to even think about another man. Besides, Michael is still here. He'll always be here.*

Memories of him flood back to the party he set up to purposely introduce her to BT O'Reilly after she told him she had a silly crush on him. Yet today, she didn't even recognize him when she walked in the door. Such crazy tricks the mind plays.

Finally, Stefen joins his daughter, "Honey, I want to turn in."

"Dad, you looked like you were having WAY too much fun with..." Lauren says mocking Deirdre's air.

"Alright you, that's enough!"

"Oh look, I see she's replaced you already by the younger set!" He turns to see Deirdre laughing and canoodling with the men's volleyball beach team.

"Well at least it takes a WHOLE team of them to do it!" He laughs. They walk back to the room arm in arm. He loves his daughter so much and wishes his wife was as loving to

her.   Even though he would never leave her, to love someone that doesn't or maybe can't love you back is draining and difficult to handle.   "You know I love your mother. It's just that Deirdre is fun to talk to."

"Yeah sure Dad, whatever you say!"

Chapter 11

"Fleeing a party, now this is different."   BT O'Reilly is mumbling under his breath. "But then everything these days are." Normally his rule is to enjoy the company of women, be playful, but tonight, he was stricken with panic. Too many people or too much noise has never been an issue for him. This new sensation of struggling to stay calm is too strange, let alone his evasive behavior with both women.

"What the hell O'Reilly?   What the hell happened tonight? Deirdre has always been good company.   Even when she's *ON*." He continues to complain to the trade winds. During his disability, she took an extended vacation just to be with him. His family liked Deirdre as she did them, everyone got along.   She was there many times on and off for weeks. He'd been especially glad she came back to visit after his Mam had left.

"And why is Lauren so *familiar*? There's more to this feeling than from the meeting at the studio and Michael's party. Her name in the dreams. What's that all about? Now I'm talking to myself.   'As long as you don't answer yourself', Mam would say. Geez, Mam, your son is losing it."

Running on the beach usually clears his mind and he needs his body to shed the anxiety.   Therefore, he takes a few

deep breaths full of the negative ions and takes off down the beach. He has the sensation of being watched and keeps looking around but sees no one. "Get a straight jacket chum. You need it." He yells into the wind as he runs faster.

It's not just the dreams, but these 'calls' circulating in his head have been happening for a few months, not understanding the why or where they come from, their impact is something he can no longer ignore. Sometimes they are whimpers, other times angry or desperate cries. They fade in and out, all the while becoming more consistent and penetrating. When he considers these voices and examines them along with the dreams, a picture of a mental ward floats into his consciousness.

When BT was released from the hospital, his mother, Helen, took care of him in his home. She had come from Ireland, with the extended family, to be with him right after his brush with death. She stayed on to help with his therapy and recuperation after the rest of them returned home when he was finally felt to be on the mend.

Independent as he is, he soon felt suffocated and the need to be alone. Helen, strong-willed and independent herself, raised her sons to be the same. Their father certainly was. An intuitive woman, she knew it was time to go home, as she saw his fullness coming back and told him so. "You'll be just fine my son," she said as she opened the door to leave.

"MAM", BT began to protest but stopped as he felt his voice crack. Instead he bent to hug her and held onto her for a while longer than usual. She stood back and looked up at him, after ending the embrace. Helen smiled at him, and her

eyes glistened with love and pride for him. She turned away toward the awaiting taxi and departed.

As BT reminisced over their goodbye he whispered to himself, "damn she's incredible." He watched the taxi pull away. He closed the door, leaned against it and asked. "Now what?"

Later he went to the refrigerator to grab a bite to eat. And there, with her usual flair, she had packed it with labeled foods. Treats and meals galore, and he checked the freezer and pantry which he saw were filled as well. A bittersweet smile crossed his face, he felt the loneliness, for she always filled a void in his life. His Mam, a wonderful and sweet woman, with a keen mind and fantastic sense of humor; she was known as a delightful person and beloved for her practical jokes.

The one-liners were to the point, always with love and a sparkle in her eyes. There was never cruelty or sarcasm to contend with, as she considered that bad form. She pulled no punches, never lacked in fortitude and you always knew where you stood with her. Mostly due to the fact she was straight-forward and always put the proverbial cards on the table. And even though her boys grew to be much taller than her mere 48 inches high, they knew she meant business when they'd get out of line just by her look.

Her talent was especially evident with her gardens. She would plant a garden in every location they lived. He had watched vegetables and flowers come up from seedlings to full grown jungle like creations. Whether from the ground or in pots, it was a delight to behold her radiant landscape

designs.   And she used what she grew, she'd cook the vegetables and placed the flowers in special spots throughout their homes.   He always liked picking just the right ones for her.

Little did he know, the last evening she was to be there, Helen had set a sweet remembrance table for dinner. Dishtowels as napkins and lemon rinds wrapped around the candles made a useful and clever place setting. Mason jars for water glasses with lemon slices were a refreshing touch and she had an old pitcher filled with loose, leggy sweet peas for a centerpiece.   Her creative spirit was on display everywhere in the mixed colors, textures and patterns in irreverent and bold ways.   With her great style, and strong personality, enjoyment was the only rule.

....

Helen O'Reilly cherishes her sons.   As her husband often said about them both: "There is an 'Irish comfort' about these boys, my wee o'Helen".   William Patrick, her oldest, known as Wills got a sports scholarship in Los Angeles, then attended medical school.   He married the love of his life, Beth, and had children while he built a thriving practice as a surgeon.

Wills practiced there until an early retirement, then moved his family to Ireland. He bought what they like to call a small castle on Inishmore, of the Aran islands.   He became the family doctor and Beth created a little museum and library. Other than missing her youngest son, living there has been a dream come true for Helen.

She is proud of them as adults, it's profound that they grew into healthy and loving men after overcoming their father's murder. She contributes this to the families in the neighborhood that helped take care of her broken little family after the love of her life was taken. The officers and firemen made sure the boys never felt alone throughout school and sport functions.

Mac's funeral was painful for all who knew him. It was a long and moving ceremony that celebrated him as the loving and caring man, father and officer that he was. Typical of the Irish parade, police and firemen from five counties around, all had tears for Mac as they walked the route.

As she stood holding the hands of her two small boys at the gravesite, they both saluted when Mac's fellow officers did. The pain that shook through all of them would linger for years. She'll never forget BT's small face as he looked up at her and the little voice that still rings in her ears. "Mam, I'm going to get the man who took my Da away."

And truly since that day, he had been preoccupied in avenging his father's death. But as a result, he became withdrawn and into himself. His quiet nature made for being kidded a lot. He learned very young what ribbing was all about. He soon started to develop a comedic nature as a security blanket.

Helen understood it was also his way of making peace with the trauma. His development as a man started with him following Mac's chums, especially Paddy Patterson. His family, of two boys also and his lovely wife, they were a comfort. The officers were always around as part of their

family and would let BT and Paddy's boy, namesakes Paddy, ride in their police cars. The boys would hang out at the police station and eavesdrop.

BT especially loved listening to the many stories the men would tell about their unsolved cases. He always liked solving puzzles and watched mystery movies. Hence through the years, Helen watched his interest in helping others overcome adversity and solving their problems when he could. He studied hard and eventually pursued a career as a PI.

Helen has been gratified that BT had inherited the same fortitude, sense of humor and playfulness from her and Mac. These traits made him good at what he does as a professional. As a man, he is funny, charming, dynamic and charismatic. Confident, with strength of character and determination he has great instincts to do his jobs.

Despite her worry over his safety, he made a good life for himself and seemed happy and fairly fulfilled. She was thrilled when he confessed to her that he'd like to pause the PI work and write a book.

Yet after all these years later, his preoccupation with revenge nearly kills him. She had hoped his declaration as a child would never come to haunt her by placing him in danger. And yet, it did. Although retired from the business, he had received a tip related to his father's death from one of his many sources which led to an ambush.

His near death experience and the lengthy time in the coma caused much anguish for the entire family. Even now after

his recovery she continues to worry over the changes in him. They give her pause; the mood swings, night sweats and terrors with yelling, thrashing in his sleep, and night sweats. He'd refuse to share what was causing them with her, let alone talk of the incident in any detail which preceded these changes in him. His response to her is only that he can't remember. She knows better and this only concerns her further.

Helen reminds herself to be grateful that her son is still here and has become stronger through the physical injuries. But she knows him too well, and she knows he recalls the scene and is reliving it night after night in his dreams.

She prays he will seek help in restoring his peace; by clearing his mind, coming to terms with the past and letting it go.   She keeps the faith that his soul will heal.   Helen couldn't stand to lose another one of her men.

Chapter 12

"What more could a man want, O'Reilly?" Deirdre's intense fervor floods through the phone to BT, early the next morning. "It's a fine Hawaiian morning, perfect temperature and an excellent Greg Norman designed, manicured course. And I know you admire his work!

"The problem is, my darling, I have been called away. Urgent business. Would you mind terribly hosting my little golf party? Lauren so needs companionship now. You know she was to marry Michael Desport? Oh, and I'm sorry you didn't feel well last night." Drilling out her exposition stampede, not letting him get a word in. Then finally pausing for a second. "Are you better now?"

"Eh, yeah, thanks." BT mumbles, trying to keep up with her. "How did you know?"

"O'Reilly, please, I'm surprised at you! You know I know everything about you! Now, you take good care of yourself, darling. And thank you for watching over Lauren and her Dad." She signs off as quickly as she began.

Shaking his head at this verbal tornado, he sighs with the usual smile he always has for her. She was at her apex when she was in control and did so with a flair, today she

was definitely on point. As he often ponders when contemplating her, there doesn't seem to be much substance and a resistance to letting him get to know her as a real authentic woman is always present. He could never get in, so to speak, and this is what he feels is missing most about her.

BT makes his way to the club house to meet the Ashlynns. Over a light breakfast and coffee, a rousing bet and bantering starts between BT and Stefen. Lauren is happy they are hitting it off so well, giving her a chance to sit back and observe them. And she secretly is ever so glad Deirdre canceled her appearance even though Lauren was ready to take on the contentious atmosphere she brings especially after her welcomed deep sleep. Perhaps there is something to her dad's resolve to change up her routine.

Sipping her coffee, she offers. "Why don't you boys ride together? I'll have more fun watching you two from afar!"

They mock their astonishment at her remark. She smiles and they all laugh. This begins an alliance that none of them will ever regret.

Lauren finds herself having a good time. To laugh and enjoy something while still in this moment of grieving, is certainly different for her. On the fourth hole, a par five, she hits a long drive.

"Maybe 220, eh Pardner? Looks like she outdrove you again! You better get on the stick, Boah!" Stefen chides BT.

"Yeah, yeah. But look, it's in the rough!" BT teases back at him.

Lauren laughs at them, gets in her cart to look for her ball. Waving off the men's offer to help her, she tracked the ball just past a huge boulder, in a cluster of trees, off to the right of the fairway. She steps out of her cart and immediately is struck by a familiar scent. It is Michael's. At once her eyes tear.

At first, after he passed, it startled her and sometimes even angered her. It meant she had to deal with the pain and loss all over again. Other times she'd be dismayed, like now, no one has been around this area for some time, yet she smells *his* scent.   From where and how? Whatever the answer, it's been damn puzzling and raises questions in herself, like, is she going crazy?

On the other hand, the frequent scents had oddly started bringing on comfort. Sometimes she even allowed herself to feel consoled knowing he is with her.   The dreams and memories can make her feel that way too. She's gradually adjusting to the realization that no one can replace him and the fact that grieving is a process. She hopes strength and contentment will come. Her goal is to function as a healthy human being, rather than experiencing life as mere surviving.

Besides today, time seems to be on her side.   Lauren likes golf; it can be soothing, even relaxing. Having a flair for the game, she finds herself doing better when she doesn't try. Getting out of her own way, with the beauty of outdoors surrounding her and her mind distracted, it's allowing for a

good game. It also gives her time to ponder the similarities of these men.

She's curiously drawn to the man playing with her father. Speculating about him last night, while she still struggles with her feelings for Michael, causes her to question her loyalty to him. And oddly, somehow they are quite similar. Even the scent is indeed similar to BT's.

Finding the ball in a small clump of pili, a tropical bunching grass designed to make the rough rougher, she addresses the ball with her five iron. Changing her mind, she exchanges it for her pitching wedge. Scooping the ball out onto the fairway within chipping distance to the hole. This impresses the men as she makes par with a two putt.

BT keeps his distance from Lauren. He is unfailingly polite, enjoys her company, and conduct of the game from afar. Although he keeps her in his sight, he does not approach her. Instead, his interaction with Stefen is genuine, and makes for a good time and distraction. Playing it safe is odd because he never felt timid approaching a woman in his adult life. Still this woman is perplexing him, and the added feelings of a strong sense of familiarity is making for a blossoming attraction.

Hole Number 15 is a par four. BT hits a straight-away drive. He pitches it up and the ball goes into the hole for an eagle-two. He leaps up and does an Irish jig, cheering. Stefen cheers and slaps him on the back. The men are exuberant, exchanging shouts of exhilaration and carrying on.

Lauren stands transfixed.   Her thoughts race back to Michael making the same exact gestures. The same yelps and the same sparkles in his eyes. Finally steeling herself, she advances and collects herself at the next hole. When they catch up to her, she bolsters herself and steps up to BT in a congratulatory manner and exclaims.   "Great shot. There's one for the Irish!"

BT is laughing and continuing the bit, says in a brogue. "Yes'm, but that shot was the luck 'o thee Leprechaun! How 'bout ye? 'ave ye a bit o'thee Irish too?"

Feeling haunted by this deja vu and casting about for a desperate and believable recovery, she forces out. "No, but I wish I were." With this, she looks straight into his eyes and they bore into her very soul. It is a look of intimacy and it's just what Michael would do.   He had done it to her many times before.

Breaking the stare, BT regains his control with a blush. "Umm, I'm sorry for that display.   I've never done that before. I don't know what got into me."

Stefen watching the strange encounter begins slapping him on the back again to alleviate the tension. With that, BT snaps back into laughing, exclaiming. "But then I never had an eagle before!"

"I was going to say!"   Stefen declares and magnanimously gestures to BT to ready his turn at the tee-box.   As he addresses the ball, Stefen stands leaning on his driver, silently chuckling at the beauty he witnessed and marveling

at the pure joy of when shots like that happen. Lauren sits in her cart bewildered, waiting for the men to tee off.

The rain begins on the seventeenth fairway. The delightful Hawaiian 'pineapple juice' makes them all laugh. For Lauren, it feels like a washing away of all her troubles and anxieties. Most main-landers would run for cover, but the three of them continue on their game with joy. It's Invigorating to them, and soon concludes a fun and eventful day on a spontaneous and adventurous note.

After the game, they have a lot to talk about at the "19th hole". The good and not so great shots, the incredible course, and the rounds of beer brought on more teasing. Relaxing and eventually enjoying an excellently prepared meal together also makes for a growing mutual admiration within the trio.

Or so Lauren thought. Because as they walk back toward their rooms BT abruptly bids them good night. She is finally relaxed and wants to keep the evening going. As she starts to protest, he graciously thanks them and leaves. It was as if he couldn't get away fast enough. Lauren is disappointed, wanting a night-cap and even a walk along the beach with the two of them.

She and Stefen are both confounded. Then Stefen surmises. "Maybe he realized the time and had a date to call Deirdre. Oh well, that sure was a fun day. And you, it was grand to see you laugh so much!" He hugs her as they walk toward their suite.

"Dad, I'm not tired. I'm going for a walk." Lauren announces as Stefen turns to their suite.

"Alright Honey, enjoy the night air. It's good to see your energy alit!"

"Thanks Dad. I do feel too invigorated to sleep. And Dad, thanks for insisting and making this trip happen. It's been interesting, weird but good too. I know you wanted me to have a change up. I think it's working. So many emotions to work through, I'm glad we're together." With that they hug their goodnights.

She makes her way to the property line overlooking the ocean. Leaning on the rail, the fresh sea air on her face, she is awed by the charge of the waves. Their power lashing at the beach below with intermittent crashing, causing magnitudes of thunderous noise.

It frees her mind to marvel at how she actually had a good time today. Despite the ups and downs of many emotions, she is happy that she made her way through them. Plus, it's only been a short time since the funeral, *It's safe to say I'm okay, at least for today. Or, should I be feeling guilty? I don't want to feel guilty or wrong anymore.*

If this day has taught me anything, golf is so much like life, that good can still happen even when it doesn't seem or appear to be so. Which brings me to what's with the confusing, intriguing, and radical mood changes of one Mr. BT O'Reilly?

As if on cue, she sees him below. He is standing at the shore-line. Lauren cups her hands and yells, "hey you..." and waves at him.

Two men approach her. Mumbling, obviously drunk. "Hey purdy laaaydy, we wanna partay with yooouuu!" Each one grabbing an arm, not giving her a chance to react, they quickly lift and whisk her off her footing.

She struggles and tries to break away. Lauren screams, "NOOOO..."

They tighten their grip on her. A hand clamps over her mouth and one sneers. "Hush little thing, we got you. We're taking a little ride."

Desperate, with the ocean pounding and the black of night, did he hear to turn and see her?

....

Rooted in the sand, BT O'Reilly hears what sounds like a woman yelling. Looking around, he sees no one and shakes it off to the ocean noise. He decides it's the damn clamoring again and turns back to the sea. Then he feels the wind shift and hears a different yell. This one is long, fearful and very loud.

There's no denying it this time, because he feels a shudder of terror run through him. Running in the direction, he reaches the hotel's parking lot, and hears a car engine racing. He peers through the darkness and is helpless to

watch two burly men pushing what seems to be a woman into the trunk of a car.

The car speeds off with no lights. He takes off for the lobby, wishing he was able to make out the license plate, let alone the make of the car. Rushing inside, BT orders the gal at the desk to call the police. He picks up a different phone behind the desk and calls his friend, the chief of police on Oahu on his personal cell phone.

O'Reilly is unsettled. Incidents like this always are difficult when witnessed. The subdued lighting around the hotel makes for a lovely ambiance but impractical for security. He was made aware of the safety record of the place, nothing violent has ever happened according to the distressed receptionist.

Preparing to give his statement, he doesn't have much to tell the police as the sirens are heard by all. But there's more, something beneath the shudder he felt is still gnawing at him. He decides to call Stefen to make sure they are both alright. His jaw drops seeing Stefen's agonized look running into the lobby.

"Have you seen her? O'Reilly, I can't find her anywhere." Stefen pants out.

"What? Catch your breath. Lauren? Where was she?" BT asks rapidly.

Still winded, he says, "She took a walk after we said good night. I started to get ready for bed, then had a bad feeling.

I went looking for her. I heard a car screeching out of the parking lot, then sirens. Now I'm really worried."

"Look Stefen, the security guards are here, the police are arriving, we will check the beach. We'll find her." BT tries to reassure him.

"Why are they here, what happened?" Stefen asks, agonizing.

"I, I saw, I think it was a woman being put into the trunk of a car." BT allows at last.

"Oh God. No, this can't be." Stefen stifles a cry. "It was her, wasn't it? I know it was her. Damn it, why? What's going on?"

"Man, I didn't see. I'm only guessing…" BT is interrupted as police officers race into the growing crowd of the lobby. Concerned guests gather as the hotel staff try to calm them. The security team confers with the police.

Chapter 13

It was a huge hangar at the Santa Monica airport. He was told he couldn't miss the brand new Piper Malibu. It was easy to see, even in the dim lighting. He strode in like he belonged there, mimicking the famous actor in his usual dress and stride.

Aviator sunglasses and ball cap lowered, he headed for the water cooler because across the way, a few mechanics stood around admiring the beautiful, sleek airplane while they drank their coffee. He took a long drink to avert them. When they glanced over, he waved in acknowledgement at them.

"She sure is a looker, Mr. Desport!" One of the men shouted out. The imposter gave a two finger salute, tapped them at the brim of his hat in response to them and took another drink. Finally they dispersed and he made his way to the plane.

"It's a damned shame to send such a beauty into the ground," he whispered to her. After putting on his gloves with a sincere gesture of respect, he ran his hand along her side, all the way to the tail section.

He began his work by removing the cover plate of the elevator rigging. He found an inner cable of the strand grouping. He scraped it enough to weaken but not cut completely through, so as not to be noticed at the pre-flight inspection that would be required before take-off. The manipulation would severely weaken the entire directional system while in the air but not cause an issue when leaving the ground.

He popped the plate back in place and left.

Chapter 14

"I want you out of there NOW.   They're not pranks anymore." Joe Kenny demands.

Deirdre's personal detective startles her enough to leave the islands in a hurry.   He explains the threats on her life are mounting and are much more serious than she took them for.

"I've arranged a plane to pick you up in an hour, be there and I'll pick you up at O'Hare.   And before you ask, I've already arranged for your luggage to be packed and sent here later." He instructs.

Breaking her off.   "And no, I'm not discussing this with you on the phone.   Believe me when I say, it's urgent you leave. You have 30 minutes to make the plane."

Before she can speak, he hangs up.   No one hangs up on Deirdre Kennsington, ever.   This rattles her because she knows now he's dead serious.   She makes the call to BT acting her utmost to not sound scared in the taxi to the airport.

Joe sees her immediately being the first one off the gangway on the airport tarmac.   She is never hard to miss, attracting

attention wherever she is. He takes her arm saying. "Not here, not now," answering her questioning eyes through her large, dark sunglasses and guides her out of the private terminal.

Deirdre is not surprised to see a policeman standing next to his running car. He opens the passenger door of his classic '40s Ford De Luxe Sedan for her to get in. Rounding his pride and joy, thanks the officer and dives in. Joe puts the car in gear and accelerates while expertly managing the traffic.

He starts in after she flips her glasses off with an expectant look. "I know the cops, and I'm not letting this Beauty run without a guard."

Deirdre rolls her eyes and demands, "I know that. I know you. Joe, what's going on?"

"You and Michael have been linked in the tabloids. *Someone* assumed you'd be flying with him that day." He begins.

"Tell me something I don't know," she laments, her voice laced with sarcasm and fear.

Now it's his turn to be impatient. "Tell me again. What happened? You tried contacting Michael, right? He didn't return your calls?"

She sighs. "Yes. No. He left a message, his voice, he was so happy, he sounded so sweet. He asked why I wasn't there, 'I understand, it's ok', he said and went on to say how

much he has appreciated me and the plane. He said he was sorry he hadn't gotten back to me but that he'd explain later. 'It's really good news D!' He said." Deirdre takes a deep breath and continues, "Damn it Joe, I *was* supposed to go *that* day. But I was too tired. I bought that thing so I'd have faster and easier access. And Michael loved her so. His enjoyment amused me, so really I think I secretly bought it for him. He always referred to it as her, I guess most pilots do. Oh god, what am I going on about?" She trails off.

"Look, I found out...uh," Kenny takes her hand, deciding to give it to her straight. "There's more to the *accident*. The plane was sabotaged. Michael was murdered. You were supposed to be too."

Deirdre stares at him. Turns away. Stares at him again. For once in her life, she is speechless. They are both silent for the rest of the trip to her high-rise apartment.

Kenny knows it was time to stop. DK, speechless? This is one for the books. She needs time to digest what he just blurted out. He had had his suspicions about the so-called accident, but needed proof before he said anything. He got it.

He has also grown to like this woman very much. She is a tough cookie alright, built a hard shell to protect herself at all costs. As a result, she seems cynical and would toss off an insult, rather than show a sensitive side or give her trust to anyone. But she has with him and has grown on him out of respect.

100

Not one to be amazed by much, he is by her.   She has allowed him to delve deeply into her past and trusts him with her life. Further still, he has come to let her in as well.

Deirdre Kennsington never returns confidences or accepts help, let alone cry. And at this moment he can tell she is fighting to not break out in sobs.   He knows if it were an acting part, she would have no trouble. But it isn't, so she's speculating how this can be real.

Kenny had been warning her for months, she didn't take the pranks seriously. But now he says they are real, that he has proof, and she finally believes him.   He has grown on her and she has learned to trust him during their time together. This is rare indeed, yet down deep she knew that day.

She learned long ago that to show vulnerability would ultimately be accompanied by rejection.   So she constantly needed to prove to herself, as a strident woman. The acting and performing became her perfect vehicles in her private and public lives.

However when it came to him, curiosity had gotten the best of her.   Ever since she had done the remake of Merle Oberon's vehicle, "The Scarlet Pimpernel", research of the period piece generated interest in her own family history. She tried to obtain her adoption papers and begin the long tedious detail work of uncovering her past. Stumped early in the search, ultimately only motivated her more.   Because strangely enough, it was looking like she was never born.

Diligently working at controlling everything, including being a perfectionist in every situation, is what has made her a fine

actress. But as a woman, cold and bitter. The irony of course, unless a give and take would be developed on her part, an emotional security could never be achieved. Many times she had the opportunity to let her guard down with Joe. But she would stop short. She found it safer to make her past the only liberty in her strict world. She was however glad she had convinced him to help her.

The day she walked into his office was a reprise of a Bogey flick. Ever dramatic, her intent was to get his attention and she had Bacall down. She heard he had a flair for the past, did her research on him and pretty much knew he was the one for the job. Her dedicated type of prep work made it unlikely she would be outdone or surprised, yet what she saw behind the old mahogany desk did just that. So astonished by his dapper expression of attire and office, she found herself tongue-tied.

Joe Kenny, a strapping man probably late thirties, sat in the old wooden swivel chair with his feet on the desk. She could tell he had a lean physique under his ever worn hat on head. The soft blue button down shirt was undone to the third. He wore his silk brown wide tie loosened with suspenders attached to the brown tweed pants. Still, what she liked the best was that his worn brown trench coat draped across the chair in front of her.

The man and the scene was complete, it was like an old time movie set. The office was cluttered, dusty with books and papers strewn everywhere. She loved it and would come to appreciate and respect him in staying true to himself and the role of an old time Los Angeles Private Detective. For his verve in research and love of the '20s,

'30s and '40s was authentic. He lived every day in keeping with his stylish threads.

Recovered quickly and certainly not to be surpassed by anyone. "Mr. Kenny I presume?" She queried in her best Lauren Bacall drawl.

Joe Kenny stood, greeted her with a tip of his hat. "That's right. Who's asking?"

"My name is Deirdre Kennsington, your reputation precedes you! Therefore, I would like to hire you." Her role maintained.

He cleared his throat to cover his guffa. "What do you want to hire me to do?"

"Genealogy research. I want you to help me with a project."

"Family history shit isn't much of a job. And to be honest, it doesn't require a PI."

"This one does. I am willing to hire you full time for your services."

"Look Lady, I have other jobs. Babysitting isn't one of them." He figured he could up the ante. He wasn't willing to admit he didn't have enough jobs to keep him going.

Deirdre picked a stack of old newspapers off the other chair, pitched them on the floor and sat down. She dropped her acting intone and got down to business. "Look Kenny, I need your expertise. There is more here than meets the

eye. What I have found out on my own isn't much. And yet is everything...*I wasn't born.* For some crazy reason, I think I can trust you Kenny and that does not happen, EVER. I won't beg you, but I'll pay dearly for your trust, confidentiality and service. What do you say?"

"Why me?" He sat heavily in his chair, pushed his hat up, with elbows on the desk, in consideration.

"I've talked to several other PIs, your name kept coming up. I don't know what you're pulling with this old time set and costume, but..."

He cut her off. "Hey, lady, this is no set. I AM the real thing. I happen to like the style of when life was REAL. This is real. I am real."

"Alright then. I wanted to be sure. I did not mean to insult you. I'm running out of time. I have a friend that is also a PI. BT O'Reilly, you may have heard of him?"

"Yeah, so what?"

"I won't ask him for help because he is a friend. Besides, he would never take my money and I can't trust a man if he won't." She admitted.

With a quiet sincerity, Deirdre slowly continued. "And, well, issues have ensued since I began this research. The truth is, there's been a few threats, I figure they're pranks. I'm an actress you know."

"I know who you are." He said flatly.

She went on. "But my agent, he's a friend really, is very concerned. He wants me to have protection, and I've finally decided he's right. I need your help. Will you help me?"

At that he stood, put his hands on his hips and his eyes bored into hers with questions.

"I am willing to offer you 120K."

He cocked his head, quizzically.

"To start, plus expenses."

He scratched his temple and let out a low, long whistle. After a moment, with a big grin. "Whiskey?"

She answered with her dazzling, famous smile.

Joe took from a desk drawer a beautiful shiner bottle of golden liquid, an old Cubs coffee cup and shot glass in which he blew out dust. Poured the drinks and announced. "Cheers!"

Deirdre smiled slightly and made mental notes. Matching glasses, Check. Cleaning crew, Check.

Chapter 15

He took the job. He wasn't sure why, it just happened. But that's how Joe Kenny lived, *things happen* he'd always say. It started an allegiance for both of them. Both loners, both hard shelled. They worked long hours and spent a lot of time together. He learned about her life, he saw only a few times how soft and caring she could be.

Deirdre told him what pieces she could remember of her past. Pieces because they were horrible memories. She was in foster care, sent to place after place and there was always abuse. A child herself, she was worked like a slave, managed younger children, cleaned and even worked the fields. The only constant in her life was sexual abuse. Beatings were regular but the rapes came to define her life. Soon she learned to use it to her advantage.

At 14, one night she was able to escape from the latest drunk. She took a bus to Chicago with her meager treasure of collected pennies and dimes. Despite all she had been through, somehow she managed to keep them hidden from all the abusers. On the bus she picked out names from a paper tucked into the bus seat. She decided her new name would be Trixie-Dixie. TD for short. It sounded bigger than her and she liked that.

She was glad she could read a little and vowed she'd learn more. She never had proper schooling as a kid, so she had to work harder to make it happen on her own. She learned early that education was her defense against her arduous and brutal life. This forged her to read everything she could get her hands on.

Odd jobs and often prostitution provided a good living and some control over her life for a few years. She was able to stay in a tiny rented room in an elderly, blind woman's home. The woman was decent to her, so in turn TD did grocery shopping, some cleaning and errands for her.

During one of the errands, TD came across a flier for an upcoming play at the neighborhood theater. She auditioned and caught the acting bug after performing a small part and *knew* her future. The few accolades she received from it, fed the attention she starved for. And she loved it.

She decided to start acting school and realized she needed to be taken seriously. Her decision was clinched when she read an article about 'acting as if'. 'Fake it till you make it' provided the gumption to continue the long hours she put in. Her small treasure continued to build.

She was good at telling stories. TD practiced her clean versions on the landlord and began doing stand-up in a few divey places. She created scenarios from past experiences that entertained many people. The darker she would go, especially the tales of brutality that she'd make humorous, engaged her audiences. Again, she was rewarded by the laughter and applause.

These stints, along with her dedicated reading and studying helped her acting and confidence. She paid attention to all the details in front and behind the scenes, observed what actors and stage hands did. She found it all intoxicating, it stirred her soul and as a result, she became a quick study of learning the ropes of the industry.

She also collected tossed out fashion magazines, learned how to dress herself better that brought her a classier clientele. She continued to work hard at both careers. After all, the *other* one allowed her to survive. Her contrived stories, manipulations of changed appearances and names kept men from finding out who and what she was.

There were a few regulars that she allowed because they weren't the sharpest tacks in the tool box. They'd pay well for the different roles she'd play out for them. They also liked their booze and drugs, which made it easier to control them. She grew up learning how men could be with their many addictions. Therefore, she personally knew to never touch the stuff to keep herself in check with self-discipline, just so she would dominate all she encountered.

Small parts in plays continued with her latest name of Trix Quinn. One of these performances caught the attention of an agent. He procured a minor part for her in a low-budget film, this in turn ignited her burning desire to be famous. Her passion for the spotlight became an obsession.

Quinn never had friends, she didn't need or trust them. She kept to herself, and had no personal life. As far as she was concerned, there was no such thing as affection, she couldn't trust it. Her extreme fear of dependence underlined

her terror of neediness. That vulnerability, she made sure, would always be covered up. But when Louie d'Langino became her new agent, things changed.

He saw through her right away and took her under his wing. Together they changed her name to Deirdre Kennsingston. He developed her, taught her how to really dress, speak and operate her movie career. She learned to trust a man because he refused to be a dalliance, instead he became her protector and confidant.

His care was real and there was no need for her dive bar and whoredom dealings any more. As a result, he cultivated a new past life for her that the tabloids swallowed. Louie made her a star. And soon both their careers grew. He became a leading producer for major studios and delivered quality movie performances.

Together they created an invincible team, a force to be reckoned with, and known for excellent work in their chosen careers. Socially, they were the Super Star couple despite their age difference. He was the robust handsome Italian and she the auburn beauty. They always dressed to the nines when out and about, posed for the reporters and signed autographs for their adoring fans.

Personally behind closed doors, they matched each other's loneliness. Although close in every way, it was unusual that neither of them made sex a factor with each other. He had many lovers, but he never thought of Deirdre that way. She felt the same about him. Any affairs they'd have were very selective and kept secret from the press. Of course there

were the write ups of each of them *cheating* on each other, but to them, it was laughable and great publicity.

All of which, with his calculated perfection, had incited devotion for them in the many tabloids. Their finances and life-styles flourished extensively. So much so, they each bought homes in the wonderful area of Pasadena which was considered the old Hollywood area. Through the years of gone, that part of the city was inhabited by many famous actors since the twenties. They both admired the history of acting, buying and refurbishing their historical mansions was yet another common factor between them. All the while, they kept their lavish apartments in Chicago.

Louie was everything to her, which in itself was a miracle. Finally, in her life, she felt a freedom she never would have imagined. Her trust issues were still formidable, but not with him. He helped her build confidence that cultivated trust within herself. Never would she look back at her old life, because the new one he made for her, she devoured.

Yet it did come back. And Louie did not like it one bit. He knew she would get hurt from diving into it. But she was a scrapper and determined. Ever since that damn film, she started in on the research. Secretly from him at first, until he found the papers laid out.

They didn't live with each other, but were free to go back and forth to the other's places. They kept no secrets, they were each other's only confidants. So he found it odd when she started locking her study.

When she walked in on him, sitting at her desk, with drink in hand, she knew she had to confess. "It started off as a small thing. Really."

He stared at her.

"Louie, come on. Don't be like that. What harm can it do?" Deirdre bemoaned her best acting part. She knew he'd be upset with her keeping such a secret, and she was right.

He got up and strode to her, smiled as he approached and said. "You know I'll give you anything you want. But this D. It's not safe for you to go there. I have a bad feeling about this. This will only bring up bad memories and maybe even worse."

"Worse? What could possibly go wrong?" She waved it off with her hand and then put it on his shoulder to assure and convince him. "I see you're worried. I'll be careful. You know I'm careful."

"Famous last words, Doll. Famous last words."

Months later into Deirdre and Joe's research, the threats escalated. She referred to them as practical jokes and shook them off as such. Louie on the other hand, saw them as real, as if his premonitions were coming true.

"Look d'Langino, you know her better than I, she's not going to give it up. I'll do everything I can to protect her." Joe tried to assure Louie many times of his concern for her welfare.

111

"From the truth? How are you going to protect her from the truth, Joe?" He asked over and over, worried about her.

Deirdre was not going to be stopped. She took it on diligently, as if it were research for a part. She was entranced with the history and characters. Louie could not convince her to stop, so he started helping Joe with the work when his time allotted. The two became good and trusted friends as a result.

As time went on, more and more evidence piled up, it made for a ride they all did not see coming. Even in Louie's wildest premonition.

Chapter 16

"'ello!" Deirdre answers her phone, trying to keep anxiety at bay. "BT, what is it? You sound frantic." Deirdre eyes Joe with distress. Listens, then says in defeat. "Yes, I understand. Goodbye."

"What's going on?" Joe asks with dread.

Pacing in her front room and her mind racing in overwhelm, she quickly blurts out. "Alright Joe, here it is. I'm going to have a huge charity ball. We'll flush them all out. They'll have to show because it's what they have to do. The society thing is their life. Isn't it? Then we'll see who is really behind all this. Michael's death will be avenged. Damn it. I have to know who is behind this. And who the hell is trying to kill me? And why? Joe, someone has kidnapped Lauren Ashlynn. I think it was supposed to be me. I'm scared Joe. Where is Louie?"

"I know you are and I'm glad you're finally admitting it. You're right, we will get to the bottom of this. But slow down, D. He's on his way. What did O'Reilly say, exactly? Breathe. You have got to catch your breath." He holds her shoulders, shaking them for emphasis.

Taking deep breaths with eyes glistening, she looks him square and explains what had just happened in Hawaii. "BT

will keep us informed, he's got a lot of help in getting Lauren back. He doesn't know about the threats to me. He only called because he said he was worried about me leaving so quickly. I've got to tell him Joe." She says crumbling and grasping onto him in terror.

"Breathe, D. Slow down. Who is this Lauren person? And what the hell does she have to do with you?" Joe's mind reels. He does know of her because of his research. He had started a theory and he needs to work it over with Louie before he discusses it with her.

"I'm not sure. I mean she was Michael's fiancé. We met on the plane to Hawaii, I introduced her to BT. She came to my party, we were to play golf..."

"D, you're rambling again. What do you mean? Slow down." Holding her at arm's length from him.

"We were on the same floor." Continuing to look at him, her eyes glazing over. "And I guess you could say we are similar in coloring and size. Sorta. I don't know, but I have an awful feeling. I don't like it Joe. What are we going to do?"

"First off, we're not going to give into panic." He states, still holding her shoulders. "I will protect you. Louie will get us more help. Relax, Doll. You've got to relax." He bearhugs her for emphasis.

"Relax? Are you nuts?" Pushing away from him and pacing again. "You look scared too. O'Reilly is scared, I'm scared. Louie has been too ever since I started the damn research.

I should have listened to him. He told me not to do this.
Damn, what have I done? That poor woman, I could have
caused this whole thing. What the hell is happening? I
thought this was just a joke when the threats started.
Pranks, everyone gets them. But this?" She takes a deep
breath and continues.

"Lauren, what is it about her? The men, BT and Michael?
Then he's killed by mistake or not and needlessly. Joe, I'm
tellin' you, there is some kind of weird familiarity about her. A
common something with her, that I feel. Oh shit, listen to me
go on. I don't have feelings for women. Damn it, they're the
competition."

She tried to laugh it off. But couldn't help what she just
heard herself say. It was the truth. Emotional isolation had
been her whole life's story. Because it was safer than
feeling. Familiar, maybe, but deep down, she could never
be all that Lauren was, she couldn't come close. It was
happening again, the old churning of her tortured soul.
"Damn it!" She protests out loud.

Joe takes her into his arms and whispers. "You need some
rest, go lie down. I'll wake you when Louie gets here."

"Oh no...what we need is a stiff drink. Don't you keep that
special golden liquid around here?" Rummaging through her
own bar cabinet, and announces. "Found it!" She gets out
two crystal glasses and begins in a high pitched hysterical
voice. "Do you remember our first encounter? Ha!" She
downs her first, handing Joe his. In a frenzy, "That cup and
you actually blew out dust from the shot glass you handed
me of this stuff! Remember that? You call this a shiner

because it doesn't have a label? What a day that was! Oh, I better get a third glass for Louie. He's going to need this too." Inhaling her second makes her choke.

Still holding his drink, undaunted by her outburst, he swallows his. At the same time dials Louie d'Langino.

Swaying, she looks at him expectantly. "Well?"

"He's on his way."

"You said that before," cutting him off with a toss of her head that makes her loose her balance.

"Crazy traffic, he said. Say, you better sit down."

"What? At this time of night?" Staggering toward him.

"It's early morning traffic, D. Look, If you're not going to lie down then we gotta get some food in you." For emphasis, Joe takes the bottle from her and walks to the kitchen. She follows him and plops on the bar stool at the lavish island in her gourmet kitchen, that of gold tones and terra cotta.

She puts her head down sideways on the cool tile, it's been such a whirlwind, leaving abruptly, hours in the air with the time change, she felt her head was going to explode.

Reading her mind, he gets out the aspirin and pours a tall glass of water. Ordering her. "Take this and drink all of it."

"Nooo…" she weakly tries to refuse, mumbling.

"Yesss, or I'll force it down you," mimicking her. Joe turns to the refrigerator and pulls out the breakfast fixings. She does as she is told and passes out with one cheek on the cool tile, arms dangling.

Louie bursts in, yelling. "Where are you?"

"We're in here."

Louie d'Langino storms into the kitchen, ready for a fight. But what he sees is domesticity and smells bliss. A stocky, handsome Italian man. Fit from his fighting days, a nose that shows one too many punches.

"Hey, sit down, you're just in time to eat." Joe tells him.

Louie points to Deirdre in question to him.

"Passed out. Fear, jet-lag, anxiety, whiskey. She's actually kinda cute there, all peaceful and quiet! Not putting on her airs and not talking so damn fast. Don't you think so?"

"Oh man, don't let her ever hear you say that! She hates cute!"

Enjoying their meal in silence when suddenly, Deirdre abruptly pops her head up with one finger pointing skyward. She exclaims excitedly, "I bet if you check the records...BT's accident was at the same time as Michael's crash...I bet his was no accident either...check it...it came to me...oh 'ello Louie...uhhh." Swaying her finger toward him, then moving it to Joe and exclaims, "isn't it weird that when I met you...I played LAUREN...HA...of all the syncs..." She folds her

117

arms on the cobalt blue tile, making a nest for her head, and passes out again.

The two men, both mid bite, turn from her to each other, staring in consternation with jaws dropped.

Joe closes his mouth first. Puts down his fork in emphasis. "Now that's something I didn't see coming! I guess we have a lot of work to do."

Chapter 17

Lauren opens her eyes as she comes to and says, "Ooh, my head..." reaching her temples. "What the hell happened? Where am I?" Trying to fight her foggy mind, she focuses on her surroundings. She removes the gag from her mouth.

"Okay, first things first, there isn't any noise...that's good, right?" She cautiously whispers to herself. She waits, listens and says. "Good, no noise. I'm talking here, out loud...ahh, am I hurt? Yes, pain is everywhere...my pounding head...damn it...okay. " She moves her hands up and down her arms and legs. Then back to her head and feels the lump. "Ohhh jeez...okay nothing seems broken."

With her eyes adjusting, she looks down at her filthy clothes and smells the stench of her, as well as her enclosure. "Okay, get a grip here...I can panic, dive into depression even...or SURVIVE. Get a grip, now. I'm going with survive and I'm going to get out of here." She says desperately, trying to keep her verve.

"Think...what happened? Remember," she commands herself while still whispering. She recounts through her foggy mind. "Okay, I saw BT on the beach...two burly men acting like they were drunk, take me to a trunk, push me in. I must have hit my head. Drugged. I don't remember being

gagged and bound though, but here's the rope burns," she recalls rubbing her wrists. She notices a cut rope at her feet and touches the gag around her neck.

"Kidnapping gone bad? Why me? Oh God, I need help... what do I do? SURVIVE...my book...I tell people to ask their source for help...HELP. Please HELP ME...okay... there's a little light coming in," she notices fixating on the window. Looking around the perimeter, she notices out loud. "A shed...fishing...by the smell of it...small room...a door... probably locked," feeling doomed again, quickly arguing, "NO. OK, maybe it's not," very gently and slowly, she begins to stand. Shaking, she rises and braces against the wall for support.

"Please get to the door." Almost stumbling, Lauren collects herself with a hand on the wall next to the old knob. "OK, please be unlocked," holding her breath as she turns it. "YES."

Cautiously peering out, she is blinded by the light of day. She stops, to let her eyes adjust and realizes she doesn't know how long she's been gone. Seeing no one, opening the door further, she steps out. Wobbly on her feet, head still groggy, she forces herself to go further. The area is seedy. Moving and bracing along the long building, she rounds a corner.

"It's a bar, and of course its name is 'Dive Bar', just my luck...," she says and grabs her head to stop the renewed pounding.

She gets to the door, bolsters herself, pulls the door and is immediately blinded by the darkness and hears, "What the hell do you want?"

Focusing on the angry man behind the bar, she makes her way to a swivel and disgusting bar stool. "Hi? I could use some water...please."

"Did you notice this is a bar?" He spouts sarcastically.

"Ohhh yes...then I'll have a...whisky...water chaser? Please, may I also borrow your phone?" She's trying to placate him.

He grumbles away and she emphasis, "THANKS" to his back.

Holding her head up, elbows on the grungy bar, she waits.

Startling her with the slam of the old rotary dial phone, he puts the glasses in front of her, demanding, "You better be paying me for these." His face twists in anger.

"Oh of course...yes...my father will pay you. Honest," she says trying to convince him.

Sipping at the water, that cools her throat, Lauren wants to guzzle it down. But weirdly a fact jogs her memory, when dehydrated, never drink fast. *Oh great.* She sips at the whisky, letting it burn her throat, and sips at the water again. *OK, steady she goes. Be still. Call Dad. Stay still.*

Holding her head in one hand, to stay stable, she continues to sip at both drinks. By the time she hears the door open behind her, she finished both glasses. Turning on her stool, she sees her Dad and BT behind him, in a glow of light. She shuts her eyes and puts her arms up to hug them as they rush to her in a bear hug.

Her dad doesn't let go and declares in a whisper, "Thank God, Lauren, you're safe. Lauren, my darling, my God. Thank God."

Stefen breaks the hug, "Can you walk?" She nods, holding on to him. They walk outside.

The bar-keep stomps over and BT smacks a hundred dollar bill on the bar. BT turns to the smiling bartender, "Thanks for helping her. Did you see anything out of the ordinary around here last night?"

"Uhh, I dunno," the bartender says. BT slaps another bill down. "...'matter o'fact, nev' saw such a purty boat out there bef'...real nice power boat. Then this morn', real early, it was gone."

"Can you describe it? Its name, color? Anything?"

Back at the hotel, the doctor on staff checks on Lauren. He confirms she's alright, despite the many bruises, rope burns and small cuts here and there. He assures them she's past the danger of concussion, and recommends rest.

Lauren has to peel off her clothing because they're stuck from sweat and grime. Only now she realizes how fortunate

she was that she had left her tennis shoes on after golf instead of her usual way of slipping on her flip-flops. She piles the mess on the shiny white marbled floor, ready for a plastic bag to go to the trash.

The shower is bliss. She lets the hot water flow and flow on her head. Horribly dirty, it seems like all the soap provided is not enough. Still feeling grungy, she scrubs herself down again. After washing her hair three times, she just stands under the water until the original water temperature diminishes. She never realized how much the appreciation of a big soft towel and comfy robe could feel.

She wraps her dripping hair in a toweled turban in her normal way and walks toward the divine smell of a wonderful array of many plates, all types of foods. "We didn't know what you'd want, so I ordered a lot of your favorites!" Her Dad remarks, trying to be cheerful.

There is hot coffee, hot water for tea, breakfast and a display of many different meats, cheeses and fruits. Pouring herself a cup of coffee, she picks up a piece of bacon. Sipping and chewing slowly as if testing herself, she feels ravenous. She sits down and scoops up eggs, toast and bacon. The fresh papaya, was nothing like she had ever tasted, so good.

Stefen and BT, at the edge of their seats, watch her closely, ready to step in at any moment. "Easy does it, honey," her dad cautions.

"Ummm, yes I know. As much as I wanted to inhale that water at the bar, I remembered not to." At this, he pours her

a tall glass of water. "Slow and easy on all of it," he reminds her.

"Okay," mumbling over her chewing. "This tastes amazing. That shower was amazing. I've always taken them for granted..." she continues to eat.

Slowing down, leaning back, coffee cup in hand, she looks at the two of them. "Go ahead you guys, eat up, there's plenty!"

The men just look at each other, watching her like they are is unnerving. "Tell me. What happened? How long was I gone?"

Stefen gives BT the nod, as he grabs a plate.

"Almost 24 hours," he says in his PI professional manner.

Stefen cuts in glaring at him and puts down his plate. Softly he says, "Not quite a day, it's about two in the afternoon now, the day after you were...uh...well, taken. I got your call about two hours ago now. Thank God we found you. You were able to escape. Oh, Lauren, I'm sorry I promised I wouldn't get emotional." He puts his hands to his face and weeps.

BT puts his hand on his shoulder and this time speaks in a calm, softer demeanor. "Will you tell us what you remember?"

"Dad, please, I'm safe now." He looks up at her, eyes wet and red.

"Yes. Please tell us what you know, that happened. But only if you can."

"Oh wow, okay. When I awoke in the shed, after coming to with a splitting headache, I checked if I was hurt. I was, but nothing broken. I figured no one was around, when I didn't hear any noises, I started talking out loud to keep sane," pausing to take a sip of water.

"Actually, I wondered what Magnum would do!" Trying to lighten the mood, at their mutual confusion. "You know being in Hawaii, the TV show?

"Fine. Alright, I remember seeing BT at the beach last night, then. Right? I was taken last night?" They nod in unison.

"I yell at him to get his attention, when these two men, acting drunk, turns out they weren't, pick me up, I yell, try to get away, but they take me away quickly. I struggle while they put me in the trunk, I had to have hit my head then because I don't remember anything till the shed."

Everyone is silent. Sitting there, looking down at the plush carpet.

"Unfortunately we don't have a lot of information," BT says. "We did find a stolen, abandoned car actually about a mile from the shack you were in. The lab is running tests. I know there were three of them, because I saw two men carry you and there was the driver. Lauren, I'm sorry I couldn't get to you in time. I didn't know it was you until...huh, by the time I heard yelling, turned and ran toward it, they were on their way...I am so very sorry you went through all that."

Adjusting his repenting, he continues. "According to your friendly bartender, there was a power boat at the dock outside the bar last night. He said it was gone early this morning, which tells me they must have fled after they realized they took the wrong woman..."

She cuts in, "That's why the rope was cut at my feet and the gag was around my neck instead of...it was horrible. Lying there in the filth, not knowing..." Lauren begins to cry, whispering to herself, *I think I'll go into that depression now.*

Stefen goes to his daughter, "Let's get you to bed. You've been through enough for now. The police will want a statement, O'Reilly here, will take care of that."

"Alright, thanks." She signals to BT in gratitude and lets her Dad walk her to her room. He tucks her in as when he used to and kisses her on her forehead. She's smiles meekly at him and falls fast asleep from sheer exhaustion.

At first it's a deep sleep lasting into the night, the adrenaline finally wearing off. But then nightmares begin to disturb her slumber in the wee hours of the morning. Making for a torment of agitation, she tosses and turns. Night sweats leaving her unsettled and fidgety, as she rouses with the dawn.

Chapter 18

It's a solemn trip back to the mainland for the three of them. With not much more information, or answers to any of their questions, they had nothing to talk about.

Arriving at LAX, they deplane and BT explains, "I am off to Chicago for business. I hope to see you both in a few days."

Stefen and Lauren look at each other then both turn to him in question. Stefen breaks the unease and says, "Sure. Yes. Thanks for your help. Have a safe trip. We'll see you when you get back. Please keep me in formed of any new developments."

"Will do. You two take care." He turns and walks toward his gate.

Lauren twists to her dad, "That was odd. He sure does shift around a lot. Anyway, how about getting me home?"

They get to her place and he helps settle her in. Lauren kisses him on the check and assures him she will be fine. He frowns, "I promise I will call you. Julie has done a fine job in stocking the place. I'm going to get lots of rest, Dad. Honest," she says trying to assure and guide him out the door.

"Alright. Keep the doors and windows locked, Lauren. I'm serious."

"Yes Dad. I love you. Now go, you've got to be exhausted too."

After attempting sleep that night, the next day she immediately sinks back into her work. More than ever, she keeps busy is her way. She doesn't have to think and she doesn't have to care about anything.

However, doing research on her next book does not keep her interest. Her mind wanders, desperately trying to avoid what she's lost and been through. Memories of the damned flashbacks nag her. She finds there is no escape in sleep due to the haunting nightmares. All of this results in becoming ill. She heaves daily and cannot eat.

Days pass since the trip to Hawaii. She refuses to talk to anyone except Julie, her assistant, and this is only to check in and lie about how she really is. Although, Stefen and BT both try to phone or see her, they are unsuccessful in getting through to her.

Lauren had called her dad as promised the first few days and convinced him that she was fine. She was busy with her book's research and needed to be alone. Stefen believed her and so he respected her wishes to leave her alone. After all, this was nothing new for her when involved with work.

Julie had stocked and cleaned her condo upon Lauren's return, so there was no reason to leave. Making it easier to

sequester herself in her home. Regrettably though, no one knows of her mounting paranoia. Causing her to have her trusted handyman change the locks and install another deadbolt.

She had let him in without him seeing her, hid in the kitchen on the normal pretense of doing her research. Conversing little as usual and had left the check for his payment near the door before his arrival.

One day, however, BT gets a frantic call from Julie, "I don't know what to do," she begins.

"You mean you have had no way of communicating with her all this time?" He says trying to contain his anger.

"Only when she calls me. We had an agreement she'd check in every day. She did and also made me promise I wouldn't' tell you, Mr. Ashlynn or anyone. I don't know if you know this, but Lauren is, well, she can be, very stubborn and willful. At any rate, she said she caught a cold a couple of days ago, and yes," Julie hears his strain to interrupt and assures him. "Anyway, she has called me every day as agreed upon.

"But when I didn't get a call today, I went to her place, tried to use my key and it didn't work. It's locked up like a drum. Oh, please help, Mr. O'Reilly. I can't get a hold of her dad, so I called you. I know something is wrong. I am worried." She says weeping in lament.

"Julie, yes, okay, I will. I'll go right over. I'll call you as soon as I know something. Settle down, girl and keep trying to call Stefen." He immediately runs out the door.

Approaching her door, he knocks, waits, then knocks harder and yells for Lauren. Just as he'd known, there's no answer. Julie was right, it looked as though she moved, except for the bright new deadbolt. Noting the obvious that it had just been installed, it wasn't there before Hawaii. Not waiting anymore, he works the locks.

He makes a lot of noise entering and shouts. "HELLO, Lauren. It's O'Reilly. Hello, are you here?"

He turns the corner to the simple, yet lovely, eclectic chic living room and sees her on the floor. Getting to her, immediately his learned medical techniques of a downed person kicks in. Checking her breath, moving his hands over her limbs for broken bones, he affirms she is passed out.

"Lauren, wake up. Lauren." Rousing her, he makes for a calm and soft tone as she comes round, "Hey you...what are you doing on the floor?"

Looking up at him, she is startled and desperately weighing her setting. She's visibly shaken and moans, "I, I don't know. What..."

"It's okay. You probably just found a more comfortable place to sleep!" He says as he's comforting her at her tremor. "It's okay, you're safe. Is it alright if I help you to the couch?"

She nods and he picks her up gently and lays her on the sofa. Then, he pulls the ottoman over to sit opposite her. Tenderly, he answers her questioning eyes, "Julie called me when she didn't hear from you today." Lauren's response is a blue tinge at her lips and she shudders.

"Lauren," he says more emphatic. "Lauren, I need you to put your head between your legs for me." She starts to fight him when he moves her to sit up and tenderly pushes her head down. "You're in shock, Lauren. You're fine, just breath, put your head between your legs, now."

BT grabs the throw and puts it over her shoulders, while combating her struggle against him. He holds her in place, reassuring her, "Lauren, it's alright. You're okay. Breathe Lauren. Stay with me. Breathe, you're alright. That's good. Nice, keep breathing. You're doing great."

As she begins to calm, his hand still on her back, he can feel her breathing getting deeper. "Good, just take another deep breath for me. Now take another. That's right. Okay, take one more deep breath, let it out slowly. Good. You can bring yourself up now, slowly. Easy does it. Nice. Feel a little better?" Pale but not blue, she sits very still, eyes glistening, questioning him.

After the shock passes, Lauren curls away from him into a corner of the couch in a tight ball and peers over her knees with a cautious glare at him. She is like a frightened child, penetrating raw fear. He reasons denial is catching up in her.

BT steps away from her, palms up, and soothingly says, "Your Dad is coming over. I'll go get you some water, I'll be right back."

He gets to the messy kitchen, food wrappings, dirty dishes and cups in and around the sink. Remembering Stefen telling him it's not unusual for her to withdraw when she's working. He finds a clean glass and fills it half way with water and takes it to her. She doesn't reach for it, only stares at him. He puts it down next to her, staying away from her as much as possible. He hears the door open, Stefen rushing in. BT puts his hand out, to slow him down.

"Lauren?" Stefen asks in concern, stunned that he seems to be a stranger to her.

"She just came out of shock, still disoriented," BT explains calmly. "Let's give her a few moments to steady herself." The two men sit at the other side of the room, trying to look relaxed as to not scare her further. In a soothing voice, he continues, trusting she will calm and loosen her tight grip, "So, Julie called you Stefen?" Nodding his understanding at BTs intent.

"I got here and found Lauren taking a little nap on the floor. We got her to the couch. Ooh now look at her coloring, I do believe we are getting better."

"Lauren?" Stefen stands. "Can I help you with some water, darling?" As she begins to unwind herself, he steps closer to her and she takes his hand. "That's it, honey." He sits next to her and helps her sip at the water. "Nice and easy, little bits will do it."

She is weary and very weak. Still distraught, yet the befuddlement is fading. She is again struck at how these two men are keeping her under surveillance. Are they wondering what the heck she's going to do next? BT hands Stefen a mug of warm soup for her.

Chapter 19

BT O'Reilly is in love with Lauren Ashlynn. Stunningly aware of this to himself, he watches her sleep, and realizes that he's been coming to this conclusion. It is his chance to get to know her better, no longer resisting his feelings, not wanting to push, maybe persuade, truthfully, court.

His profession had made for rescuing people, that's how it always was. But now, things have become different and difficult with all the excess baggage in both their lives. He decides to be persistent in his attempt to get through to her. At that, she smiles up at him, slightly embarrassing him.

Reaching for a Kleenex, she notices a vase of flowers on the night stand. "Thank you for the flowers," she says. Over her previous trepidation, feeling safe, she is pleased he's here.

"I'm glad you like them. Your Dad didn't want to be outdone!" Smiling and waving over to the dresser where a huge bouquet sat on the surface in all its glory. Handing her a glass of water with a straw, he says, "Do you think you can take a few sips? You must be thirsty."

Feeling relieved she wasn't acting scared, he says. "Then maybe get some better sleep? You've been through the mill

with that fever and..." Her confused look cuts him off. "It's past, you're good but you look like you're fading fast."

"Okay, thanks again."

"I'll just go in and clean up the kitchen. I thought I'd make my Mam's famous chicken soup." He declares as he gradually backs out of the room. "Well then, I'll see you later. Sleep sweetly." He can't take his eyes off her.

In this moment, Lauren is very aware of how nice he looks, the little encounter with him, and the simple joy of it. She is still at odds with what's happened and doesn't remember very much, except for the old fears coming back. She feels sticky from night sweats, but too tired to shower. *Dad and BT looking at me like they're on guard again, when was that? This time in my own living room. I'm looking forward to getting answers.* She drifts off to sleep once more.

Once they settled her and got her to bed after the shock, they both decide to stay with her tending to the intense fever. They take turns switching cold compresses, putting ice on her lips, and watch in concern at her moans and shivers. When the fever broke finally in the early morning, Stefen held his shift and sent BT home. Later that day BT was back, refreshed and ready for his turn.

Lauren awakes hungry. BT already has her soup covered on a tray with toasted bread triangles, and a glass of ginger ale. She lifts a piece of the bread, with a questioning smile on her face.

"My Mam would always cut them fancy like that when we were sick," BT responds as he blushes slightly.

She grins up at him and takes a bite.

"Will you try the soup or shall I feed you?" He asks with a wry smile.

"Remarkable as it seems, I think I can do it!" Feeling like she can finally put spunk in her voice, she remarks, "It's great timing you had this ready for me, like you knew when I'd awaken." He nodded with his crooked smile.

"This does look terrific, thank you for making the tray look so pretty!" Lauren toasts her ginger ale to him. "Smells nice too. After this, I need a shower. Will you wait for me?"

"You bet, I thought we could play some games if you're up to it later."

"I think I'd like that. Was Dad here too?"

"Yeah, we took turns watching over you. He left early this morning to get some sleep. He'll be back soon."

Lauren ate the toast triangles, after dipping them into her soup. Once sated, she moved the tray away. She slowly tries to bring her legs around the side of the bed, shoving off the covers. Spinning slightly, she holds onto her head as BT comes to her from his chair, grabbing her elbow.

"Easy. Stay still until the spin stops."

She looks up at him, as if he were a magician, reading her mind. Feeling safe in the moment felt good, even though it is an odd feeling to being safe with him. "OK, it's passed. I'm going to stand up now," she announces with strained vigor.

"Are you sure?"

"Yes, I really can do this!"

"Alright, but I'm going to be right outside waiting for you. Call out if you get shaky."

Lauren plays annoyed with his seriousness and slowly walks to the bathroom. "I'm closing the door, but for a few inches. I trust you will not come in unless I call," she says smirking up at him.

"I will be a gentleman, I promise. But I'm serious about you getting shaky in there, call out if you do, alright?" His voice is earnest.

"Yes, ok." She smiles and takes her time, sitting on the toilet, peeling off her clothes. Holding onto the sink to steady herself, she sees why he's so worried. A pasty, grey stains her face. Lauren's hair is greased down, making weird tuffs that stick out and black circles outline her eyes. "Oh god!" She says alarmed at her appearance.

"Lauren?" BT exclaimed.

"No, I'm ok, I just saw myself in the mirror. This isn't pretty."

"You'll feel better after the shower. I laid some sweats out for you just outside the door."

Carefully, she steps into the shower and soon embraces the lovely hot water that overcomes her. Staying under the perfect flow feels like heaven, washing off the illness, hopefully fears and anxieties too. Shampooing her hair and washing her body three times is a tremendous corporeality as she strains to stand steady.

Gradually, she finishes and gently towels dry, wrapping her hair in the infamous turban. Stepping to the door, she calls out, "I finished and I'm going to get the clothes, will you step out of the room now?"

"You're sure?"

"Yep."

Seconds past and he announces, "I'm closing the bedroom door, it's safe to come out!"

Lauren makes her way to her living room. The couch is ready for her with pillows to prop herself and blankets. A TV tray at the ready with a glass of water and plate of toast triangles welcomes her. He stands at the kitchen door watching her closely.

"I'm good, walking slow! Thanks for the new place to rest, it's so inviting!"

"You're welcome. I figured I'd change your sheets on the bed while you rest there."

Bending to sit, moving ever slow to lie within the pillows, "Aw, this is nice. Yes, clean sheets would be wonderful!"

For days, BT cooked, cleaned and made home-made meals for her. He made getting well fun, explained it was what his mother had done for him and his brother. She also found when he smiled at her, it was warm and it made his eyes sparkle.

Stefen dropped by several times, and the three of them laughed and shared funny stories. He apologized for not giving her fun times as a child. Her father would sometimes sneak her to the circus or park for a few hours. But that was rare indeed. Only when her mother was away, he would play games or help her do a puzzle.

Lauren has fun with them and enjoys the laughter together and being playful. It made her actually relax without thinking something else had to be done. Monopoly, Yahtzee and laughing at their different ways of going about jigsaw puzzles made for good times. She sees similarities between BT and Michael, but decides not to perplex herself with them. Lauren chooses to enjoy the present moments.

Time goes on and she becomes stronger. It is time for Stefen and BT to explain what happened to her. Taking turns, each tells a different portion of the incidents. Describing how she had been in denial, getting ill from the fear and disorientation she experienced and how it all made her body break down. They asked her if she remembered how she locked herself in and when they got to her, she was so ill from fever and frightened that she hadn't recognized either of them.

"I'm stunned, no, shocked that I can't remember any of this." Stunned and trembling, Stefen takes her hands.

BT, relating to her ill at ease, explains, "Lauren, these are all signals of disbelief in reality. Ignoring your inner self allowed you to blank out the horrors you went through. This is normal, your mind was trying to protect you from the inner torment."

"I don't want to believe this, it's too incredible. But I'm trusting you both," as their conviction astounds her. Lauren questions them. "These truths, facts, why...I mean, what are we going to do about this?"

Stefen embraces her and declares, "We've been working on it, but for now getting well is your priority."

She looks at him with her burden, turns and sees in both men their earnest, making her somewhat reassured. Reasoning with all they expressed would be a slow process and she realizes she has some choices to make. Not sure how, but she has to become willing to face her fears. Obviously forging ahead has not worked so far. Perhaps, as she spouted in her book, one step at a time is the answer.

"Well then, this sure has been enlightening. I have work to do. On me," she says at their questioning eyes. "I have a lot to think about, I know I need a lot of rest. I want to be able to trust myself again. I need time on my own for a while. I promise I will stay in contact with you both. I promise," she expresses to their stringent faces giving them her most earnest and convincing smile. "It's time for you two to leave."

Lauren assures them that she will abide their demands of being constantly monitored. Mulling over her new and old burdens for days, she decides to go back over all her old books on the subjects at hand. Reading her own, reminds her that she already has the tools to come to terms with her life.

She then does the scariest of all. Allowing to sit and be still with herself and all that has transpired. "I am remembering *the flutter.* It has come back to me. Writing the book, I'd feel it, the words would flow as if transcribing. It is also a healing balm of mind, heart, soul and body. Being congruent, is listening to my own inner-ness. I want to be happy. Oh Michael, I love and miss you so. And I know you want me happy, healthy."

Sobbing and rolling into a ball on the bed. Remembering him. Loving him. "You loved me so much...I know that. You taught me to love and trust myself, at least for a time."

Unwinding, lying on her back, arms and legs outstretched, she announces to her bedroom, "I AM WILLING TO BE WILLING TO CHOOSE LOVE, PEACE AND JOY. I CHOOSE HAPPY. THANK YOU FOR THE POWERS THAT BE...I CHOOSE HAPPY. Farewell Michael and all that you were, I am trusting you are at peace in your new home. I love you and always will."

Lauren had done depression. Denial too. Grieving takes time with all the many steps. Gleaning from her own book and others, she makes the decision to try to be still. Use the positive mantras when the negative, sad and fearsome thoughts flood in...*Peace, Be Still. Let Source, Let Go.*

Over and over again, a jillion times a day, because that's what it takes to make her way through.

Gradually, with lots of ups and downs, she allows the processes of 'willing to be willing' by the sheer virtue of execution. Her will and stubbornness put to good use works in recovering, resolving and even the beginnings of replenishment.

Upon returning to work, she actually feels better, despite tiring easily. Although she would always wear sweats while working, now she dresses for the research at hand for the new book and continues to journal. Being under strict instructions to not overdo by the men and her assistant, she continues to work part-time and builds her stamina. Besides, she'd never know when they'd surprise her by showing up to check on her.

. . . .

Meanwhile, as prayers are answered, there is no peace for the one still working at the truth of his murder and her being truly loved.

Chapter 20

"You sure look beautiful," BT remarks trying to restrain himself from taking her into his arms when she opens the door at his arrival.   Playfully trying to recover, he adds. "Fresh as a daisy!"

Lauren hopes she'd see him today, she had bought a new sundress. The spring colors show off her slight tan and she feels pretty. "Well, hello to you and thank you very much!"

Striding in, he asks, "Are you ready to dance?"

"Care for some lemonade?"   Smiling while pouring him a glass, she adds, "And what is this about dancing? I don't do that well."

"Some friends of mine are having a party at my house and I'd like you to come with me!"

"But if you do have other plans, I would *try* and understand. Even though I would be *mortally wounded*. I know it is short notice, but honestly, I didn't know they were doing this till a few hours ago.   *And* it really would be *terrific* if you would accompany me.   *Ohhh*, please say you will. So, I can prove to them I'm not really down and out, that I can get a date!"

Emphasizing his mock pleading with her while using his most charming smile.

"Oh jeez, thanks a lot! I would just would *love* to be your last-minute date," she laughs teasing him back, and matching his mocking. "Alright, if I *have to*, I guess I do owe you a favor," she says complaining. "Okay you, here's the deal: only if all debts are paid in full!"

They break into hysterics. "Let me get freshened up, I'll be back in a flash!" She gets her purse and sweater. Waiting for her, he realizes how refreshing, easy going and how much he appreciates how she keeps things simple. Definitely different than Deirdre, in looks and temper.

A memory occurs to him, when Deirdre had become ill, he surprised her with a bouquet of flowers. The surprise backfired. She refused to see him until she was completely well and with an imposing force, spat, "I'm not one to be put off-guard, and I'm certainly not presentable for anyone. Especially you, Mr. O'Reilly. I will take those, thanks." Grabbing the flowers from him, left him bewildered to say the least.

Not that the two women could be compared, but he found himself comfortable with Lauren and excited to be with her. Struggling with the love for Lauren Ashlynn, yet not quite sure why he could be with a woman he hasn't known that long. Admitting he misses her when he's away from her. Happy when he is with her. And although had never been much for telephone conversations, he found himself calling her several times a day to hear her voice. Of course, under the pretense of the mandatory check ins.

Wondering about those dreams, trying to justify, whispering to himself, *"Some sort of premonition? Waiting for someone like her? It could explain the 'familiarity', huh, and what of the nurse-maid role? What is this all about O'Reilly?"*

Walking to his fire engine red, '94 Camaro with T-tops off, Lauren says admiring, "Nice car!"

He opens the door for her, explaining, "Thanks! I never liked the body styles until they changed it to this in '93."

As she's getting in, he's aware of her quiet sensualness and that he wants to touch her. *"Ah, better change the subject, chum!"* He tells himself.

Getting in himself, "How 'bout that architecture, eh?"

At her puzzlement, "I hadn't taken the chance to admire your newer condominium complex before. The pastel colors and design remind me of the Jamaican islands. Or, what I'd imagine them to look like. I haven't been there. You?"

Shaken and fighting a surge of distress, "Ah...yes. Michael...we went there. He asked me to marry him... there..."

"Oh God, Lauren, I'm sorry. I didn't know. I don't mean to hurt you."

"It's okay, I...I'm working at letting the anguish go. Reminders are bound to come up. Besides, it was a lovely time. You might want to go sometime," trying a cheerier note.

145

"You know actually, that reminds me, I've noticed that through these weeks of your recovery, well, it's as if you've been replenishing yourself." At her bewilderment, he attempts to go on, "It, well you, jeez, I'm sorry, I'm not usually one to stumble over my words! What I am trying to say, is well, my Mam, she is always about the 3 Rs. Relax, Resolve and Replenish," sighing that he finally made his way through that statement.

Lauren is once again taken aback; this man keeps bringing up familiarities. Odd wording, arresting and personal phrases that are hers, even Michael's. She looks out the window, her hair blowing, refreshing her face as tears sting her eyes. Willing herself to stay in the moment. *"It's a pretty day, I'm in a beautiful car being driven to a party, I'm wearing a pretty dress of colorful flowers and comfy sandals. All is well here, now…"* repeating again, staying still in the moment.

She turns to him, "Thank you BT for this invite and ride. Thank you for all you've been doing for me these last days. You really have helped remind me of the sweetness and the good sensations of life. It's been a difficult road, but I'm moving one step at a time. I have to say though, I'm not sure I'm up to meeting new people. I…"

"Hey, I know. There's only a few friends and they are very welcoming. They will be easy on you, I promise!"

The sky begins to change colors as it does in the later afternoon of summer and the ocean breezes begin their magic waltz. BT explains further about his friends enjoying his home for parties. They clean, set up and clean up

146

afterwards, it's been a win-win. And because he is not considered the host, he assures her he will take her home whenever she wants to go.

He proceeds to converse, hoping to deflect her grief with the history of his brother and family. BT bought his home from his brother many years ago. A custom house that he built in Santa Monica to grow his family. As an excellent doctor and fine surgeon, he built a thriving practice. Then he and his wife decided to move to Ireland to be with Helen, and sold the practice.

BT always loved the home because of its rustic, warm and roomy charm. They had made it a loving family home, welcoming to all and a joy to play with his niece and nephew. The panoramic view overlooking the ocean was never bad either, especially making it a favorite retreat for all.

His expressions indeed help change her mood and soon they arrive. Lauren walks into a most spacious living room, a cabin feel of knotty pine walls and high vaulted wooden ceilings. The room overlooks a huge patio that faces the beach through the floor to ceiling bay windows and sliders. Moving closer she spots what might prove to be her escape, if necessary, a curved walkway to the sand.

A few people scurry around, getting ready for the guests to arrive. Friendly and genial, BT leads her through to the adjacent and enormous kitchen where others introduce themselves hurriedly.

The kitchen is modern, yet keeping the old charm of the rest of the home. Its generous space is open for the

entertainment and room for all who gather in the kitchen. The large, dark green, granite island provides a sink and work area. The same knotty pine base has room for several bar stools on two sides. The kitchen window opens onto a long counter that provides access to the bar and patio areas.

Opposite the sea view, at the kitchen's back wall, is an open two-door width archway that shows off a spacious and informal dining room. To the left at the corner, Lauren's curiosity is peeked at the incredible old time, antique, swinging bar doors. BT is happy with her obvious admiration of his home, but it's her striking regard for his favorite doors, that delights him.

He invites her to push them open and she announces with astonishment: "You have your OWN PUB!"

The massive bar curves behind the dining room to the opposite wall. A gracious old thing, carvings telling stories of long past has undeniably been lovingly preserved, maintaining its history. The glass shelves behind, are filled with beautiful liquor bottles and glasses of all types. Most likely any drink one could imagine, could be made at this incredible bar.

Quant Irish mementos and historical artifacts collage the emerald green walls. Bar stools of carved old wood adorn three high-top copper tables and at the bar. All making for a walk back in time. That is except for the several bright green neon shamrocks placed here and there.

"This is my favorite room!" He exclaims waving his arms around. "My family and I brought a lot of this from Ireland.

148

Even these old glassed windows," he explains pointing to the northern windows that overlook the sea. "My Mam's favorite, are these old glassed French doors," he praises lovingly.

"They are exquisite. This whole room is," Lauren pauses in admiration. "An incredible display of love for you, your family and ancestry. I am honored to be here. It's amazing. Your home is amazing, so homey, welcoming and loving, just like you explained. But this room...it takes my breath away!"

Opposite the bar, the doors lead to the L part of the patio that overlooks the sea. Walking out and around to the kitchen window, she sees the effort given in the design to entertain. Another huge island of river rock gives way to the sink and work area of tile and a glass composition of lovely sea blue, green and teal waves. The stainless, hulk of a BBQ built in near the sink area for easy clean up.

BBQ roaring with ribs, chicken and tri-tip smells delicious. People bustling at turning the meats, talking, laying down appetizers of many kinds makes for a festive gathering. It's plain to see this enormous ringside of the main patio area was designed for such.

Tables with umbrellas and cozy, cushion chairs in the same color scheme make for a comfortable cafe feel. Outlining, jutting brick and stone work provide cushioned benches. Several types of palm and Italian cypress trees completely border the area as hundreds of potted plants and flowers adorn throughout making for a tropical paradise. Different sized pots add dimensions of eclectic textures and colors that please the eye. Some are stacked on other pots to

149

make lovely groupings, all of which make for a staging magic that provides peace as the theme.

Steps down offer the magnificent pool and gazebo spa, both matching the tile and glass of the BBQ island. The entire site and home were certainly designed for pleasure and enjoyment, all being surrounded by the phenomenal view of the Pacific Ocean.

As the party comes into full swing, Lauren finds herself having fun and sharing it all with BT is a delight. She is welcomed with open arms by his friends and truly feels comfortable. All having fun with laughing, mingling, drinking and eating. BT usually at her side, and embarrassed the few times he was needed for hosting duties, makes time for her wanderings. She doesn't mind and assures him so, many times.

"Look, Big Guy, I have been to parties before. Why, I have even mingled with people I didn't know before! Now do your thing and stop apologizing. I am having fun; your friends are being very nice to me. Really, BT, stop fretting!" She pushes him away, with a sweet smile.

He leaves, she muses at his acting the hurt puppy. Sipping her wine and strolling the patios, she discovers lovely, funny and antique garden art treasures all throughout the gardens and plants. Surprises delighting her with each encounter of the attention and love put into the entire expanse.

She notices the enchanting pathway that leads to the ocean is edged on either side with ice plant and one of her favorite

pungent geraniums. "Hmmm, we have got to go down there later," pondering to herself, "It's hard not to like this guy."

BT is concerned and doesn't want to leave her alone, keeping an eye on her however, sees she seems to be enjoying her own personal tour of the place. His Mam would be tickled to see her adoring her work.

At twilight, thousands of tiny lights enhance the entire open courtyard, even the trees edging the property lines are filled with the same glimmers. Several spot lights illuminate certain trees and big plants. The whole place is lit up in a sparkling splendor as she hears: "DINNER IS SERVED!!!"

Chapter 21

Delicious lip smacking, finger licking ribs and potato salad, just like Lauren likes them made. Let alone the plethora of great salads to choose from, then there are fruits, more cheese platters and many deserts laden for the feasting. Several tables hold the foods decorated in summer BBQ fair. BT takes a seat next to her with his own plate piled high. She chuckles at him and he retorts, "What? I'm really hungry!"

"I can see that! I am too, this is all so delicious. BT, I'm having such a fun time. Thank you. I seem to be doing that a lot lately...thanking you!"

"That's okay, I don't mind!" He mumbles as he chews.

Laughing, she continues finishing her own plate. "I'm going in for one of those delicious looking brownies with caramel, oh yum!"

At the table of deserts, she spies her quarry, when she notices him glancing over at her again. All the times, they were apart today, he would do that often. His concern and care for her is quite obvious, making her feel embraced by him. And that's when it hits her like a ton of bricks, the old, nagging feeling of Michael.

Swaying at the impact, she holds onto the table. A woman she hasn't met, holds onto her arm, "Are you okay? You look like you've seen a ghost," noting Lauren's face, she changes tack, "Maybe it's the thrill of all these desert choices!" She acts kind to give her an out.

Lauren smiles meekly in agreement, "Thanks, I got a little dizzy is all." She leaves the table, scanning for BT, he left his spot and detects he is out of her sight. She slips away and heads for the beach. His guests are absorbed in their conversations.

She makes her way to the end of the pool terrace, towards her right. Dusk is turning into night quickly, yet the stoned pathway is courted by thousands of tiny lights that make for a magical encounter as the ocean lures her. Despite the ensuing panic, she has to slow her track as the walkway twists back and forth due to the severe steepness of the hill.

Making many turns, she feels salt in the air. She tastes it on her tongue and tries to breathe deeply because she knows she's heading for the onslaught of anxiety.

Finally, she comes to the end of the path. Taking her shoes off in the sand, she's drawn to a tiny patio just off the passage. It's obviously a part of his property because it sits directly below the house. A little secret veranda attaching to a shed. The funky door has a sign that reads:

MOONDOGGIE'S O'REILLITY

Lanterns and more of the tiny lights decorate the area. A few benches are placed specially for watching the sunset.

She sits down and stares into the moonless night. The crashing waves help to drown the party noises and her bubbling cries.

Feeling very alone, her thoughts are sad and her vision is intense of Michael. So quiet is his approach, she is startled when she senses BT watching her.

"What's wrong? What happened, Lauren?" He asks concerned, yet keeping his distance.

"I, I was admiring your view, your home. Everything here is wonderful, BT. Thank you for inviting me," she says wiping her tears in the shadows.

"May I join you?"

"Please." She motions for him to sit next to her. "It's lovely here. I just can't get over it. How fortunate you are to live here. It truly is beautiful. The details are delightful." She speaks sincerely, changing the subject and quick to cover her crying.

"I got concerned when I couldn't find you. I thought maybe you had taken ill, again. I hope this hasn't been too much for you. I just wanted you to get out and enjoy something new. You were so good about resting, even being cooped up. I hope you're alright." Lauren knows he knows something is very wrong, as she keeps trying to cover her face.

"I'm sorry I worried you. I was curious as to where the path led."

154

Looking intently at her, she finally looks his way. She fiercely tries not to cry and immediately turns away. The ocean is endless and so is the moment.

"Are you thinking of Michael?" He asks, not sure he wants to hear the answer.

Overcome, she nods and the tears flow and then she starts uncontrollable sobbing. It's as if he gave her permission to relieve her emotion. He holds her shaking body and offers his handkerchief, as she bawls into it. She is bewildered by a man who embraces her while crying over another man. Still, she can not stop the torment of loss.

After the sobs turn to weeping, BT asks with a quiet patience, "Tell me about him. I want to know how you felt when you were with him. I want to know you, Lauren. You have become very important to me."

Lauren's tears subside and she wipes her face, breaking from his embrace. She grabs for tissues in her pockets because his handkerchief is drenched. BT stands up to give her a moment. He steps over to the shed door, opens it, and turns out the lights.

BT covers her shoulders with a towel and places the other over her lap. All he wants is to hold her till the pain leaves from her trembling body, but knows it doesn't work that way. Instead, he sits close and waits for her to begin.

Lauren starts slowly and speaks in spurts of different times she shared with him. There is no order or measure of time, for she skips around in her tales. She sobs at times and just

as quickly laughs at reliving her memories. Her emotions run rampant and she is completely honest with him. Lauren holds nothing back and tells him things that she never told anyone, but Michael.

She goes on for hours, until she becomes calm. Her throat dry, even hoarse. She smiles meekly at him and asks, "I know that was a lot. I haven't talked so much in well, forever. Oh BT, thank you. I guess I really needed that. It's such a relief, sorry to unload. Damn it." She gets up, pulls the towel closer to herself and turns to him. "Are you willing to tell me more about you?"

He stares at her and adjusts himself in his seat. He motions her to sit back down and proceeds to say things not many others know. He is shocked that he talks so much about himself. He describes his family and precious mother. He laughs as he speaks of her gruffness because she had to raise her two ruffian boys by herself.

Finally, they sit silent for many moments, mutually trusting and comprehending all that was said. Then, BT puts his arms around her. Released of emotions, Lauren hugs him back and wonders if it's possible the sky could turn a deeper black.

BT whispers, "Lauren, it's almost dawn. I have a guest room where you can sleep. Otherwise, I will take you home as promised."

"I'd like to stay, thanks." She takes his hand and they stand together.

They walk back up to the house slowly. It is eery because the tiny lights are no longer on. He knows the path by heart and guides her carefully to the top. There are notes everywhere thanking BT for the party and miraculously his home was set clean. He leads her to the guest room. According to the layout of the house, she figures she is above the small patio they just left.

While holding her hand, he can't help but notice how soft her skin is. He remembers how strong and hearty her handshake was when they first met, and decides it is a good combination. With their fingers intertwined, he notes how long hers are in his hand.

Standing in his mother's room, he feels his desire warming. Wanting her, he resists. Instead, he kisses her fingers while staring into her eyes. With that, he smiles and turns toward the door. "Please make yourself at home, you'll find what you need in the bathroom and that drawer there," pointing to an elaborate, detailed dresser.

"So, there's the key!" Pointing to it in the door lock on her side. With a mischievous smile, he walks out of the room.

Lauren stands alone in the lovely room. She thought BT would make love to her. *Why is he is so much like Michael? Isn't that what they do in the movies? This isn't the movies Lauren. Oh my God woman, get some sleep!"*

Looking around the room, she understands more about BT and his mother. He loves her very much and most strikingly, it is nice to see a healthy and strong relationship, so unlike her own.

He explained earlier that Helen had done this room a long time ago when she lived with her elder son and family. Done in an old-fashioned posey, flower-type print with early American maple furniture. Simple, comfy and warm, Lauren loves it. The large dark pink flowers against the blue and green background on the wallpapered walls, carry onto the bed and large, over-stuffed chair. Making for a perfectly easy place to read in the corner with a tall Tiffany lamp stand.

Although used as a guest room, he has left everything the way his Mam designed it. He promised her he would keep it the same so she would want to come back.

Lauren searches and finds extra shirts and socks in the top drawer. There are boxed toothbrushes, paste and an assortment of toiletries for guests. Slipping into bed, she feels safe and comfortable. Adjusting the pillows, already the sky is gray, and she is fast asleep.

Later that day she awakes, feeling refreshed. Maybe it's the room, the ocean or maybe BT, but she feels alive. Stretching and feeling the blood coursing through her, she pads over to the ajar French doors. They open onto a pretty tiled balcony of terra cotta.

She spots the same geraniums from down below, only in pots everywhere. A little green ice cream table with its lone chair is positioned to watch the sunsets. "Helen must have enjoyed this spot, I wonder if you have a spot like this in Ireland facing this one?" She asks the plants that need pruning.

They are ragged from lack of care. She automatically begins pinching the ends, picking off the old flowers and stems. So many varieties, their fragrances all different, are such a delight. Although they are being watered, she can tell they certainly miss Helen's TLC. "You poor babies," she coos and enjoys the fragrances they produce from being loved.

She's so busy, she doesn't notice BT's watchful gaze from down below. Drinking his coffee in a favorite chair, watching the sea. Under the slated-wooden pergola, he reaffirms he is enchanted by her. Because she is tending to his mother's flowers? He does not know. He does know that no other woman has slept in that room, and yes, he loves that she is tending to his Mam's flowers.

Helen would be proud. She often made funny remarks about BT's women. "How can they care for you and a family if they can't tend to God's green earth? Darlin' you find a lass that cares for these plants, and you will have ye'self a good wife!" He smiles at her words.

He finds himself going over the things Lauren told him that morning. Her loss was overwhelming, and he wrenched at the pain he saw in her face. That troublesome feeling of familiarity had come up many times during some of her stories. He also found that he was remembering parts of dreams, he had tried to sort out before but could not.

Things are getting more confusing and uncomfortable because he knows some of the places and feelings she spoke of.

He was a man of usual simplicity and answers came easy, but these worries of his own sanity did not set well. Although everything had changed after the accident, BT finds learning to deal with this new disorder is not easy. Fortunately, he finds doing simple chores help to stop the incessant clatter in his mind. At least the endless questions stop for a while. He decides to finally make breakfast at noon.

Chapter 22

"Adversity and pain are growth factors. We have choices, always. One way or another we're going to have to face life. Either now or later, it's easier when you pick now. God put us here to live, to learn and to love. The sooner you *get it*, son, the better off you are." Lauren remembered what Helen told her son.

Helen relayed this at several troublesome times to him, it reminds Lauren of her own writing in her book: *Face the fear, it's the only way. I did that with him last night. Being able to talk and communicate emotions. Being real, is such a freeing treasure. Michael sharing and now on Mr. BT O'Reilly. Wow, this is fascinating that this is happening now. And that sign on the door, Moondoggie's O'Reillity, what a hoot of a play on words and so the truth! I love the synchronicity.*

Lauren loves that he shared so much with her. Lying in her own bed, she goes over the bit of history: after the death of his father, he was all about an undercurrent of revenge, even as a kid. This, in turn, built his career and writing books became cathartic.

After he survived that horrible accident, BT found he was afraid he didn't have anything left. He tried to be light-

hearted, but couldn't help be serious when he said, "I was completely empty. Fear became paramount, just to survive. Everything felt different, I have even felt I'm not me. It's as if, weird to say, there is someone else living in here." He pounded his chest. "Pretty nutty, huh? I don't know, Lauren, I am kinda weird at times. Life is scary, but what other choice is there, except to pick up our worlds and go, walk the journey?"

The next day, after sleeping through the night, miracles on miracles, she gets back into her research work completely. This business, she started from nothing. One book and she hit the international market. She is proud of her accomplishments and is beginning to feel well with the world.

BT has a lot to do with these new feelings. She allows him to be her only interruption. He has done so much for her, mainly helping her to see a second look at life. Destroying herself over the loss, tragedy was not going to get her life on course or make for changing the reality of the situation.

She recalls how nice it was holding his hand that night. He was tender and caring, and listened. He said she is important to him. *Man, he sure did take good care of me during the flu 'bout and I can't get over how much fun I had recovering!* She laughs to herself. Life is taking a new road for her, by decision and gratitude.

"Oh, the diversions of him, back to work, girl!" She commands and forces herself to concentrate.

Thoughts continue to permeate her, BT would come bounding back into her mind. Her heart was finally melting of the cold and dire hurt. Sometimes she'd feel as though she were a child looking for a dear, lost toy. At other times, she feels her body opening and wanting pleasure.

She certainly cannot deny his rugged good looks. He is taller than Michael, his broad shoulders emanate his strong masculinity and oh, he is very sexy.

"Julie must have made a fresh pot of coffee," she smells the air trying to change the subject. Sighing and remembering the scrumptious breakfast he made her that morning. "Ah, he cooks too! Boy, now I'm going nutty!"

Reasoning with herself, she says out loud, "It was so good though. I even had seconds! He sure looked funny when I asked. Then sitting there, sipping coffee, while he cleaned up! BACK TO WORK. NOW! Never mind, it's not happening!"

"Hey Julie, I'm going out. I'll see you later!" Excitement running through her as she adorns her necklace and shoes, then grabs her jacket and keys. Taking a chance and feeling free, "Let's see what happens," she muses, starting up the car. Driving the busy streets of Santa Monica to BT's home, she considers his wonderful home. He didn't give her a tour of the whole house, but he mentioned his office is a side entrance off the living room.

. . . .

It was something Deirdre said about her own investigation that got BT thinking. She was justifying herself in the hire of another PI when the information started coming in. The snowballing of facts and ideas flying at them, what Joe had related, made for much to go on. Deirdre being afraid after all the threats. This had become personal.

The combination of frustrations and putting pieces together were a part of the business. He loved the mysteries and would become consumed with the cases, this is what made him good at what he did. Although he promised himself he was retired, there were too many connections to be happenstance. Besides, he never really quit looking for his Da's killer, hence the ambush.

They had associated how evidence and coincidences mounted. Deirdre's theory that the kidnapping was for her, still makes his skin crawl. That Michael's crash was murder and Deirdre was to be too, is almost more than he can bear. Then they left the big one for last, they made him aware of the *time*. The ambush that drove him into a coma and Michael's death.

Studying his notes and so very deep in thought, he doesn't hear the knock on the door nor its opening. Feeling a presence, he looks into the eyes of the woman he loves— the last person he expected to see.

"Hi!" Lauren says smiling. "I just happened to be in the neighborhood. Thought I'd drop by to see you." She laughs poking fun at the hour drive it took her.

"I'm glad you did!" He says covering some of his notes and standing to greet her.

"Actually, I was hoping I could take you to a late lunch. Are you free? Even though it looks like I'm interrupting you."
"Well, not really. I have this huge back log," motioning to his cluttered desk.

"All your efforts in helping me to regain my health and mentality. I wanted to prove to you that you are an excellent coach. I am working on spontaneity here, so if you don't let me buy you lunch, well, I'll be forced to accept the fact your lessons don't work. Now, you wouldn't want that, would you?" She starts walking toward him slowly. Seducing him with her manner and eyes and then bending over his desk with a sensual pleading for emphasis.

He is intoxicated by her and he knows there is no way he can continue his research after this display of hers. He plops down in his chair, leans back, twirling his pencil in hand and considers her. Playfully he says, "Since you put it that way, how can I resist?"

Lauren moves around to him and kisses him on the cheek. "Now that's what I wanted to hear!" She takes his hand and leads him out the door. He leads her to his car and opens the door for her. He drives them the short way to his favorite spot, a French cafe.

After retrieving her from the car, they walk hand and hand, enamored with each other. The tables are under a trellis full of hanging wisteria. As he pulls her chair, she delightedly remarks. "This is charming and I love that smell."

They sit, she looks about while he is taken with her. That her sense of fun and demeanor would let her surprise him like this is such a difference.

"It sure is hot, how can you look so refreshed? Those ceiling fans aren't doing much, may I help you with your jacket?" BT stands as he tries to make conversation covering his infatuation.

She laughs softly and stands. "Yes, thank you. You are gallant!" Lauren is pleased with herself that she is able to turn the table on him a bit. She had been in such awe of him, now she can tell he is befuddled. Besides, it feels good to feel the vibration of life again and to express herself.

He pulls the cream, colored blazer off and finds her shoulders are bare except for the thinned, spaghetti-straps. She is wearing a black linen dress with tiny, white polka dots, a red posy of geraniums is fitted on a ribbon, around her neck, below her collar bone. This makes her cheeks glow. He notices her toe nails match and are barely covered by the high-heeled sandals that bring her closer to his height.

"I thought it would be fun to accentuate your car! Besides I enjoy geraniums like your Mam!" Seeing his eyes drawn to the posy and her toes.

Chapter 23

"You are putting me in the trick-basket, lady! That's a fact, and now I am going to stop staring at you!" BT O'Reilly declares, breaking his stare at her.

Lauren smiles at him and silently wonders if he knows she is naked under her dress. She isn't sure she wants something to happen yet. She does know they are becoming closer and feeling freer with an undue intimacy.

"So, tell me, did I strike a chord when I convinced you into lunch? And what pray-tell, is a 'trick-basket'?" She inquires, laughing.

"Yeah. You're good at this, now I know what it feels like to have the tables turned! I guess I have been talking you into quite a few things lately."

"Okay, good. You admit it!" Changing the subject, she asks, "Do you come here often?"

"As you noticed, it's a short distance, so yes and the owner is a friend of mine. In fact, you met him the other night at my party. His name is Jack Perdot. He not only owns the place, but he does the cooking too. He's a character and it shows in his culinary creations! Good coffee drinks, too."

Suddenly, his mouth is dry and he marvels at her beauty. The sunshine filtering through the lattice radiates her face making her hair glisten. He has to take a long drink of water and tries to cool off his thoughts. Finally, he asks, "So, what are your plans for the rest of the day?"

"I took the day off from work, I thought you'd be proud! I brought my suit, I'd like to go to the beach. Would you care to join me?" She refuses to reveal that she can't stop thinking of him and that is the real reason why she couldn't work.

The waiter walks up, placing a bowl of peanuts on the table.

"Shall we order?" BT asks. Understanding her puzzled look, he explains, "Jack is a baseball fanatic. He named his restaurant, Joie de Deux, because of his two favorites. 'The Joy of Two,' being a French lover of baseball!" Grateful for the change in subject, he finds himself at a loss for words again. He is actually bewitched by her, not many do this to him.

"Is the 'Chicken a'la Orange' salad served cold?" Lauren asks the waiter.

"Qui mademoiselle. Today it is served on a bed of ice!"

"Good. That's what I'll have and a draft beer, please."

"Very well, and you sir?"

"Nice choice," he agrees not looking into her eyes on purpose. Addressing the waiter, he says, "I'll have what the lady is having."

"I can see why you like this place, BT. Who would have thought a French cafe and baseball? What a concept, I like it!" She giggles.

"Do you like baseball?"

"Oh yes, very much."

"I thought you would have ordered wine with your salad." She knows he's testing her.

"Wine is lovely, I do so enjoy it. But with the peanuts and baseball, this heat, you just got to have a beer! Speaking of which..." She points to the waiter carrying their refreshments.

Lauren takes her icy mug and holds it to toast, "Thank you Mr. O'Reilly. I am most grateful to you!"

Embarrassingly, he returns her toast, "Cheers!"

She sits back, feeling fresh and asks, "What do your initials stand for?"

"They don't," he responds matter-of-factly.

Mischief dances in her eyes and she looks quizzical. The cool substance going down her throat helps condone her

sensuality and playfulness. She can't keep her eyes off him and as he smiles at her, she asks, "What?"

"You have a mustache!" He leans over and wipes it off with his thumb, ever so slowly. Again, needing to change the subject he gulps down half his beer and nervously wipes his mouth with the back of his hand.

Sensing his anguish and feeling awkward herself, she suggests, "Maybe this wasn't such a good idea. You seem preoccupied and I did interrupt your work."

"Lauren..." pleading with her, but is stopped by Jack.

"Ah, look who is here! My friend and his enchanting guest!" He exclaims and sets the salads down. He takes her hand to kiss it and is grateful his friend is interested in someone finally.

BT smirks at him, "Always the charmer to the ladies and not a single look my way!"

Ignoring the remark, Jack continues. "Mademoiselle, how are you today? It is good to see you again, Lauren!"

"Very well indeed, it's nice to see you too!"

Turning to BT, "Alright, my friend, you win! I'll order you more beers." He mock salutes him, with a grin at his leave.

An airplane flies by and Lauren looks up to watch. Being so close to the beach, it tows a suntan ad banner.

"Do you know much about airplanes?" BT asks.

"No." She's thrilled that she is not hurt or offended by his question like she could have been. "Just very sensitive. Before I met Michael, I always looked up to see them fly by. I enjoy the noise they make. Besides, he loved them so."

"I noticed you watch them a lot. When we played golf, you looked up at them." He wanted to kick himself for bringing up the subject of airplanes and Michael. Her eyes reveal her mood is fading fast and he is wrestling with how to stop it.

Astonished that he watched her there, makes for all of a sudden her falling into a tumble of emotions, and she doesn't know how to stop it. Lauren sips at her beer but it doesn't stop the oncoming doldrum. She draws designs in the mist on the mug with her nail not looking at him and trying not to think of anything.

"Lauren," BT reaches for her hand. "I'm sorry, I..." not knowing what to say.

"No. Look, it's not your fault. I get stuck sometimes. I see an airplane or a picture in a magazine. It can be a word, anything, they set me off. It is very hard shaking the depression. I'm the one that is sorry."

Jack returns with fresh beers and is perplexed. "Why aren't you two enjoying my salads?" Seeing their change in faces, he asks, "You two, what has happened? My delightful salads are not good? You have only picked at them, should I take them back?"

"Oh Jack, no please, it is very good." Lauren stumbles to be enthusiastic.

BT stands abruptly, finally clear as to his direction. "Jack, it's always a pleasure. Thanks for the grub, but we have to go." He shakes his shocked friend's hand vigorously, helps Lauren from her chair and grabs her jacket.

His strides are long and fast and she can hardly keep up. He pulls her along and she yelps. "Hello? Excuse me? Can we slow down a bit? I AM wearing heels here...where are we going MISTER MAN ON A MISSION?"

"Get in!" He exclaims practically jumping over the hood to get to his side of the car, starting the engine before she's settled in.

Chapter 24

They rush into his office while Lauren tries to catch her breath, then gapes at him as he plunks her into a lovely upholstered, leather chair. She looks at him standing behind his desk, waiting for him to speak, but he just stares at it. He sifts through manila folders and searches through the mess of papers, as if he's looking for something important.

Meanwhile, she glances around and admires the beautiful library styled room. Funny, she didn't notice anything about the room earlier. The twin chair, next to her, is piled with more folders and news clippings. The handsome antique desk of dark mahogany wood sits in the middle of the nicely sized room, all done in the calming hues of deep greens. Her comfortable chair is large, plush emerald with a high back and fat arms.

BT O'Reilly looks over his organized chaos and gathers his thoughts for the information he needs to tell her. The how is what stumbles him now, breathing slowly, he looks at her. She is so pretty and small sitting in one of his favorite chairs.

He is concerned for her and her welfare, and still doesn't know how the hell to tell her all that he needs to. Finally, gently, he speaks up. "Lauren? You're probably wondering why I brought you here, so fast. Plopping you in that chair

like that." He's embarrassed at the thought and says. "Ah, yeah, sorry about that. I...well I...I have a lot to tell you. We haven't talked much about what happened to you. I told you what I knew back then...it's just that there's more. Uh, a hell of a lot...and as you can tell, I'm having trouble with where to begin."

Lauren jumps in. "Ohhhkaaay. Let me begin by saying, I trust you. I feel comfortable sitting in this lovely room with you. As a matter of fact, I must have been preoccupied earlier to have not noticed it!"

With that, he completely takes over the stage. Speaking very fast and rattling off details of the case he's working on, he has been compiling and collecting information for quite some time. Some specifics sound familiar to her and some don't. Lauren isn't following much of his discourse and finds she half listens to what he says.

And so as he continues with the barrage of ideas and theories, her mind becomes a blur in his wake. She hears bits and pieces that are becoming more familiar and sounding true. This makes her feel unsettled, almost sick to her stomach. His statements continue to fly fast and furiously, she holds onto her belly when she is stopped short.

"Michael's death was not an accident...Deirdre was being set up...the kidnapping was meant for Deirdre..."

Sputtering at this bombshell, she demands. "Just what are you saying?" Then immediately flashing in anger, she

screams, "ARE YOU COMPLETELY OUT OF YOUR MIND?"

Suddenly, she feels as though a huge gust of wind propels her to the wall, hanging there, spread eagle. She's helpless. Stuck by its sheer power, holding her suspended. Her breath is gone. Stupefied and numb, she stares at him in disbelief.

Without warning she finds herself calm. How odd it is to watch from what seems to be afar, as if she is out of her body? She cannot hear anything, even though she sees his mouth moving. She sees herself in the chair, in his office and looking down at her lap at the polka dot dress. Incongruently though, her hands are clenching the arm rests.

It could be a normal situation; two people talking across a beautiful mahogany desk. A delicious looking man thumbing through papers. Often looking up at his client with compelling eyes. Fully knowledgeable of his case and records. Excitedly telling her of his discoveries, evidence falling into place.

She, the beautiful client, flirting with him. Walking around his desk, looking at his things placed on the credenza, picking up this or that. Studying the fixtures that tell one about another; the old baseball, pictures of families and dogs. A saxophone sitting in the corner, it's not dusty, so he must play it regularly.

Once in a while, she'd lean over to break his attention. Arrange her hair to fall in his face and let him smell her

perfume. Perhaps tantalize him by sitting at the edge of his work area. The old trick of crossing the legs slow and seductively, while playfully tossing the baseball.

Sadly, this isn't the case. This isn't a fun time, he is serious and accusations are flying. Her mind is buzzing. It is probably shutting down right now. Maybe diverting her to a nicer place. To hide, run or whatever it takes, so she doesn't have to comprehend what he is saying. Panic is constricting her throat.

Desperately attempting to assemble her mind, from somewhere, she does not know, she is thrown back into herself. Jarred into the reality and hears from her mouth, "STOP." This surprises both of them, but somehow grounds her back into her chair.

Lauren wants to leave, but she cannot even stand, let alone get out of the chair. She figures she is having a breakdown and like the few she had before, reasons very soon, all functions will stop. So, she waits. Nothing happens.

He is looking at her funny, kind of like he and her Dad did before. Maybe she is looking at him funny too. Perhaps she is going crazy, and that is why her mind is mush. Yet, she hears *should I tell him to call the looney-bin service to take me away? Hell, I can't even talk. This is nuts. Yes, I am nuts and soon this all will be over.*

Dangerously, the words in her head are not helping. She feels her mouth open as if to speak, but nothing comes out. She closes her mouth, then opens it again to try to speak.

Nothing happens. Her old terrors are coming back and they were taking her breath away. She begins to gasp for air.

He is kneeling beside her, pushing her back down. "Lauren, put your head down between your legs. Yes, it's okay, you're going into shock. Breathe. That's right, breathe nice and steady. Good. Slow and easy. Just breathe."

She steadies herself. He gets to the sideboard, that was made into a bar. Filling a glass of water, he carries it to her and declares. "Oh God, Lauren, I am sorry. I was going too fast. I haven't allowed any of this to set in." She looks up at him, visibly shaking. "Try and sip this. It's water, just a sip," he puts the glass to her lips.

He finally notices the black despair in her eyes, pits sunk into her ghastly white mask of a face. He grabs his Mam's Irish woolen throw from the sideboard's drawer and covers her. Back at the bar, he pours an Irish neat. Then one for himself and bends to her.

"Here, drink this." Her hand convulsing, he puts it to her lips. She takes in a sip. "Try a bit more," and she does as told. Only shivering now, she takes the glass and downs the rest. He hands her the water and she sips at it. He adjusts the caftan around her and takes the little glass to refill them both after downing his.

Once again, he kneels at her side as she sips at the new whiskey. Lauren hands him the water glass and settles back into her chair. Grabbing onto the throw, she doesn't look at him, but stares straight-away.

He gets up and props himself against the desk, facing her in line of her stare. "I have been inconsiderate. Lauren, please forgive me. Can you hear me?"

She makes no acknowledgement of his presence. She only continues her blank stare. He walks back to his desk, leans back in his chair and watches her sip the whiskey. *Look at what you've done, throwing everything at her like that. I am, or at least I have been a professional.* He internally berates himself.

Things had gone well at lunch, but he felt lost with her. Out of touch, then all of a sudden, he *knew* what he had to do. The pieces started falling into place for him, telling her what he knows, sharing it with her made sense because she is apart of him now. That was what was missing...he needs her to *help him*.

But he let his own excitement take him over, spouting off all the details and he hadn't even warned her. She had no idea of what was happening, and she had already been through so much. He reasoned though, knowing the facts would help her. But her naivety had kept her separate from his world, he could only hope he hadn't destroyed what little left she has of her semblance.

He watches her as she gains some control. Slowly, color creeps back into her face. Such a beautiful face. Adoring her as her eyes soften and he wonders when he is going to make love to her. He smiles in spite of himself. *You're a gawddamn dog.* He blasts himself.

She tries to muster a smile but her lips don't listen to her. They maintain a stiffness, except when sipping the delicious amber liquid. It helps settle her mind and bearing with each swallow. Breathing easier, she begins to relax. Blinking her eyes, she finds him looking at her in that funny way of his.

"When you think you are able, I will take you home. I'll arrange for your car to be delivered to you tomorrow." He says sadly as he stands. Then he turns away from her and looks out the window. He feels dead inside.

Chapter 25

Lauren holds her cup of coffee with both hands, standing in her studio. Hoping the rays of the morning light will wash away yesterday's aftermath.

Her favorite room is painted in a light lime green wash that carries a splash of soft coral that fades into the green, in a wave surrounding the suite. Such a fine place, she had made it into a haven, an alcove overlooking the Santa Monica hills behind the condominium complex.

What she enjoyed when she discovered the place, was that the builder didn't like square rooms, he made wall space by making it look like the walls turn. Because of the different shaped rooms, lots of corners and good-sized cubbyholes were created.

Lauren's studio is upstairs from the living area. It was intended to be the master bedroom and bath, but she designed it to be otherwise. Because of the skylights in the bathroom, she created a small green house. Plants of all varieties hanging, standing in tall and short pots in a colorful array of Mother Earth.

Everything she likes to dabble and enjoy is in this large room; passions spent and abundantly fulfilled. Custom pins

made at the flat drafting table and sold to help get her by in her early career. In a corner, facing the side windows is set for painting. These too were sold in galleries back in the day. A nook area holds her small TV and VCR, tapes for exercise and golf instruction along with a stationary bike and workout mat.

Up against the balcony and sliding glass doors is her desk, to enjoy the outside while writing and researching. She doesn't dabble at this. As a matter of fact, it has become her life's work and lively hood. She worked long and hard for many years, making a name for herself. Formulating her success in writing a bestselling book, making herself proud. Especially so, because she never used her family's status or money, breaking from them long ago. This is all hers.

Looking around her favorite room now, it occurs to her that she is good at a lot of things. Maybe superficial at best. Her talents abound, yet her life is a complete mess. Michael led her to love and enjoy life but now she is left with less than she had before. Hurt, devastated and lonelier than ever, her broken life has fallen all around her. "And now the terror of murder, how do I deal with this?" She demands aloud.

She sits down in front of the glass and puts her coffee cup down. She lies down and looks up at the high-vaulted ceiling painted in a cobalt-dusky blue sky with glow-in-the-dark stars everywhere. This is so she can see stars all the time, which remind her she belongs to the universe.

She talks out loud to herself that begins the long difficult task of looking into her life. Again. "It seems like a deja vu, I just did this, what, weeks ago? Right. Never mind, let's try it

again. I've got the time. Julie is downstairs looking after me, so let's begin at the beginning, just like my book says."

Lauren sees an image of her mother and shudders. Cold and unfriendly thoughts of Joseanne, but her grandmother, even worse. Milicent the Formidable. Considering her father, warmth and humor, how did they ever make it and why? Joseanne and Stefen Ashlynn.

"Dad, why didn't you *save* me from them? Doesn't every little girl *know* her Daddy will save her from the wicked witch. I had two of them. Where were you?" Her anger is startling her. She's wanted to ask him so many times through the years.

He was there for her often. Just not enough and there wasn't enough comfort to go around. How odd that this is coming up now? "I had always thought of you as my hero. But you weren't. You aren't. No one is, damn it. So, who is going to save me now that I'm all grown up? Who is going to save me from *me*? Well, doesn't this put a new hole in the fence?" She tries to laugh at her attempt of derisive humor.

Not much to go over, remembering but minuscule sections of her childhood and teens. Always shy. Except when nervous, she'd over compensate. Force conversations and generally not be herself. "Isn't that a cliché? Who am I?" Rolling on the floor, she starts laughing and crying anxiously.

She sits up suddenly and interrogates: "JUST WHO ARE YOU? WHO THE HELL AM I EXACTLY?" She shatters the silence, as life is shattered already. "IT ISN'T GOING TO

182

HURT TO MAKE SOME NOISE. A LOT OF NOISE." She yells and stomps her feet.

Julie runs up the stairs. "Oh God Lauren, are you alright?"

"Sorry, yeah, sort of. I'm having a major temper tantrum!" She realizes the honesty in that statement.

"Julie, I know this doesn't sit well with you. After all, you've been seeing my behavior quite crazy and radical. But you know, this time I really am okay, I just have to flip out and figure stuff out. Please, you don't have to stay. Honest, I promise to call if I need help. Honest."

"Promise. Really promise me. Or I'll call your Dad!" Julie threatens. She stands in the doorway, watching her, hands on hips to prove her deliberation. She knows this woman and has seen her through a lot in the years. She understands how Lauren operates, how she'd get into her research and sequester for days.

There is something stirring in Lauren that Julie recognizes and this makes her feel better. Because that inner drive of Lauren is forming out of all the anguish she has seen her go through. Still concerned however, with everything of late, she says, "I'm going to call you in a few hours, you better answer."

Lauren assures her by walking over to her and hugging her. "There is something changing Julie. I appreciate all you've been through with me. Especially of late. I promise I will answer, better yet. I will call you! Now go, you need a break from all this drama."

Julie leaves, Lauren smiles to herself with gratitude that she has been an incredible friend, confidant and trusted assistant. She hears her lock the door downstairs as the exhaustion of pain and the fatigue of confusion swarms her. In remedy, she flips on the CD player. Genesis is singing, "...I think I'll change my life today..."

Lauren starts moving to the rhythm of the music and sings the chorus, "'...I think I'll change my life today...'

"Change my life...change what? My past? Growing up? Everything had to be always quiet. It had to look good, nice, and be fine. But nothing was good. Nothing. No one was happy. None of us were or are. What is that all about? Precisely. What's it about? I'm going to find out. And if it does kill me? Hell, what do I have to lose? I've been dead most of my life, except with Michael. DAMN IT. WHAT A WASTE."

"I'm tired of fighting and being mired in all this old, regimented mess of my past life. Release the resistance and use my energy to create solutions. Don't both take the same amount of time and attention anyway?"

She stops and looks in the floor mirror, an idea starts brewing. Even though arguments ensue in her head. "Just do it, damn it!" She exclaims to herself. Before she can change her mind, she calls Julie and leaves a message: "I've decided to go to BT's for a few days. He has more information on all this crap that's been happening. I want answers. You can reach me there. Thank you, Julie, for doing all you do for me, caring and supporting me. I appreciate you."

184

Lauren packs a bag, showers and changes into jeans and picks an old favorite T-shirt of Michael's to put on. She wants something close to her that smells of strength. Something friendly.

She drives and within a few miles, second thoughts repeat in her head. "You're being rash. Turn this car around and go back." But this time and just as quickly, she recognizes the voice. "Mother, I AM NOT LISTENING TO YOU ANYMORE! Aaaah, YES!" Lauren yells into the wind. Gathering her nerve and finally understands what the books say about 'old tapes' running in 'the monkey brain'.

"And I even wrote about this stuff! Damn, it does take cycles to make our way through the jumble of the past." Remarking to the wind, she turns on the radio and turns it up loudly.

Chapter 26

"YOU SHOULD BE SHOT."   BT yells reassessing his mistakes. "Your behavior was inexcusable, mister. You are a deplorable man, a wild animal obsessed…" He paces his office.

After driving Lauren home, BT returned to his office.   He couldn't sleep. He couldn't rest. He couldn't eat. He went for the Irish. And again. Now, he tries to doze on the couch, to no avail.   Even the whiskey doesn't work, but he continues in hope it will.

Alcohol induced, bowled over with confusion of his own making, he tries to focus on Michael Desport. There is a connection. "Oh yeah, there's a connection alright.   The woman I love. Loves him. He's dead and she's still in love with him. That's just great."

Agitating himself only more, he forces reason through the haze with more Irish. His dreams and Lauren. The name "Lauren" in his dreams. Then he meets *her*. A pilot in his dreams.   Michael was a pilot.   He was killed in a plane crash.   In the dreams, he crashes.   "Now, I'm getting somewhere! I'm Michael and he's me! Yeah that explains it all…"

"GET A GRIP.   God, please don't let me lose it."   He demands aloud.

BT O'Reilly isn't a man that fears for no reason.   He is straight-forward and reality based.   Fear is considered a safety guard, protecting, not allowing him to get cocky.   He can manage and control his life.   It is his forte.   Or at least it used to be.

Repeating his attempt to reason, he slows his thoughts down.   Reevaluating the last hours with her; he allowed an old rookie problem get the best of him.   He got carried away with excitement and it was the beginning of the end.   It led to carelessness and neglectful insight.   Let alone hurting someone who has become so dear to him.

He walks to his desk and sits down.   He turns to the window and takes the ball into his hands.   It endeared him to his father.   The old man caught it for him at Wrigley Field.

It was a perfect summer day.   The sun was hot but no one seemed to mind.   The Chicago Cubs were tied and the sellout crowd were on their feet.   Bottom of the 9th and a 3-2 count.   He was only three, but he would remember this day for the rest of his life.   He knew that then.

The crowd was thundering as the pitch was thrown.   Da caught the Cub's home run while everyone screamed.   The big, burly man picked up his son and twirled him around.   He squeezed him so hard the boy spilled orange pop over both of them.   They laughed and cried at the pure pleasure of it all.   BT smiles as if he can see his Da's face in the baseball.

Their beloved Cubs pulled it off, but Da was the real hero. It was no wonder his tombstone said so.

"What am I going to do Da?"

Forcing himself back to the present, he turns his chair to the desk and puts his feet up on it and passes out.

Waking with a splitting headache, he gets up to take something for it and makes coffee. At his first drink, he twists to see Lauren. Standing in the doorway, she looks like she trying to be courageous and bold, with her hands on her hips. So, astonished he catches himself from tripping and falls into his chair, spilling his coffee all over his undone shirt.

Lauren announces, "I need to know what you know about Michael. I will hire you if I have to. But I have to understand what is happening. It is important that you tell me, again, all the facts, theories and all that is involved. My life, I feel, is at stake here. And I aim to be a part of it. I will not take a back seat any longer and you are not to treat me with kid-gloves.

"I know I have acted as a protected child and I am naive in many respects. Last night, I was shocked beyond recognition. But not now and it doesn't mean I won't be able to take or handle the truth. You have to tell me everything and be completely honest. Why on earth did you remove the protective sweet-coatings and blast me with those details yesterday?"

She pushes the same big chair she sat in yesterday close to his desk and sits down. A show of reclamation. As if that

would prove she had overtaken her fears. Set with determination, she is ready to prove her readiness. Situating herself to face him at his desk, she takes out a pad of paper and spreads several pencils in front of her. Leaning toward him, she is intent to listen.

Wiping at his shirt, he knows she's trying too hard. But he also knows it's what she has to do to fortify herself. He is glad. He wants to protect her, he wants to share everything with her. Paradox after paradox. He asked for a second chance and he has gotten it. He swears he will not mess up again.

"Okay. But I have to warn you, this won't be easy. There are a lot of things you aren't going to want to hear. Or learn for that matter. It's going to be a long and sorted process. There are no short-cuts here or fast and easy answers. There are too many missing pieces and I don't have many answers.

"I don't mean to sound harsh or patronizing, but Lauren, *this is going to be tough.* All the paper, pencils and determination aren't going to cut it. Maybe you should think on it some more."

He marvels at her strength and resolve to come back and tackle the trauma. But to act courageous is one thing, to hold out and try to function under siege is quite another. To take the knocks and stand up to the fear constantly, can take her down. He doesn't want her downfall on his hands.

"I know. I have thought of that and the consequences. This has not been a snap decision. I've been rustling with things

for a very long time. I just didn't know how to go about it. Yesterday was very scary, but then I've been scared of my shadow most all my life. I trust you BT O'Reilly, and I believe in you. I'm not exactly sure why, but I do. Your sign downstairs, 'O'Reillity', I'm for it."

BT likes her verve, she'll need it and he will be there for and with her. He can't help the feeling that the siege she will confront would be better if it consisted of guns upon a fort. Rather than the emotional roller coaster she is about to embark.

What he does not realize is his own emotional torment and the connections he will confront.

Chapter 27

"Your grandmother was a gangster's moll back in the 1920's," BT begins.

"Ohhhkay, you have my attention," she says. Lauren isn't too surprised, what with how awful and formidable the old bat is.

"But first, we need to discuss so many things. It's important...so that...well, we need to get things cleared up between you and me. I am sorry and ashamed I was such a brute yesterday."

"I'm working through that, so calm your miserable self!" She tries to make fun and lighten his grimness. She really does care for him, but sees that was too harsh considering his crest fallen look. Lauren knows he appreciates the banter to be fun, yet realizes she overstepped in that he is hurting. So much so, he still hadn't changed his coffee stained shirt.

"Ouch, I guess that's a start...yeah...alright...then second, I know you are determined to stand up to your fears, but like I said, this is going to be really hard and extremely difficult. There are a lot of horrendous details in this old information. I won't be able to protect you from the truths."

191

"Well, as you may know, in order to heal, we have to go through the pain. And because I have a lot of experience managing expectations, I have to do this. I have to walk the talk. I wrote a book on it, for God sake! Not talking is a guarantee of not changing and I am not willing to NOT see this through. So, if you figure all this begins with my Grandmother, then so be it. I like history and I know it's important to start at the beginning sometimes," she says not letting him in on her earlier declaration. "So, what do you have?"

"Well then, just remember, you don't have to believe the messenger to believe the message! Besides, it wasn't easy to dig up the dated details and yet Joe did an amazing job on ol'Milicent."

BT commences the long and tedious process of explaining the bygone life. He cites from Joe's reports that Milicent allegedly set up this particular gangster, he was shot in a raid. She became a very powerful woman. But a woman's power in those days had to be behind a man.

This was fulfilled by using Archibald deTournay's naive young nephew, Archie. He wanted to learn the ropes, and being deeply in love with her, she could oblige to this, keep her secrets, retain her anger and control.

....

SHE RAN AWAY AFTER STABBING HER UNCLE 23 TIMES. HE HAD HIS WAY TOO MANY TIMES WITH HER, SO SHE VOWED THEN, SHE WOULD NEVER HAVE A MAN TOUCH HER AGAIN. HER ANGER DEVELOPED AS A SMALL CHILD. A DEAD MOTHER FROM BOOZE, A FATHER THAT

SOLD HER OUT TO SUPPORT HIS OWN HABIT. WHEN THE COURT WAS FINALLY BROUGHT IN, SHE WAS TURNED OVER TO HER UNCLE WHO APPEARED TO BE A FINE, UPSTANDING MAN OF THE COMMUNITY.

BY THE TIME SHE TURNED 12 SHE KNEW ALL ABOUT TERROR AND THAT'S WHEN SHE LEARNED TO USE ANGER TO KEEP HERSELF ALIVE. STABBING HIM FELT SO GOOD, THAT'S WHY SHE COULDN'T STOP HERSELF. AFTER STEALING HIS WALLET AND STASH, SHE BARELY HAD ENOUGH MONEY TO GET TO CHICAGO.

AFTER BEGGING FOR FOOD AND DESPERATE TO SURVIVE, SHE SNUCK ABOARD A SMALL BOAT WHEN NO ONE WAS AROUND. FINDING AN OLD COAT, TROUSERS AND A CAP, PULLED DOWN OVER MOST HER HEAD, SHE COULD MAKE OUT AS A BOY. SHE FOUND HER WAY TO THE ENGINE ROOM, WIPED GREASE ON HER FACE AND MADE HERSELF FAMILIAR WITH THE REST OF THE BOAT. BACK TO HER ORIGINAL HIDING PLACE, BEHIND BARRELS AND FISHING NETS, SHE FELL ASLEEP.

COMMOTION AWAKENED HER, BOYS AND MEN WHISPERING, A MUFFLED MOTOR, FLASHING LIGHTS. BARRELS BEING MOVED ABOARD AND THEN SHE COULD FEEL THE SEVERE DARKNESS OF THE HUGE MICHIGAN LAKE. SHIVERING, SHE STAYED IN HER SPOT. LATER, THE WHISPERING STARTED AGAIN. THIS TIME BARRELS WERE MOVED AGAIN, FEAR SHE'D BE SEEN, SHE DARED NOT MOVE.

BUT SOON THE PEOPLE WERE GONE. CURIOSITY GOT THE BEST OF HER AND SHE CLIMBED OUT OF THE BOAT AND SNUCK TO FOLLOW THE BOYS. JUST WHEN HER COLLAR WAS PULLED UP SHORT, SHE TRIED TO SCRAMBLE AWAY BUT HE WAS TOO BIG AND STRONG.

THE CIGAR SMOKE GAVE HER AWAY, AT HER CHOKE, HE PULLED OFF HER CAP. HER HAIR FELL DOWN AROUND

HER SHOULDERS AND HE LAUGHED A BIG HARDY HOWL. SHE FOUGHT AND CLAWED AT HIM, SO HE THREW HER IN THE WATER. SHE SANK IMMEDIATELY, BUT SOMEHOW TORE HER WAY TO THE SURFACE. SHE SCRAMBLED TO GET OUT OF THE GREASY FILMED WATER, HEAVILY WEIGHED DOWN BY THE BIG WET CLOTHES, SHE EVENTUALLY TUMBLED ONTO SHORE.

THROUGH HIS CONTINUOUS AND SARCASTIC MOCK OF HER, HE ORDERED THE BOYS TO TAKE HER UP TO THE MANSION, HAVE HIS MAID CLEAN HER UP AND HAVE HER PRESENTED TO HIM.

DRESSED IN THE FASHION OF A STRAIGHT, THIN SILK, HE MARVELED AT HIS NEW DISH. SHE WAS MADE TO BE PRETTY WITH MAKE-UP AND HAIR DO, BUT WHAT HE LIKED ABOUT HER WAS HER FEARLESSNESS AND SPUNK. IT WAS OBVIOUS THAT SHE WAS A RUNAWAY, BUT SHE WAS RELENTLESS, THAT SHE HID ON A BOAT AND FORCED HERSELF OUT OF THE LAKE, THAT TOOK GUMPTION AND MIGHT. HE LIKED THAT. WHEN HE ASKED HER NAME, SHE SPOUTED 'MILL'.

"YOU HAVE MOXIE, GIRL, I LIKE THAT! MILL RHYMES WITH WILL, A FINE BOY'S NAME. THAT'S WHAT YOU'LL BE!"

IF HE HADN'T BEEN THERE WATCHING HIS SHIPMENT COME IN, HE WOULD HAVE MISSED THE LITTLE SPY. HE FIGURED SHE DIDN'T KNOW WHO HE WAS, BUT SOON SHE'D GET IT, HE COULD TELL SHE WAS A SMART ASS FOR HER AGE. HE DECIDED TO TAKE HER IN, BECAUSE HE KNEW SHE'D COME IN HANDY. FIRST, SHE'D NEED TO LEARN THE INS AND OUTS OF HIS BUSINESSES, AND THE BEST WAY FOR THAT WAS TO MAKE HER HIS SLAVE.

HE WASN'T MUCH INTERESTED IN SEX, HE LIKED THEM YOUNG, BUT HE HAD A LOT OF OTHER DOLLS FOR

THAT. HE HAD ANOTHER IDEA FOR THIS ONE. DRESS HER AS AN INNOCENT BOY TO DO HIS DIRTY WORK, THAT ONLY A YOUNG LAD COULD GET AWAY WITH. SMARTLY DRESSED WITH KNICKERS, SHINED SHOES AND A STROKER HAT, HE CLEANED HER UP TO APPEAR VIRTUOUS. ARCHIBALD HAD HER TAUGHT TO PUNCH WITHOUT MAKING MARKS OR SHOWING BLOOD. THE ILLUSION PROVED QUITE USEFUL.

HE ALWAYS HAD THAT GUT FEELING OF WHO WOULD BE TOUGH ENOUGH FOR THE JOBS. HE SET HER OUT TO VALIDATE HERSELF, IT DIDN'T TAKE LONG TO PROVE HIM RIGHT. SOON HE MOVED HER UP TO COLLECT HIS "PROTECTION TAXES." SHE BECAME BETTER THAN SOME OF HIS MEN, ALTHOUGH HE NEVER DISCUSSED THE SECRET DETAILS OF THE BUSINESSES WITH HER, HE DID EXPECT HER TO WORK HARDER THAN THE OTHERS.

SHE WASN'T OUTRAGED BY THE VIOLENCE THAT COLLECTIONS DEMANDED. AS A MATTER OF FACT, SHE ENJOYED THE MERCENARY OF IT ALL, AND SO DELIVERED BRUTALITY WHETHER IT WAS NECESSARY OR NOT. SHE WAS PREPARED TO DO ANYTHING SHE'D HAVE TO, JUST TO MOVE UP IN HIS RANKS. SHE MADE HERSELF TOUGHER AND THAT GOT HER IN CLOSER WITH THE "BOYS," WHICH ALLOWED HER TO ABSORB MORE AND MORE OF THE BOOTLEGGING AND PROTECTION BUSINESSES.

SHE WAS DETERMINED THAT ONE DAY SHE WOULD HAVE IT ALL. THIS WAS HER SPECIAL PROMISE SHE MADE TO HERSELF. SOMEDAY, NO ONE WOULD EVER CONTROL HER AGAIN. SHE EVEN FIGURED THIS GANGSTER WAS EXACTLY, NO, VITAL, TO GET HER TO WHERE SHE NEEDED AND WOULD BE.

AS THE YEARS WORE ON, SHE WAS ABLE TO MAKE MORE OF A POSITION FOR HERSELF. THIS ALLOWED

HER A NICER ROOM AND SOME FREEDOM OF THE MANSION. SHE EXPLORED AND FOUND SECRET PASSAGES THAT LED THROUGHOUT THE HOUSE. IT WAS THEN SHE WAS ABLE TO DISCOVER THE KEY TO HER FUTURE SUCCESS.

SHE WAS ABLE TO INFILTRATE THE BOSS' MOST SECRETIVE INSIDE INFORMATION AND SLOWLY SHE DEVELOPED MORE AND MORE ACCESS. EACH NIGHT, HE WOULD HAVE A DIFFERENT DAME AND EACH NIGHT THEY WOULD DRINK THE BEST, UNCUT LIQUOR THAT NOT MANY HAD THE PRIVILEGE OF TASTING.

HE ENJOYED THESE EVENINGS IMMENSELY AND LOVED TO BRAG ABOUT HOW SUCCESSFUL HE WAS WITH THE LADIES AND HIS BUSINESSES. HE WOULD TELL HIS SECRETS AS STORIES AND REVERED PUZZLES SO HE WOULD GIVE CONVOLUTED DETAILS OF WHO WAS TO BE KILLED OR WHERE THE NEXT SCORE WAS.

HE HELD A HIGH RESPECT FOR THE TANGLED GAMES, SO EACH ONE WOULD BE DIFFERENT AND NO ONE PERSON WOULD KNOW THE WHOLE PICTURE. HIS FAVORITE SAYING TO THE DAMES WHEN THEY ASKED TOO MANY QUESTIONS WAS, 'SPEAK EASY DOLL, I'M TALKIN' HERE. THIS IS MY PARTY.'

MILL WOULD GET TO HER HIDING PLACE EACH NIGHT WHERE SHE WOULD LISTEN AND REMEMBER EVERYTHING. SHE WAS SMART ENOUGH NOT TO WRITE ANYTHING DOWN, BESIDES SHE DEVELOPED A QUICK AND SAVVY MIND. HER MEMORY, BECAME AN IMPERATIVE STEEL TRAP, ALL FROM WHAT SHE LEARNED IN THE DEALINGS AND NUMBERS OF THE BUSINESS. SHE ALSO ASSIMILATED FROM HIM THE EXEMPLARY WELD OF CONTROL; THEREFORE, SHE KNEW ONE DAY SHE WOULD HAVE HER OWN LIFE OF NOT JUST CONTROL, BUT POWER.

NOT MUCH COULD SURPRISE HER, BUT WHEN SHE TURNED 16, HE GAVE HER A PARTY THAT WOULD SHOW HER OFF. HE WAS STUNNED BY HER BEAUTY, HOW SHE HAD GROWN AND FILLED OUT. HE NEVER PAID ATTENTION TO HER AS A FEMALE BEFORE BECAUSE SHE WAS A HARD WORKER AND THE BOY CLOTHES SHE ALWAYS WORE.

BUT NOW HE WANTED HER. HE WANTED HER IN THE WORSE WAY. HER YOUTH, SMARTS, AND IN HIS OWN, WAY. SHE WAS TO BE HIS AND EVERYONE WAS GOING TO KNOW IT. HE ORDERED THE BEST OF EVERYTHING. HE EVEN SMUGGLED IN THE CHAMPAGNE FROM FRANCE, 'JUST FOR YOU', HE TOLD HER.

SHE KNEW BETTER THAN TO FEEL SPECIAL, BUT IN THE DAYS PRECEDING THE PARTY, HIS COMPLIMENTS, ENDEARMENTS, THE FABULOUS DRESSES AND JEWELS WERE TOO HARD TO IGNORE. BECAUSE HE NEVER TOUCHED HER IN A SEXUAL WAY, SHE WENT AGAINST HER BETTER JUDGEMENT AND HOPED HE'D BE WHAT A GOOD FATHER WOULD BE LIKE.

THE NIGHT WAS BEAUTIFUL. CLEAR SKIES WITH A BRIGHT MOON. TINY LITTLE LIGHTS DANCED EVERYWHERE IN THE SLIGHT BREEZE. THERE WAS MUSIC AND HORDES OF PEOPLE THAT DANCED ALL TYPES OF SHIMMY. AND OF COURSE, LOTS AND LOTS OF BUBBLY, THE DELIGHTFUL CHAMPAGNE FLOWED.

WHAT COULD IT HURT TO ENJOY THE CELEBRATION? IT WAS IN HER HONOR AFTER ALL. HE TOLD HER HE APPRECIATED ALL THAT SHE HAD DONE FOR HIM AND BECAUSE SHE HAD NEVER HAD A BIRTHDAY PARTY BEFORE, HE WANTED TO DO SOMETHING NICE FOR HER.

SHE WORE THE MOST BEAUTIFUL PALE PEACH SILK AND BEADED DRESS SHE HAD EVER SEEN. HE HAD THE DRESS DESIGNED IN PARIS AND SHIPPED IT OVER JUST

FOR HER. IT WAS A STRUGGLE TO TRUST HIM, YET THE LUSH EXTRAVAGANCE CONTINUED SO SHE DECIDED TO ALLOW HERSELF A LITTLE HAPPINESS AND FUN.

NATURALLY, SHE DRANK THE DELICIOUS BUBBLY, AND DANCED WITH ALL THE HANDSOME MEN. SHE WAS THE LIFE OF THE PARTY AND WAS TREATED WITH THE UPMOST RESPECT. AS THE NIGHT WORE ON, THE BOSS WAS BY HER SIDE MORE AND MORE. HE DANCED WITH HER AND BECAME POSSESSIVE OF HER.

HE WHISPERED IN HER EAR HOW BEAUTIFUL SHE WAS, THAT HE WAS SO PROUD OF HER. REPEATING HOW GRATEFUL HE WAS TO HER FOR ALL THAT SHE HAD DONE FOR HIM. THIS MADE HER FULL OF EXCITEMENT, ACTUALLY HAPPY AND GIDDY. SHE KEPT DRINKING THE TASTY WINE AND LOVED THE ATTENTION. IT WAS ALL SO WONDERFUL. NEVER, HAD ANYTHING BEEN DONE FOR HER LIKE THIS. THUS REMOVED ALL OF HER INHIBITIONS AND CAUTIONS.

INTO THE NIGHT, HE BECAME MORE ENRAPTURED WITH HER. SHE COULD TELL HE WANTED HER AND SHE BEGAN TO WANT HIM. BESIDES, SHE HAD TO, DIDN'T SHE? AFTER ALL, LOOK AT ALL HE HAD DONE FOR HER; RAISED HER, THE EDUCATION AND NOW THIS EXTRAVAGANT SHOW. DIDN'T SHE OWE HIM, ISN'T THAT HOW IT WAS DONE? SHE WATCHED HIM WITH ALL THOSE DAMES HAVING SEX. SHE WONDERED WHAT IT WOULD BE LIKE AND FOUND HERSELF JEALOUS AT TIMES OF THE OTHER WOMEN.

HER TINY NIPPLES STOOD ERECT UNDER THE SHEER MATERIAL, AS SHE VIBRATED TO THE MUSIC. HIS FERVOR WAS ABOUT TO EXPLODE AS HE FONDLED HER EVERYWHERE. SO YOUNG, PERT AND THAT SMOOTH, CREAMY SKIN. SHE WAS HIS AND NO MAN AGAIN WAS GOING TO DANCE WITH HER, LET ALONE TOUCH HER.

HE WAS ENTICED BY THE WAY SHE GIGGLED IN HIS EAR. DRINKING AND SPILLING THE LIQUID ON THEM AS THEY DANCED. THE WET DRESS OUTLINING AND CLINGING TO HER PERFECT CURVES. HE NEEDED TO GRIND HER AGAINST THE GROUND.

NOT BEING ABLE TO TAKE IT ANYMORE, HE GUIDED HER THROUGH THE VERANDA, INTO HIS PRIVATE GARDEN. OUT OF SIGHT OF THE OTHERS, WITH ANOTHER BOTTLE OF CHAMPAGNE IN ONE HAND AND MILLIE ON HIS OTHER ARM, HE LAID HER ON THE COOL GRASS. HE DRIBBLED THE COOL DRINK ON HER THROAT, HE LIKED THAT IT TICKLED HER, SO HE LICKED THE PRECIOUS FLUID FROM HER SWEET SKIN.

HER HEAD SWAM BUT SHE WAS HAVING SO MUCH FUN. HE WAS BEING SO NICE TO HER AND SHE LOVED THE SWEET THINGS HE TOLD HER. THE KISSES WERE NICE, ESPECIALLY ON HER THROAT. SHE ACTUALLY LOVED HOW HE HELD HER AND SHOWED HER OFF. NO MAN HAD EVER MADE HER FEEL SO SPECIAL AND CARED FOR.

HE WAS HERS NOW AND NO OTHER WOMAN WOULD BE WITH HIM AGAIN. SHE 'KNEW' HE ONLY WANTED HER. HE MADE HER BODY FEEL SO GOOD. HIS KISSES WERE SO HOT THAT ONLY THE AIR AND DRINK COULD COOL HER. ALL OF IT MADE HER FEEL POWERFUL. THAT SHE COULD HAVE EVERYTHING NOW. SHE KNEW SHE WAS HIS AND LIKED IT.

THE EXCITEMENT MADE HER FEEL HOT AND DIZZY. AND THEN, HE STARTED TEARING HER DRESS OFF. WITH EACH RIP REMINDED HER OF ALL THOSE OTHER TIMES BEFORE. HER MIND STUMBLED, HOW COULD THIS BE? SHE WAS SO SURE...HE WAS NOT LIKE THE REST. BUT NOW HE WASN'T BEING SWEET TO HER...HE WAS RAPING HER.

She was so woozy, she couldn't stop him or her head from the spin. The ugly pain was back again. Then there was nothing, no feeling except for the sickening, familiar blackness, like wet fur covering her entire being and mind.

She awoke with daylight on her face in his bed. Her head felt split open with stars leaving it. It was a continuous attack on every part of her body, she felt like ground meat. She barely made out the bowl at the side of the bed, lunged for it and heaved. Again, and again wrenching the dryness of her soul. Passed out, she awoke again, but this time in her own bed.

Later that night, she awoke back in his bed. She was wearing a beautiful satin nightgown. Candlelight and flowers were everywhere. She sat up and tried to orient herself. He walked in looking dapper in his sharp suit and sickening smile from ear to ear.

"Hey baby, I didn't think you were going to make it. But after you slept all day and stopped making sick, I wanted you back with me. What do you think of the place? I had the maids clean you up and fix the joint. I figured you'd want to see everything look nice."

She couldn't say anything, her voice was gone and her throat hurt terribly. She wrapped her hands at her throat and pleaded with him in a weak smile that he'd understand.

"Don't worry sweet cheeks, and whoa are they! You are mine. Only mine. My Millie." Leering with the look of a wolf. He began ripping his clothes off and pounced on her for the kill.

She laid there, willing herself not to be sick and scream. Cigar smoke made her green. He hurt her as he contorted her body every which way. But within minutes he was done. Sitting up against the massive head board, he reiterated that she was only to be his. And he decided she could have some say in the rule of his empire.

She tried to be still, because she was in such pain. Millie let what he said sink in. She tried to remember what had happened last night. Everything was a blank to her, so she only smiled as sweetly as she could at him, hoping he would pass out any moment, as was his MO with the others.

Within a few months she knew what she had to do. When he was gone, she swore a man would never touch or get close to her again. It was so hard to believe that she 'allowed' herself to feel happiness, to believe he was different. And that she let him 'play' her like that, actually let him next to her. But she had to admit she was responsible. So with that, it only strengthened her vow, and as disgusted and sickened by it all, she would make her bitterness and resentment define her future.

She secretly planned 'her' empire; to rule with venom, leave others raped and made to pay dearly her prices. Cruelty was her motto. No one would get in her way or ever stop her again. Not even the baby she now carried. This baby was his, and its only purpose would give her the power and control she needed over him and his boys.

After his death, his nephew Archie, came into rule. But he was young and green and, so in

LOVE WITH HER. WHICH OF COURSE WAS TO HER ADVANTAGE. SHE KNEW EXACTLY HOW TO CONTROL AND MANIPULATE HIM WITHOUT HIM OR ANYONE ELSE KNOWING WHAT WAS HAPPENING TO THEM. HER DOMINION TO INFLUENCE HAD BECOME AN ART.

ALTHOUGH SHE HAD BECOME KNOWN AS 'HIS MILLIE', THE DAY AFTER HIS SHOOTING, SHE DECLARED WITH A SOLEMN FACADE, "BECAUSE MY HEART ACHES AT THE LOSS OF OUR DEAR BOSS, I WILL NO LONGER BE REFERRED AS 'HIS MILLIE'. I UNDERSTAND I HAVE TO BE STRONG TO CARRY ON; THEREFORE, YOU ALL WILL REFER TO ME AS MILICENT DETOURNAY. THAT IS ONE L. DO YOU UNDERSTAND?

"WE ARE ALL GRATEFUL TO ARCHIE FOR STEPPING IN DURING THIS HORRIBLE TIME TO LEAD US THROUGH TO OUR BRAVE FUTURE. OF COURSE, WITH THE UNDERSTANDING THAT THIS BABY OF 'THE BOSS' IS THE TRUE HEIR OF THIS EMPIRE." SHE HELD HER STOMACH IN EMPHASIS, SHE KNEW HOW TO USE DRAMA EFFECTIVELY. HER BEAUTY, AND DUPLICITOUS SOFT SPOKEN DEMURE, HAD THEM EATING OUT OF THE PALM OF HER HAND.

Chapter 28

"What I'm about to tell you all started with the phone call I made to her after you were safe. I had called Deirdre after you were kidnapped. When you were free, I let her know. I couldn't help but notice you and your Dad were perplexed about why I left you at LAX to fly to Chicago. It's just that I didn't know any of this until I got there. She wouldn't discuss it over the phone and implored me to get there as soon as I was able."

"Hey, we wondered but we also figured you and her are friends. Besides, it wasn't, isn't our business of your relationship. At any rate, I'm here to listen to your story." Again, Deirdre is the subject. Lauren holds her opinion of *her* to herself. Hurt as she is, remembers he told her that he had feelings for her, Lauren. She stiffens straight in the chair as mixed messages circle overhead.

He sees he's losing her interest, that her demeanor condenses and stutters. ""She's been a friend for a long time. Look, I know this all sounds crazy, but please hold your judgement and let me try to lay down the groundwork of all this."

They exchange uncomfortable glances. Not knowing what else to do or say about that, he begins. "Okay, it all started

with Deirdre searching out her parents, because she was orphaned as a toddler. There's a lot of details, but I'm going to fill you in with more of a bullet point timetable.

"Roadblocks compelled her to spend money and hire a detective. You see, each time she would talk to someone, or go to certain places, she would get an unusual call. Sometimes threatening, sometimes just a warning. So, when she hired Joe it was mainly to protect herself. Deirdre isn't one to stop at anything. She always follows through to the end, whatever she starts.

"Joe was able to do a lot of research with unlimited funds. He collected bits and pieces of facts that began to snowball. As you know, the dollar can be a great inducer for people to talk, so he gave it away on her behalf. There were many bitter people who wanted to tell their stories." BT talks faster as Lauren's eyes glaze over.

"These accounts led to your grandmother. She set up The Boss and arranged for him to be taken down by a rival gang. It was quite the scandal, but she was completely left out of it. She played his grieving gal who was pregnant and because he was happy about his heir, he changed his will to excessively provide for her and the child.

"She became Milicent deTournay, the most powerful woman of her time. Despite the fact she had a girl, it did not stop the businesses in growth. She was able to increase what the old boss had created into millions. An actual empire. Her savvy kept her alive by upholding her rule behind her "boys" and they were loyal to her. What went on in that mansion, not many people knew."

Lauren can't help notice his eyes when he speaks of Deirdre. They gleam, it's obvious he likes talking about her, that he is proud of her is certain. So much so, his emotions run high. Lauren is really getting sick of this woman. Everywhere she'd be, *she* would turn up.

Looking down at her hands, as if they would give her courage, she asks, "Excuse me, but just what does *Ms. Kennsington* have to do with me? First, Michael. Then the airplane ride to Hawaii and now even my father is infatuated with her. This old-time story about my horrid grandmother...and you...obviously your relationship with *her*. BT, I feel like a fool. I thought, well you said you are having feelings for..." She breaks off, not looking at him.

"Lauren, please. I do have feelings for you. You have come to be important to me." He finally understands why her mood changed so dramatically. Damn, he sure could be slow sometimes. He hurries to explain, "It's just that, that phone call after you were safe. That's when she told me of the threats on her. And what with the work she had done convinced her, well. Well, that you were, uhhh, are a part of this."

Seconds pass, she tries to continue, "It appears you are making a connection with me and I don't understand why." Lauren finally looks him in the eyes, pleading her wish he would stop talking about *her*, yet wrestles with knowing she needs to hear the truth anyway. She prepares herself.

BT takes a long time to answer. He gets up from his chair and turns toward the skyline out his office window. He

struggles with how he is going to tell her the rest of what he knows and to keep it in some kind of clear order. Instead, he walks to her, bends down to be at eye level, takes her hands, looks straight into her eyes, and delivers. "I don't know how to tell you this without bowling you over like I did yesterday. So, I'm just going to say it, I, we believe Deirdre is your sister."

Chapter 29

BOOM, Lauren hears in her head. She yanks her hands away and grips the seat arms. As emotions churn, she hangs on for the waves of panic. They seem to be in shorter spurts now, maybe because she is finally doing something, like acting toward her life. But this, this is all too much.

She forces herself to look back at him. Lauren's fear is spinning out of control, but questions him despite it and asks. "I know you said this was going to be tough, but sisters? There's really proof for this? And from your eyes, there's more, isn't there?"

He nods and stands, sits next to her in the accompanying chair. "Yes." He wipes his brow with the back of his hand and continues, "Lauren, there is a lot more. The research is far reaching. Touching many lives. Including mine." He lets that last line hang.

Lauren pushes herself back into the chair hard, not taking her eyes away from his. Anguishing over how she signed up for this, confusion repeats as she braces herself once more. She pushes through, "Do you mean your accident? I don't know what to say. You. Do you mean Michael and you too? Because I have got to say there are too many similar,

uncomfortable I might add, actions and expressions you share."

"How? What do you mean?" It's BT's turn to be caught off guard.

"Damn. I don't know." She gets up and starts pacing. At least this helps slow the boiling panic in her stomach. Hot tears burn behind her eyes but she keeps moving as an idea begins to niggle at the back of her brain.

"Okay, I just may be one snowflake short of a blizzard," Lauren builds momentum in a nagging theory as she continues to pound the lush carpet.

"Michael believed in reincarnation. It was very real for him. He talked of it a lot and would cite lots of examples of the studies he researched." She stopped talking and went to the window to look out. She didn't see the landscape, she looked into the fathoming facets of her mind that is bringing about a hypothesis.

The tears flow out and she cries, "He said he, we would always be together. That there was no way we couldn't be. He said our love was that strong. A soulful experience whether you prefer the words metaphysical or mystical. It didn't matter because he knew it to be true. I believed him. I still do, damn. This is tough." She puts her hands to her face and cries more.

BT sits back in his chair. He's rattled and stunned but stays quiet.

Finally, Lauren drops her hands and turns to him, tears running down her face. "It's just that you so remind me of him. It's really uncomfortable how similar you two are. And yet, there are differences too. You both are kind, funny, the sense of humor," she ponders a moment, "so akin.

"I jumped subjects. Sorry. Did you mean the accident? Will you tell me what happened?" Lauren digs in her jeans to find a wad of rumpled Kleenex.

BT is now completely bowled over at this display of comparisons. "I don't know what to say. I'm flattered? I'm confused."

"I know. I know. Me too. But I got to say, and I can't believe I'm saying this. Clarity is forming by the moment, even though I know I'm still in for it. I'm ready for the 'blow me down' moment'!"

Lauren continues. "Look BT, I'm not going to let fear keep me from being happy. I know I have to go through the pain to heal. You appear to have. It works right?" Pleading with him to agree, to help keep her conviction.

"Sure? Yeah, I know you're right. Actually, reincarnation? I'm not into that."

"It's not that you're *in to it*, it just is. And that's what makes sense here."

"Eh, Lauren I don't know. But I do understand, sort of. It's just that with all the more to explain to you, well Lauren, I

need your help. There is so much more, I really need your help with all this. As for the accident. It wasn't."

Her jaw drops.   She closes her mouth and attempts to speak.

"I know. Like I said. There's a lot more. Before I tell you, will you agree to help me?" He goes to stand near her at the credenza by the window.   He takes her hands again in emphasis. He really likes her hands.

....

Chicago is not far away enough to prepare her for what she is about to hear and do.   Confronting a woman she hardly knows for proof that her life is completely upside down. But she saw the softness in BT's eyes when he took her hands. When he told her about her alleged sister and how he implored her to help him. And how he does have feelings for her.

The L1011 makes a graceful landing.   They de-board and leave O'Hare without incident.   The late night is beautiful. Stars bright with hope, the city lights shinning of welcome. BT holds her shaking hand with ease and reminds her to breathe deeply. He invites her to enjoy his native city. The taxi takes them to "Magnificent Mile" and they pull in front of the Ritz-Carlton.

"Ah Mr. O'Reilly, it is so good to see you again!" The night manager exclaims.   They shake hands, he tips his hat to Lauren in greeting and guides them to the elevator.

"Everything is set for you, I hope you enjoy your stay." At that, a bellman appears with the keys and escorts them to their rooms.

He opens Lauren's door and gestures her to enter a room of flowers. They are everywhere. A slight breeze pesters the lace curtains and soft sounds of an enchanting evening tread through her memory.

She turns around to find the men gone. Immediately she is awe struck at the sense of deja vu. Michael.

"All we need is High Tea and this will be a rerun," she whispers to herself. So much for clarity and the bravado she held in LA, as fatigue and the familiarities smack her in the face with uncertainty and distress.

The bellman appears at the adjoining room door, "Is everything to your liking Madame?"

"Yes, thank you very much."

BT follows him, grinning as if he found the pot of gold. "Thank you!" He resounds shaking the bellman's hand.

"Do you like it here?" He asks her as her front door closes quietly.

"Very much. It is so nice of you to bring us here. The room is beautiful." Lauren is trying very hard to stay composed.

She seems so sad. Her mood has since plummeted after all they discussed before the flight. He knew this trip would be

tough, but he hoped the luxury would soften it and please her. BT is struggling too, not knowing what to think with all she said of Michael. He puts on a good show however. He figures if they both can relax enough to sleep well tonight, they can be fortified for their drive and what's to come tomorrow.

A light rap at the door announces his other surprise.

"I took the liberty of ordering a late night snack for us!" He exclaims and opens the door. Room service has carts of what else, High Tea deliquesces.

Lauren smiles weakly and plops down to stop her faint-of-heart. After the men leave the room, he pours the opened champagne and hands her a flute.

Holding her glass out to him in a toast. "This is lovely, BT. Do you enjoy High Tea often?"

"Actually no. But I thought you'd like it," he says as he clinks her glass. He hopes the display cheers her up, he wants her happy again.

"I do. It's just that..." His eyes, they look so much like Michael's. His expression, the inquisitive and mischievous smile combo gets her. "Oh, I am so sorry."

"Don't be. What's wrong?" BT is confused and concerned.

"Michael used to do the same thing. I feel as though I'm seeing a ghost," she confesses.

"In me?"

"Yes," she says quietly, nibbling on a cucumber sandwich to cover her tearing face.

Chapter 30

JOSEANNE DETOURNAY CAREFULLY FOUND HER WAY AND QUIETLY SLIPPED DOWN THE GARDEN STEPS. WHEN SHE FELT SHE HAD ENOUGH DISTANCE FROM THE MANSION, SHE RAN HARD TO HER SECRET PLACE. AN INCREDIBLE AND MASSIVE DITCH PROTECTED BY AN IMMENSE NATIVE BLACK WALNUT TREE.

THE OLD BRANCHES, HEAVILY WEIGHTED DOWN WITH BIG LEAVES AND FRUIT, ENCIRCLED AN AREA OF UNDERBRUSH. THIS MADE AN ELABORATE AND INTRICATE ROOT SYSTEM THAT CREATED SEPARATE AREAS. SHE LOVED THIS HIDE-AWAY AS A CHILD AND MADE 'ROOMS' FOR HER 'PLAYHOUSE'. IT WAS ALMOST AN UNDERGROUND CAVE, WITH WALLS OF HARD, PACKED DIRT AND ITS SOFT PADDED FLOOR OF LEAVES.

IT WAS A STILL BLACK NIGHT FOR A SECLUDED HAUNT. HER HEART POUND SO LOUDLY SHE WAS AFRAID THOSE EVIL PEOPLE WOULD HEAR HER. FINALLY, SHE REACHED THE SPOT AND HUNCHED DOWN TO WAIT JUST UNDER THE SECRET ENTRANCE. AT LAST SHE HEARD HIS FOOTFALLS. HE NEVER RAN TO HER. CONFIDENT, AT SEVEN YEARS, HE WAS ALWAYS IN FULL KNOWLEDGE OF WHAT HE WANTED.

HE HAD CHIDED AND DARED HER TO MEET HIM, "YOU'RE NOT TOUGH. YOU'RE A SCARED LITTLE MOUSE, I DOUBLE-DARE YOU TO MEET ME TONIGHT. SNEAK OUT FROM UNDER YOUR GUARD. HA, THERE'S

NO WAY YOU'LL BE THERE!" HE WALKED AWAY FROM HER, LAUGHING.

HE MADE HER MAD. SHE WANTED SO MUCH TO BE BRAVE AND SMART LIKE HE. HE EVEN SHOWED THE ADULTS HE WASN'T SCARED OF THEM. HOW SHE ADMIRED HIM. SHE DIDN'T WANT HIM TO GET THE BEST OF HER, SHE WAS THE SAME AGE AND SHE DID NOT WANT TO BE SCARED ALL THE TIME. BUT NOW, SITTING IN THE COLD, BLACK NIGHT, SHE WONDERED WHY SHE LET HIM CON HER INTO THIS.

WHEN SHE SAW HIM, SHE KNEW WHY. HE WAS TALL AND FULL OF SECRETS. SHE WANTED TO KNOW WHAT THEY WERE. SHE WANTED TO BE LIKE HIM, SURE OF HERSELF AND CERTAIN.

"SO YOU DID SHOW UP!" LAUGHING AT HER.

SHE STARED AT HIM, FIGHTING THE STING OF TEARS. DESPERATELY TRYING TO BE TOUGH. BUT HE KNEW HOW TO INFLECT HER DAMAGED PRIDE. SHE WANTED TO RUN AWAY.

"AREN'T YOU THE TOUGH ONE?" HE SMIRKED, CHIDING HER ONCE AGAIN. HE DIDN'T TAKE HIS EYES AWAY FROM HER. HE KNEW HOW TO INDUCE FEAR, IT MADE HIM FEEL POWERFUL. HE LIKED HER WELL ENOUGH, BUT HE LIKED PUSHING HER MORE, THE RICH LITTLE GIRL. MAKING HER BODY TREMBLE EXCITED HIM. HE LIKED THE AFFECT HE MADE ON HER. AND MOST OF ALL, HE LIKED TAUNTING HER.

HE BENT DOWN TO HER AND FIXED ON TO HER EYES. HE COULD READ HER TERRIFIED, LITTLE MIND AND WANTED TO AGITATE IT MORE. SO, HE KISSED HER MOUTH VERY FAST. IT WAS FOR THE REACTION, BUT HE WAS CURIOUS TOO.

STARTLED SHE JUMPED UP TO LEAVE. HE GRABBED HER, PULLED HER INTO THE ENCLOSURE AND PUSHED HER DOWN ONTO THE GROUND. HE SAT ON HER TO STILL HER. HE LOOSENED HIS GRIP AND ENJOYED HER TORMENT. SHE LAY THERE, NOT KNOWING WHAT TO DO. THE TEARS CAME NOW AND BURNED HER CHEEKS WITH EMBARRASSMENT, ALL THE WHILE SHE TRIED TO AVOID HIS MENACING GAZE.

OH, HOW SHE LIKED THIS LOUIE ARMANT. HE MADE HER LAUGH AND SHOWED HER THINGS LIKE FROGS AND MUD. HE WAS FUN FOR THE MOST PART, BUT HE SURE COULD BE MEAN AND ALWAYS FOUGHT FOR HIS OWN. SHE KNEW, DOWN DEEP, HE WOULDN'T REALLY HURT HER BUT TONIGHT WAS DIFFERENT. HE HAD NEVER BEEN THIS ROUGH WITH HER BEFORE AND IT SCARED HER.

HE WAS FROM A POOR FAMILY. THE SOLE SON OF HER GRANDMOTHER'S GARDENER AND HE ONLY CAME EACH SUMMER TO BE WITH HIS FATHER. WHEN HE WENT TO SCHOOL, HE LIVED WITH HIS GRANDMOTHER.

HE NEVER SPOKE OF HIS MOTHER, EXCEPT ONCE. HE SAID SHE DIED FOR HIM, AND THAT MADE HIM SPECIAL. WHEN HE GREW UP, HE WOULD BE VERY RICH LIKE HER. SHE DIDN'T UNDERSTAND WHAT HE MEANT BUT KNEW BETTER THAN TO ASK.

FINALLY, LOUIE EASED UP ON HER AND EXCITEDLY ANNOUNCED, "LET'S GO LOOK FOR SOMETHING!"

"WHAT?" SHE WHISPERED. CATCHING HIS EXCITEMENT, SHE LOOKED AT HIM HARD.

"FOR SECRET STUFF. WILL YOU DO IT? OR, ARE YOU CHICKEN?"

"Her eyes blazed at him, "No. I'm not a chicken, I can do it."

"OK, Josie. That's good!" He smiled winning her confidence. He scooted over so that his back was against the ditch wall. She followed him and he pulled her to him so her back pressed against him.

"First, I will teach you to drive. You steer and I'll push the peddles."

"What are we looking for?" Excited in adventure, she held her hands up to steer on the make-believe wheel.

"Now, we'll only know it when we see it. Let's go." He pulled her closer to him with a jolt. Her little body pushed on him and he began to feel a strange and warm sensation in his pants. He made engine noises and moved his feet at the air peddles. His hands explored her shorts.

He made her feel funny there. She tried to squiggle away but that made him squeeze her harder and hurt. He made the engine noises louder in her ear and pushed at her while he pulled her back even more against him. She kept steering right and left, hoping she was making him happy. She tried to do good for Louie and tried to ignore the funny feelings down there. She didn't want to disappoint him by doing something wrong.

"Do you see it yet, Louie?"

"I think maybe it will be here pretty soon. You're doing real good Josie. Keep steering, I have to work the gears and the peddles. It's a

Chapter 31

"So, you're Sweet 16, but I know you've been kissed!" Louie declared. He liked to reproach her in his usual way as often as he could.

"Yes I have and by much better boys than you," she returned the cut.

His expression changed to that of dismay, he wanted her for real this time. They had continued to explore each other's bodies as they grew up. With each year the need became more insistent. Sneaking off became habitual and addictive for both of them. They shared secrets of discovery and it made them closer in numerous ways.

They enjoyed laughing and teasing each other. Skinny-dipping at night and running through the woods naked allowed a freedom they never were able to experience at any other time in their lives. Even their talks gave them each importance. Their dreams were given a chance to grow and develop.

He was late getting back this year from school. He knew she was mad at him, he wanted to soothe her temper. She had become much stronger through their years together. He was proud that he had taught her fearlessness. She became a good opponent for him and it only

MADE HIM WANT HER MORE. ASIDE FROM THE FACT SHE HAD FILLED OUT INTO A BEAUTIFUL WOMAN.

HE TOOK HER DELICATE HAND AND KISSED IT SOFTLY. HE TURNED ON HIS CHARM, "FORGIVE ME, IT IS YOUR BIRTHDAY AND YOU LOOK SO BEAUTIFUL. WILL YOU HONOR ME WITH YOUR PRESENCE TONIGHT FOR A BIRTHDAY SURPRISE?"

"WHAT ARE WE LOOKING FOR THIS TIME?" SHE WAS ANGERED BY HIS CHARM, BECAUSE HE ALWAYS KNEW HOW TO BEGUILE HER. BUT SHE DID WANT HIM TO TOUCH HER, IT HAD BEEN SO LONG. OH, HOW SHE ACHED FOR HIM. AND NOW, BEFORE HER STOOD A MAN. HE HAD GROWN INTO A MAGNIFICENT, TALL AND SEXY ROUGE. HIS LUST FOR HER BURNED IN HIS EYES, SHE KNEW IT WAS FOR HER.

"COME ON JOS, I ONLY HAVE YOUR BEST INTEREST IN MIND. YOU KNOW I WOULD NEVER HURT YOU. BESIDES, WE WERE JUST KIDS THEN!" AS IF HE READ HER MIND.

SHE HEARD HER MOTHER CALL. HER EXPRESSION IMMEDIATELY CHANGED TO DESPAIR. SHE COULD BE COURAGEOUS WITH HIM, BUT NEVER WITH HER. STILL, SHE GOT EXACTLY WHAT SHE WANTED. HE DID PUT ON THE CHARM FOR HER AND SHE KNEW HE WAS ENTHRALLED AS TO HOW SHE HAD GROWN THIS LAST YEAR. HER EXCITEMENT AND ANTICIPATION GAVE HER AWAY, "YOU BE A GENTLEMAN AND I WILL BE THERE!" SHE EXCLAIMED BREATHLESSLY AND RAN OFF.

THE PARTY WAS ELABORATE AND THERE WERE HUNDREDS OF PEOPLE. ALTHOUGH IN HER HONOR, THERE WAS NOTHING FOR HER TO DO. SHE DIDN'T RELATE TO HER PEERS. THE ADULTS WERE STUFFY AND THE CAKE WAS AWFUL. SHE SHARED NOTHING IN

COMMON WITH ANYONE, THEY WERE SO BORING. EXCEPT FOR THE THOUGHTS OF HIM.

SHE DELIVERED HER MANNERS PROPERLY. POLITELY DANCED WITH THE MANDATORY SOCIETY AND PERFORMED THE REQUIRED ETIQUETTE. HER MOTHER WAS HER POMPOUS SELF AS USUAL. SHOWING OFF EVERYTHING SHE OWNED, INCLUDING HER DAUGHTER. NOTHING AS PRECIOUS TO HER AS HER WEALTH.

JOSEANNE DID LIKE GETTING DRESSED FOR THE BALL AND SHE ENJOYED THE RICHES OF GIFTS AND STATUS. SHE UNDERSTOOD THAT NOTHING COULD EVER COMPETE WITH THEIR MONEY. IT MADE LIFE EXCITING AND LUSH. TRIPS AND ANYTHING EXPENSIVE WERE HERS FOR THE ASKING. BESIDES, IT TOOK THE COLD STING AWAY OF THE OLD BATTLEAX THAT WAS HER OPPRESSIVE MOTHER.

HOWEVER, DANCING WITH OLD, DRUNK MEN SICKENED HER. THE PRICE FOR STATUS WAS IMPERIOUS AND IT MADE HER THINK OF HIM. HER DESIRE MOISTENED AND THIS AGGRAVATED HER TO NOT BE WITH HIM. SHE COULDN'T GET OVER HOW MUCH HE HAD GROWN IN ONE YEAR. HIS LONG, BLACK HAIR SEEMED DARKER, INVADING HER MIND. HIS SHOULDERS HAD BROADENED INTO A VIRILE STRENGTH. SHE LICKED HER LIPS IN ANTICIPATION OF HIM.

PEOPLE BEGAN LEAVING THE PARTY, AND JOS DECIDED TO LEAVE DUE TO A HEADACHE. SHE WAS GLAD THIS PLOY WORKED WITH HER MOTHER. BUT SHE KNEW IT WAS ONLY BECAUSE THE GRAND DAME WAS PREOCCUPIED WITH HER IMPORTANT GUESTS. THE ONES THAT STAYED INTO THE NIGHT. THE FINANCIAL GAINS SHE COULD CONDUCT AND SOCIETY IMPRESSIONS SHE WOULD CONTINUE TO PRODUCE.

Sneaking out wasn't as difficult as she thought it would be. She didn't want to appear overly anxious, so she coolly walked toward their rendezvous. She wanted to keep the control with him. But when she saw him, it slipped a slippery slope.

He stood before her in all his naked glory. Dripping wet from a midnight swim. He had previously placed candle lanterns on the built in 'shelves' of the tree's elaborate root system and scattered flowers throughout their precious, secret area. To be sure they were protected and the lights wouldn't show, he had walked the perimeter several times from different angles.

"For your birthday!" He announced proudly, his arms outstretched in display showing off his achievements. He boldly walked up to her and put his hands on her shoulders. He jammed his tongue into her mouth and found hers. Then he bit it.

The pain caused her to jump. She tried to yell and pull away, but he held her tighter. She fought him with all her might. He pushed his tongue in further. She tried to knee him, but he was much stronger. He wrapped his leg around hers to control her. He nibbled at her neck and pulled her hair back.

"You look incredible tonight," he said biting her lip as he wanted to rip her dress down the front. He stopped abruptly and beamed down at her. "I promised to be a gentleman, so how do I get this off of you?" She was his now. Completely still and powerless to his will. He pulled her down onto her knees with him and

SLID HIS HANDS WITH THE DRESS DOWN. THERE HE RESTED AND HELD HER BUTTOCKS.

HE LICKED HER NECK AND SUPPLE BREASTS LIKE A MAD DOG AFTER BLOOD. HE BIT DOWN ON THE HARD-PINK STONES AS HE SQUEEZED HER ROUNDED CHEEKS. SHE WANTED TO BE FREE TO SCREAM IN ECSTASY. AND SCREAM SHE DID INTO HIS CHEST. SHE DUG HER MANICURE INTO HIS BACK AND DREW BLOOD.

INVIGORATED MORE, HE PUSHED HER ONTO THE COOL, DAMP LEAVES. HE FORCED HIS HEAT INTO HER FLAMING MASS. STABBING HER OVER AND OVER AGAIN, SHE HUNG ONTO HIM FOR THE RIDE. SCRATCHING AND CLAWING HIM, SHE CHEWED ON HIS LIP.

HE FORCED HIMSELF DEEPER INTO HER, CAUSING HER TO YELP WITH TREMENDOUS PAIN. BUT HER PASSION AND LUST OVERCAME IT AS THEY RODE EACH OTHER IN A BOILING FRENZY. THEY TOOK AND STOLE ALL THEY COULD FROM THE OTHER, AS IF IN REBELLION OF THE WORLD. THEY PUMPED EACH OTHER FOR THE REIMBURSEMENT OF LOSS, ANGER, DEFIANCE AND NEED.

Chapter 32

MILICENT DETOURNAY HAD INSPECTED HER DAUGHTER'S ROOM AND BATHROOM PRIVILEGES REGULARLY. WHEN SHE TURNED THIRTEEN, THE GRAND DAME ENFORCED AN ARDENT EXAMINATION EVERY MONTH. CONTROL AND COMPLETE AUTHORITY WERE DEMANDED BY ALL UNDER HER EMPLOY.

ALTHOUGH HER ANGER WAS IMMEDIATE, SHE DECIDED HOWEVER TO CHECK AGAIN IN TWO WEEKS. HER CRITICAL EYE TURNED THE EVIDENCE SHE NEEDED, AND IMMEDIATELY REACTED WITH HER COLD AGGRESSION. NOT CARING ABOUT HER ONLY DAUGHTER, SHE TORE INTO HER WITH BLATANT DEFIANCE AND HARSHLY PUNISHED THIS PIECE OF THRASH WITH SATISFACTION.

"YOU PESTILENT, WHORING BITCH. YOU HAVE SQUANDERED YOUR LIFE AWAY. YOU HAVE RUINED YOUR PERFECT BODY FOR STUPIDITY AND LUST. YOU ARE TO LUST FOR POWER, YOU FOOL. NOT SEX. YOU WILL LEARN TO GET YOUR PRIORITIES STRAIGHT.

"YOU WERE JUST GIVEN SOME FREEDOMS AND LOOK HOW YOU REPAY ME FOR ALL YOU HAVE HAD. YOUR COMING-OUT BALL WAS A COMPLETE SUCCESS AND THIS IS HOW YOU THANK ME?

"YOU WILL STILL BE MY WAY, TO MY MEANS. THIS WILL BE TAKEN CARE OF, MY WAY. DO YOU HEAR ME, YOU INSIDIOUS MAGGOT?" ANGER COURSED THROUGH HER VEINS. EVER DILIGENT IN HER UPMOST CONTROL, THIS

WOULD BE TAKEN CARE OF. SHE DIDN'T WAIT FOR JOSEANNE TO RESPOND AS SHE CONTINUED THE RAMPAGE.

"YOU WILL NOT HAVE ACCESS TO ANYTHING ANYMORE. YOU WILL BE WATCHED AT ALL TIMES BEHIND LOCKED DOORS, UNTIL THAT DESPICABLE THING INSIDE YOU IS BORN. IT IS MINE AND I WILL DO WHAT I WILL WITH IT WHEN IT IS TIME. DO YOU UNDERSTAND?

"YOU ARE NO LONGER FREE TO TALK OR WHISPER. THERE ARE TO BE NO NOISES FROM YOUR MOUTH. YOU ARE NOT TO LOOK AT ME, ALWAYS YOUR HEAD IS TO BE KEPT DOWN.

"YOU HAVE HAD YOUR DAY IN FREEDOM AND DESIRE, NOW YOU WILL PAY FOR IT. IT WILL TAKE YOU THE REST OF YOUR LIFE, AND YOU WILL PAY DEARLY. YOU HAVE ALWAYS BEEN OWNED BY ME AND YOU WILL ALWAYS BE MINE.

"YOU WILL MARRY WHO AND WHEN I SAY. IT WILL BE FOR THE EXTENSION OF MY FAMILY. YOU WILL HAVE CHILDREN WHEN I SAY AND NOT BEFORE. IS THIS COMPLETELY CLEAR? YOU MAY AFFIRM THIS BY A SIMPLE NOD." CALMLY, SHE WAITED FOR THE EXPECTED RESPONSE. NOTHING OR NO ONE COULD EVER GET TO HER. SHE WAS COLLECTED AND INCISIVE IN HER DELIVERANCE. MILICENT WAS IN HER ELEMENT AND SHE THRIVED ON IT.

"NOW, YOU WILL GET TO THE BASEMENT. THERE, YOU WILL LIVE WITH THE MICE AND COCKROACHES. FITTING, AS THAT IS ALL YOU ARE. ALL EXTRAVAGANCE, ALL LUXURY IS NO LONGER A PART OF YOUR LIFE. YOU WILL HAVE THE BARE NECESSITIES. I WILL PROVIDE THAT FOR YOU, IN CAPTIVITY, AFTER ALL.

"YOU WILL LEAVE NOW. I DO NOT WISH TO SEE YOU ANYMORE AND YOU ARE NOT TO MAKE ANY ATTEMPT TO COMMUNICATE WITH ME UNTIL THIS IS OVER. THEN, I WILL CONSIDER WHAT YOU WILL DO. LET YOUR IMPRISONMENT BEGIN!" MILICENT RIGHTEOUSLY THREW HER ARM IN THE AIR, DISMISSED THE LIFE WITH RESOLUTE POWER. THE SERVANTS WERE ORDERED TO TAKE THE GIRL AWAY. IT WAS DONE.

JOSEANNE HAD ALWAYS AGONIZED HOW HER MOTHER COULD HAVE SO MUCH HATE FOR HER. EVEN THOUGH IT NEVER DID ANY GOOD OR CHANGED ANYTHING, SHE WOULD CRY HERSELF TO SLEEP EVERY NIGHT. FROM THE LONELINESS AS A KID FOR AS LONG AS SHE COULD REMEMBER AND IT CONTINUED AS SHE GREW UP.

SHE PERPETUALLY FELT IMPRISONED IN HER BEAUTIFUL ROOM, SCHEDULED AND RESTRICTED IN HER COMINGS AND GOINGS. IT WAS ONLY THOSE RARE SUMMER LATE EVENINGS SHE WAS ABLE TO ESCAPE TO SEE LOUIE BECAUSE MILICENT ENTERTAINED FREQUENTLY AND THE BODY GUARDS WOULD ENJOY THEIR OWN CARD GAMES.

NOW AS A TRUE PRISONER, IT ACTUALLY WAS NO DIFFERENT THAN BEFORE SHE REASONED. AT LEAST THERE WAS NO ILLUSION. LIVING IN THE DUNGEON, HER CLOTHING AND NICE THINGS GONE MADE IT CLEARER TO HER THAT MILICENT WAS ALL ABOUT THE BEAUTIFUL PICTURE FOR THE WORLD, KEEPING SECRETS AND UGLINESS HIDDEN.

SHE CONTINUED TO CRY HERSELF TO SLEEP, BUT NOW WOULD AWAKEN WITH SICKNESS EVERY MORNING. PERHAPS DYING WOULD BE BETTER THAN THIS, IT WOULD REALLY UPSET THE WOMAN'S PLAN. AS ALIVE, SHE WAS ONLY A COMMODITY. SINCE SHE WAS HORRIBLY ILL, IT COULD BE A GOOD SOLUTION. SHE

FILLED HER MIND WITH DEATH AND KEPT A LOOK OUT FOR SOMETHING THAT WOULD ACCOMMODATE.

THE CELL WAS DARK, DIRTY AND COLD. SHE CONSTANTLY HEARD THE RATS SCURRYING AND THE MASSIVE COBWEBS ABOUND, IT ALL MADE HER SKIN CRAWL. JOSEANNE WAS DESPERATE WITH SICKNESS AND DEPRESSION, SHE ASKED MARIE TO HELP HER KILL HERSELF.

MARIE WAS THE YOUNGEST SERVANT GIRL AND HER ONLY REAL FRIEND. SHE TRIED, WHEN POSSIBLE, TO SNEAK HER SOMETHING CLEAN TO WEAR, AND SPECIAL FOOD. BUT SUICIDE, SHE WOULD NOT BE A PART OF. "OH NO, MISS JOSIE. YOU HAVE MUCH TO LIVE FOR. YOU HAVE A SWEET BABY OF LIFE INSIDE YOU. THAT LIFE WILL MAKE EVERYTHING GOOD. YOU'LL SEE.

"I KNOW THIS IS HARD FOR YOU, BUT YOU WILL SEE THAT LIFE WILL BE GOOD. SOMETIME, SOMEWHERE. LIVE NOW. FIND IN YOUR HEART WHAT KEEPS YOU WARM AND THEN HOLD ON TO IT ALWAYS. NO MATTER WHAT." SHE WOULD ALWAYS WHISPER VERY QUICKLY. ALWAYS LOOKED OVER HER SHOULDER, BECAUSE SHE NEVER KNEW WHEN SOMEONE WOULD CHECK ON HER WHEREABOUTS.

SHE OFTEN CAME AND HELPED JOSEANNE TO STEADY HERSELF. THE THREAT OF FOOTSTEPS TORMENTED THEM BOTH. STILL MARIE CAME. A CONSTANT FRIEND DELIVERING SUBSTANCE AND A SPARK OF LIFE.

WITHIN WEEKS, JOSEANNE FELT THE TINY STIRRINGS INSIDE HER. IT WAS A FULFILLMENT SHE NEVER KNEW. WITH LOUIE, THERE WAS ALWAYS THE CRAVING FOR LIFE. WANTING, BUT NEVER SATISFIED. WITH THE GRAND DAME, IT MEANT FIGHTING THE COLDNESS, NOT JUST THE ROOM BUT THE HATRED THAT EMULATED.

228

However, this child, somehow, struck something new for her; balance, a strength that produced life and care. Joseanne had never known how to be content until now. Despite her surroundings and abuse, she could rest, be still and felt curiously safe with the growing life inside her.

Marie helped teach her this. They spoke in guarded whispers of the sweetness of life. No matter how things looked, it was within that mattered. No matter what. Despite her fears of working there, her inner compass of love was true and forthright.

Together, they had cleaned the dingy little room. Milicent allowed this along with clean water and decent foods for Joseanne because she needed her to be healthy after the birth.

Other than that, Milicent relished in the girl's torment. She certainly did while she was pregnant. Therefore, this message was relayed everyday upon the inspections from Gertrude or Cloresent, Milicent's horrible assistants. They were mean and reveled in carrying out the nasty orders of continued punishment and harassment.

Near the last month, one day Marie ran breathlessly to Josie. Fighting her tears, she explained she heard muffled voices. "She plans to kill the baby. Drown it, as soon as it is born. What can we do?"

Joseanne's contentment turned bleak. The baby kicked inside her as if hearing what was said. Instinctively, she reached down to her bulging stomach and rubbed her hand across the vast

AREA. "WE ARE GOING TO BE JUST FINE, LITTLE ONE. MAMMA HAS A PLAN." TEARS WELLED IN HER EYES AND TRIED TO SOUND BRAVE.

"MARIE, I WILL ESCAPE. YOU HAVE TO HELP US. IT'S THE ONLY WAY," SHE WHISPERED.

ALARMED, MARIE BURST INTO HYSTERIA. "HOW? HOW ARE YOU TO ESCAPE?"

JOSEANNE REFUSED TO ACCEPT THE DESPAIR SHE SAW IN MARIE. SHE LOOKED AROUND AND AS IF IT WAS THE FIRST TIME, REALIZED THE TINY WINDOW ABOVE HER HEAD JUST MIGHT DO THE TRICK. SHE WAS TALL AND LANKY, HER BELLY WAS ROUNDISH, BUT PROBABLY COULD FIT, IF SHE MANEUVERED JUST RIGHT. "MARIE, YOU HAVE GOT TO GET ME SOME LARD AND SOMETHING TO DIG WITH. IT'S GOT TO BE SMALL ENOUGH SO YOU CAN SNEAK IT TO ME. NOW DON'T YOU WORRY. PLEASE GO AND HURRY, MY FRIEND." SHE WAS DESPERATE FOR HOPE.

Chapter 33

MAC O'REILLY WAS THE TYPICAL 'GOOD OL' CHICAGO, IRISH COP'. HE WAS HONEST AND A FAIR MAN. EVERYONE THAT KNEW HIM LOVED HIM AND HIS FAMILY. HE LOVED HIS WIFE AND SONS. LOVED HIS 'BIT O'IRISH' AND BEER. AND HE LOVED HIS CITY. HE WAS A MAN THAT LOVED LIFE AND LIVED LOVE. GENUINE THROUGH AND THROUGH.

HE WAS WORKING HIS REGULAR BEAT, WHEN HE HEARD A SCREAM. HE PULLED HIS CAR OVER AND JUMPED OUT, ALMOST BEFORE THE CAR STOPPED. HE RAN TOWARD THE CORNER, GUN DRAWN. MAC FOUND THE SLOUCHED FIGURE OF A BEAUTIFUL, YOUNG GIRL.

ENCIRCLING THE AREA, IN REGULAR POLICE FASHION, HE REALIZED SHE WAS IN LABOR. SHE DRIPPED WITH PERSPIRATION AND SCREAMED IN PAIN. HE QUICKLY SIZED UP THE SITUATION THAT SHE WAS SOON TO DELIVER, BEING THAT THE LAST SCREAM WAS FIVE MINUTES AGO. OBVIOUSLY ALONE, AND PROBABLY A RUNAWAY AT THAT.

MAC PICKED THE GIRL UP AND MADE HIS WAY BACK TO THE CAR. HER PAIN AND FEAR WAS UNBEARABLE, ALMOST CHOKING HIM WITH HER GRIP. "PLEASE DON'T LEAVE ME...PLEASE DON'T LEAVE ME." SHE SOBBED INTO HIS NECK.

"IT'S ALRIGHT LIT'DARLIN'. YOU AND THAT BABE WILL BE JUST FINE. BUT I HAVE GOT TO GET YOU TO THE

HOSPITAL AND YOU'LL BE MORE COMFORTABLE HERE IN THE BACK SEAT. NOW, MY NAME IS MAC O'REILLY, AT YOUR SERVICE! I WILL NOT LEAVE YOU, SO DON'T YOU WORRY." WITH THAT HE SQUEEZED HER HAND AND WINKED HIS GLEAMING CHARM. CLOSED THE DOOR, JUMPED IN BEHIND THE WHEEL AND SPED OFF.

MAC PUT ON THE SIREN AND DROVE AS FAST AS SAFETY WOULD ALLOW. "HOW ARE YOU DOIN' M'LUV?" LOOKING AT HER IN THE REARVIEW MIRROR.

SHE SCREAMED HER RESPONSE. "AH, WELL RIGHT ON TIME! OK, NOW YOU HOLD ON LASS, WE ARE ALMOST THERE." BUT SHE SCREAMED AGAIN AND YELLED A'MIGHTY. THERE WAS NO MORE TIME. AGAIN MAC PULLED THE CAR OVER IN A HURRY. JUMPED OUT AND RAN AROUND TO HER. HER LEGS WERE UP ALREADY AND THE BABY'S HEAD WAS CRESTING.

"ALRIGHT M'LUV, YOUR LIT'DARLIN' IS COMIN'. YOU BREATHE, EVERYTHING IS ALRIGHT. I AM RIGHT HERE WITH YOU, NOW PUSH." MAC O'REILLY HAD DELIVERED MANY BABIES IN HIS TIME. BUT WORRIED ABOUT THIS POOR GIRL, ALONE, AND THEIR FUTURES. IT WAS TOO COMMON A SCENARIO AND IT MADE HIM SAD.

TEARS WELLED IN HIS EYES AS HE WRAPPED THE BABY IN HIS JACKET AND PLACED HER INTO JOSEANNE'S ARMS. "THERE YOU GO, MA'AM, YOUR BRAND NEW BABY GIRL!"

JOSEANNE SMILED UP AT HIM THROUGH HER WET EYES, THEN DOWN AT HER PRECIOUS BUNDLE. "DEIRDRE!" SHE EXCLAIMED. "DEIRDRE IS YOUR NAME. A NICE IRISH NAME, AFTER THE NICE IRISHMAN THAT BROUGHT YOU TO ME."

"OH, THANKS TO YOU! NOW LET'S GET YOU TWO TO THE HOSPITAL."

THEY ARRIVED QUICKLY AND HOSPITAL PERSONNEL MET THEM. THEY HELPED HER ONTO THE GURNEY AS MAC TOOK THE BABY. HE HELD HER HAND AS SHE RODE ON THE CARRIER, GRINNING AT BOTH OF THEM. "NOW, DARLIN' THESE FINE FOLKS WILL TAKE GOOD CARE OF YOU. I WILL START THE PAPER WORK FOR YE. AHHH, HERE'S MADGE, SHE WILL GET YOUR WEE DARLIN' A CLEANING!"

"THANK YOU, MAC. THANK YOU SO MUCH FOR EVERYTHING." BESIDE HERSELF WITH HAPPINESS, FORGOTTEN, WAS HER MOTHER AND ALL THE HORRIBLE TIMES SHE SPENT IN HER LIFE.

MAC BEAMED WITH PLEASURE, "HEY YA MADGE, HOW YE DOIN' LUV? I WISH I HAD A CIGAR TO GIVE YOU!" AS HE HANDED THE BABE TO HER.

"OH MAC, YOU ALWAYS SAY THE SWEETEST THINGS! CUTE BABY, HUH?"

"YEAH, A WEE LASSIE SHE IS! WHAT CAN I DO TO HELP THAT GIRL?"

"WHAT'S HER NAME?"

"THE BABY'S NAME IS DEIRDRE! ISN'T THAT A CHARMIN' NAME? D-E-I-R-D-R-E."

"YES MAC. BUT YOU'RE NOT MUCH HELP, WHAT'S THE LAST NAME?" MADGE SMILED BACK AT HIM.

HE SCRATCHED HIS HEAD, WHILE HOLDING HIS CAP, EMBARRASSED, HE REMARKED, "NOW ISN'T THAT A GOOD ONE? I DON'T KNOW!"

Mac O'Reilly whistled out to his car, proud and happy. Excited to give Helen and the boys a kiss. Life was good and he was glad to be a part of it.

He started the engine and looked around to pull out into the traffic. He saw the gun. There was no time to do anything about it. All was dark.

Once Josie was in the room, a nurse cleaned her up and gave her a new bed-gown. She seemed nice enough and explained the baby was being cleaned. "But for now, you need to rest because you're so anxious and tired. Take these pills to sleep, then you will see your baby. She needs to sleep too." Quickly, she felt very sleepy.

. . . .

She awoke in her own bed. The room was the same as it had always been. Everything seemed beautiful and the sun was shining. Marie came in with a tray of breakfast. Was it a dream? "I was dreaming!" She exclaimed to her friend.

Marie did not say anything, she didn't even look at her. Milicent followed the servant. "Well, don't you look happy! That's an excellent way to start the day. You need to tell Marie what clothes you want to wear for your trip, so she can pack everything for you. You leave tomorrow, just like we decided. You best get busy, you don't have much time." With that, she left the room.

Stunned, Joseanne turned to Marie. There was nothing she could read on her face. "Marie?

What is it? What's happened? I was dreaming, wasn't I?"

Marie delivered the tray and said, "I am not sure Mademoiselle, please tell me what clothes you choose for your travels."

"Marie? Please look at me. What's going on?" Sensing trouble, she looked under the covers, and her belly was flat. But it should be, right? And why was her mother being cordial? Everything seemed in order, but why wasn't her friend looking at her? She got out of bed. Her head started to pound and her legs turned to mush. She fell to the floor. Marie rushed to her.

"Oh please get up. Get back to bed. Take this slow," she whispered with agonizing fright. Marie tucked her mistress properly in bed. Joseanne was bewildered and could not make out the confusion. Marie continued to shake her head to alert her to not ask anything more.

"Well, young lady you are looking fit and ready for travel." Gertrude pounded into the room. "Is Marie doing her job? Make sure she stays on her toes, there isn't much time. That shopping spree you had yesterday, should certainly help in making your choices. Aren't you just the lucky one, always being taken care of?"

Gertrude was always pompous. Her mother's assistant, they were perfect for each other. Joseanne responded in her regular, obedient tone, "Yes, Madame. I am just extra tired this morning. Thank you for your concern."

235

THE WOMAN LEFT WHILE MARIE HEADED FOR THE CLOTHES ROOM. JOSEANNE LAID IN BED AND TRIED TO CALM HER SPINNING HEAD. SOMETHING WAS DEFINITELY WRONG. SHE COULDN'T REMEMBER ANYTHING, BUT WAS STARTING TO SENSE HORROR. SHE DECIDED IT WAS SAFER TO NOT ASK MARIE ANYTHING ELSE. SHE KNEW THAT THE GIRL WOULD BE IN BIG TROUBLE, BESIDES SHE WAS AS PALE AS A GHOST WITH FEAR. WHAT WERE THOSE DARK PATCHES ON HER FACE AND NECK?

THE NEXT DAY SHE WAS PUT ON A TRAIN, BOUND FOR NEW YORK, ACCOMPANIED BY CLORESENT. SHE WOULD ATTEND SCHOOL THERE AND WOULD NOT BE BACK FOR MANY YEARS. CLORESENT LEFT HER AT THE DORM STEPS. NOTHING WAS SAID OR EXPLAINED. NO GOOD-BYES, ONLY THE COLD, HARSHNESS OF BEING ALONE IN A WORLD THAT NO ONE CARED FOR HER.

SHE BEGAN A LIFE IN A PLACE SHE DID NOT KNOW. THERE WERE TIMES SHE TRIED TO REMEMBER WHAT HAPPENED TO HER. CONSTANT WERE THE HORRIFIC NIGHTMARES, NONE OF WHICH MADE SENSE. SHE HAD REALIZED THAT TIME HAD SLIPPED BY HER AND LAPSES OF MEMORY BECAME A VAST DUST BOWL. WITH NO EVIDENCE OR UNDERSTANDING, IT BECAME EASIER TO STOP THE QUESTIONS. HENCE, LIVE A COLD, EMPTY AND BITTER LIFE.

Chapter 34

"My precious, are you all right?" Joe filled me in, you know I'll do anything I can to help you. But first, let me hold you." Louie rushes to Deirdre, with open arms and heart. The two men had carried her to her bedroom after they ate their breakfast. Then set up her dining room as their 'war room' for research.

Deirdre Kennsington had slept for hours, and awoke hungover. In her mentor's arms, she sobs. Feeling like her whole life has split open, she has a wretched ache within then retches into the pale he provides. Her head pounds after the whiskey and anxiety. The tears flood, forcing out all the dread of coming to terms with the truths of late. This is excruciating for her.

Fighting intimacy and feelings all her life has been her only salvation. Being addicted to stimulation and drama as her passion, is what has kept her alive. Damn it, has allowed her to survive.

Stopping any closeness or feelings had made her a steady, controlled fixture. But now, crying like a baby in this man's arms, all of her control is completely gone. She is left with raw humanness, she cannot do anything else but feel.

"Oh my dear, it's okay. You keep crying. Get it all out. You have so much to cry over." Louie says tearing up himself. He provides a damp washcloth for her and is stunned by his own emotion. Always one to be strong and even pompous when needed. It is difficult to understand his confusion with this woman. They sit on the edge of the bed. He embraces her close.

Always the lover, strong-willed and self-righteous, he has always gotten his way. But with her, he never wanted it that way. Even in the beginning. She was young and aggressive, sexy and willing to do anything to get what was necessary. He admired her, and she reminded him of his youth, but he was immediate in his response to her, that their relationship would not be of sex. Of a mentor regard only. Her Trixie image needed refinement, a lot of work and the name had to be changed. It all happened as he prescribed.

Through the years, their relationship deepened. Respect for each other was done with integrity and honor. When she brought Joe Kenny onto the scene, it was difficult at first for him. He couldn't understand why she revealed so much of herself to him. But he came to trust and like him.

She developed an addiction to the past, he wanted it all to die and be left alone. He knew hers wasn't good and his childhood was not anything to relish either. The best schools were not an option for him. His life was poor, being raised by his grandmother after his mother died at his birth. His father worked at *that* mansion for the wicked witch, then he killed himself. Fedrico Bellisimo was a distant memory to

him. He grew up not having respect for him and that's why Louie changed his name.

Deirdre cries herself to sleep. Louie lays her down and covers her with a blanket. Sweetly, he bends over and kisses her forehead. He is glad and thankful that she is actually sleeping. It's unusual that it's peaceful, she has never slept much but for a couple of hours at a time. He quietly leaves the room and shuts the door.

He finds Joe pacing with worry. Intently puffing on his cigar, hat still on. Noticing Louie's inquisition, "Oh damn, I think better this way. There are so many pieces still missing. She wants to force it all out into the open, like an old movie. We can't protect her with all those people."

"I know. I'm worried too. But you have given me an idea!" Louie stares through Joe as if he could see his thoughts manifesting on the wall behind him.

"Well, are you going to let me in on it? Or do I have to pretend I see it on your movie screen?" He sarcastically questions him.

"Sorry Kenny! I'll pull all my favors in, we'll make this a ball no one will ever forget. A costume party set in the twenties. I'll get extra security put on Deirdre. They'll all be dressed as Keystone Cops, she can have one on each arm. She'll play that to the hilt! No one will be the wiser that we have so much security to protect everyone incase Milicent has something up her sleeves. I can already see the guest list that D has in mind! The secret service will be there too.

"I'll get D's event planner right on it, he'll love this and will make it really authentic! 'Cold tea' as they called hootch in the day. The moonshine will be legit! Speakeasy sections, people can dress up as racketeers, grifters, and the Molls can show off their flamboyance keeping with the time. We can make up 'clams' instead of real dollars that will be exchanged at the gaming tables, which will bring in more charity money."

Joe watches his mind buzz with the ideas, no wonder he is a master at what he did in the movies. Deirdre shuffles in blurry eyed, rubbing her head and makes her way to the kitchen. She plops down on her stool. The men follow her and Joe immediately starts on making her eggs.

"Hey, you good?" Kenny asks.

She grunts.

Louie puts his hand on her shoulder as Joe puts a cup of coffee in front of her with two aspirin. "We've been going over ideas for the ball. I figure you already have a guest list in mind? I was just getting ready to call Ro~Lond." Louie starts.

Deirdre nods. In a scratchy voice she says. "Actually, I'll do that. Will you jot your ideas down for me? Have we heard from BT yet?"

"They got in late last night. They should be over here soon," Louie walks into the dining room for a pad of paper, pen and walks back to her, sitting next to her.

"I'll get the ideas down for you now."

"Joe, that smells good!" Louie says as Kenny puts the plate in front of Deirdre. Joe refills hers and Louie's coffee cups.

"Not sure I can eat though," she groans and holds onto her flat stomach.

The men both look at her and say at the same time, "Eat!"

"OK, OK. You don't have to gang up on me. I'm hurting here."

They smile. Joe makes a plate for Louie and himself. In between bites, Louie gets back to his list. Clears his throat and begins. "Security. We will need a lot. Let's arrange the men and women security guards to be dressed as Keystone Cops. They can wander about as being playful, especially on each of your arms, D. The guest don't have to know they're there to ensure everyone's safety. Besides, it's an extra precaution that Milicent doesn't have any surprises up her sleeve."

Joe and Deirdre agree with a salute.

She surprises herself by eating more than she thinks she can. "Alright, let's get this show on the road. I'll take a shower and then call The Extraordinaire Ro~Lond. See you two later, then you can fill me in on the latest info." She grabs the list from Louie, plants a kiss on his cheek. Joe, puts his finger to his cheek. She beams, struts over to do the same to him and makes her way to her room.

"Kenny, this party, it's going to bring up a lot of emotions for a lot of people. I know you've done a lot on the old bitch and her daughter." Louie has followed Joseanne's life in *Variety* and other showcases, she seemed well enough and often wondered about her. The two of them were so vital and wanted much, both rebellious in their own ways and lusted for life. Now she is a married socialite and he a self-made movie mogul. It will be interesting to see her again. They walk into their 'war room' as Louie continues.

"As a matter of fact, I think I better tell you that I knew this Joseanne deTournay when I was a kid. My dad was the gardener at the mansion. Every summer I would stay with him and play with her. After her sixteenth birthday, though, my father was fired and sent away. But, I was also told he committed suicide. There weren't any definitive explanations, and I never did hear what really happened.

"That woman was a real tyrant and besides I didn't care much about anything then. I was a kid, and very angry. I didn't know what to think about my father. My nonna, she was a piece of work, I couldn't wait to get out from under her. Anyway, the poor man couldn't take it I guess. I've been thinking about him because of all of this. I don't suppose you've been able to get anything on him, have you? Damn, Kenny. What is it? You look like you've seen a ghost." Louie proclaims in alarm.

"I believe I just have." Joe takes off his hat and starts pacing again. Rubbing his forehead, he turns to Louie, "Oh man. You're one of those missing pieces, d'Langino! Or should I call you..." Joe watches Louie's face change from concern

to astonishment in a flash.   He always continues to be amazed how actors can do that, so quickly.

"What the hell?"

"Joseanne got pregnant back then.   You changed your name, so I could't find out who the father was, until now!"

"But...that means...you're trying to tell me that Dei..."

"Yes, man. That's exactly what I'm saying," he cuts him off. "Milicent made some big mistakes back then. She must have thought she took care of everything. Paying off and threatening a lot of people to cover up the event. It looks like she even went so far to have a cop killed. And damn it anyway, he was O'Reilly. I haven't let BT in on this yet," Joe lets this sink in a few beats and squeezes the bridge of his nose.

He continues. ""There are so many to this day that hate her, many who would love to take her down. She hurt too many people and they would love nothing better than to have revenge.

"The way I figure it, she had a lot of businesses going down, back then. Too many shipments were coming in at the same time. Her resources were thinned to the hilt and she couldn't be on top of things as well as she usually could. She was always a master in control, cover-ups and her business world. As it slowly declined, she arranged Joseanne to be married. Milicent made sure she, herself, was taken care of for life. It proved to be quite the prolific merger for the Grand Dame.

"You see by that time, times had changed. It was important to keep her secrets, to protect her status and crimes. She couldn't keep the mob-type businesses going anymore even if it was under the radar so-to-speak with the feds. The proper social decorum was up most important, so she made sure to paint some of the businesses as legit.

"She hates men, but marrying Joseanne off was a great asset that allowed the protection of her addiction for wealth to keep on. The Ashlynn family's money made for a new income for her. So, she was able to let a lot of her security go, the usual businesses ended as she aged behind heavily, protected and closed doors. She's become quite the enigma and recluse."

"Poor Jos, she was always afraid of her, that's for sure. She was afraid of all the guns around. Was told they were to protect her from the dangerous outside world. She was very naive and I...well, I was...I was a rough kid, not one that I'm proud of...Deirdre. My God. I had no idea." Louie slouches in his chair, taking in all that he has heard.

Looking back up at Joe, he asks, "Her name, why did she change it to that?"

"She said you and she came up with it, that it had a nice ring. The irony is, when I spoke to a nurse that was there at the time, she told me of the good ol'cop that brought her and the baby in. How proud of that name he was. Everyone liked him. Even the crooks. Him being shot in cold blood there at the hospital was a big shock to all. The city had a huge parade for him. Whoever did it, I figure they knew he couldn't be bought so they just killed him and it was also to

save time. Remember Milicent needed this to be cleaned up quickly." Just as he finishes, they hear D's door open.

"Hey, why so glum, Louie?" Deirdre comes barreling in, remarkably recovered from just an hour ago and excited.

"And you Joe, ohhh, I know that look!"

"What?" He pleads mockingly. Then retorts, "It's the look of brilliance!"

"OK! That's a gimme, Joe! We know you are brilliant indeed! So, what's going on, I want to hear the latest. But Louie, first tell me what's got you in such a dislodge?"

Joe is still standing, guides her to the sofa as they both sit down. He turns to her, looks at Louie, then back at her and begins, "D."

"What's going on? Out with it," she demands

"We have something new to tell you and I think you'll like the latest news!" Joe is excited, he turns to Louie once more.

Louie sits up in his chair and blurts out, "I'm your father, D."

Expressions fly on her face. Her eyes dart between the two of them. She is still for some moments then stands up. She grins, eyes glistening and traverses the distance to Louie, he stands to meet and hug her. They embrace, crying and laughing in contagious delight.

Joe makes his way to the bar refrigerator and pulls out a bottle of champagne. He makes it pop and they look over at him. "Finally, something to celebrate!" He exclaims.

Chapter 35

"What do you mean a ghost? I don't understand Lauren."

"It's just that you two are so similar. I don't understand it either. But almost every move, jester and sometimes your voice change is exactly like Michael. If I didn't know better, I'd think you were twins.

"I am sorry BT. I don't want to hurt you. I have grown to care for you very much. And that's why, well that's why I spoke of the synchronicities. I know this is all crazy. Maybe I am crazy. But it's gotten beyond coincidental, and I don't even believe in that. Actually, that's not true. I, I didn't and then I did and now I do. I learned about synchronicities from him." Lauren sips her champagne, then reaches for a glass of water. She begins to pace.

BT doesn't want to hear this. He keeps hoping she'll stop making references of him. It's making him really uncomfortable. It's as though she's trying to see more into it or make him like Michael.

The problem is, he knows there's some truth. Everything has been amiss for months for him. The near death and coma had certainly taken its toll. In his dreams and life of late, he has come to understand who Michael really was and

really, he can't fight the common occurrences or thoughts any more either.

Something is really strange and disturbing about all of this. His instincts are kicking him to solve this mystery, it even feels like Lauren is forcing his hand. What with her and her family's past coming into focus. He is bound and determined to find out what is happening. He hopes none of them get killed in the process.

"Look, Lauren, I know there is so much here that's confusing and that's why we're here. But Michael and I are two different people. He is dead and I am alive. And I love you, Lauren. I love you very much. I want to be with you and share life with you. But I sure as heck don't want a ghost in our way. Lauren, I am here, he is there." He holds her hands and looks intently into her eyes.

"I know that. I know he's dead, but you don't understand. It's not like that. It's not that he's in our way, he's in YOU." She grips his hands and returns the intensity. With this statement, Lauren becomes very calm. Calmer then she has been in a long time.

She continues, "Listen, I know this sounds crazy, but I read somewhere, well, somehow souls get mixed up. If the body dies suddenly, the soul can get stuck. Confused and disoriented. But if something is wrong and things were not taken care of, they need to stay. They have to finish business. He believed that reincarnation is benevolent in that it is the journey of the soul.

"In this way, with what little you have told me of yourself since that accident, the information Deirdre has shared with you, I can't help believe *he is here.*" She sees his disbelief, then his eyes adjust to a recognition she hasn't seen before. Lauren is spurred on with a steadfast confidence.

"Now wait. Hear me out. Look, I'm not one for this kind of stuff. If it hadn't been for him and his stories. It does seem far-fetched. But the problem is, it makes sense. Doesn't it? BT, what? What's happening?" She feels his body shudder.

He pulls her over to sit down. "You've made your point." He assures her.

She lets out a deep, pent up breath. She takes another breath, looks him in his eyes and sees they are brighter now. She waits.

"It's time. I haven't told you, I was going to. I just didn't know when or even how. I don't know how to begin."

"We are both analytical people, so let's look at the facts. Tell me what happened. You said it wasn't an accident. When did it happen? What happened, I mean what was the accident? If I'm not mistaken, there's a timing thing here. It was when Michael died, right? I'm right, aren't I, I can see it in your eyes. Please."

"Alright." He signs, takes a breath and explains, "I've had haunting dreams, about being a pilot. Crashing. Uhhh, let me back up." He talks of his Da, him being killed when he was four. He promised he'd avenge his death. Even when he quit the PI business, he still searched for clues because it

was an unsolved case. I was set up, an ambush. Knocked out, went into a coma.

"Afterwards, are you ready for this?" He tightens his hold on her hands and finally admits out loud. "In the nightmares, as I'm in the plane diving into the ground, I'm yelling pull up, pull up...Lauren, I will never leave you." He studies her face.

She is intent, her eyes are jetting all around. She gets up and begins to pace again. Matter of factly, she asks, "You have never been a pilot, have you? And you hadn't known anyone by my name, am I correct? Even at the studio, you didn't know who I was. You were only being nice to me. Michael's party, same thing."

She doesn't let him answer and continues quickly, counting off the facts, "Michael was an excellent pilot and told me many times he would never leave me. I always thought how odd it was when he said it. It was as if a resolution, not like a common comment a lover tells the other.

"In Hawaii, after you made the eagle, you apologized because you had never jumped liked that. Michael was a regular at it. You had the same sparkle and jaunt that he did. As a matter of fact, you have reacted in like many times and have looked bewildered afterwards.

"That night of your party, we spoke all night? A number of times, you looked as though you had seen a ghost. Did any of my stories sound familiar to you?" Searching his eyes, feeling strong, she has a very strong sense of balance.

Pieces are falling into place and she isn't running or hiding. The more she speaks, the more resolute she becomes.

"Yes, but I didn't tell you about them," he says in a puzzling response. Remembering how fragile she was then and surprised how calm she is now.

"I knew it! You gave me that same quizzical look he always did. You're doing it now! When I would explain something, that he already knew. Like deja vu. We constantly laughed at those things and finally stopped questioning them. We decided to accept the episodes as the way it was. Proof that we belonged together, as sure as rain." She is proud of herself, it is all becoming totally clear to her. She needs to assure him that these thoughts are not a threat to him.

"Don't you see BT, I have fallen in love with you too. Not in spite of Michael but because of *him*. I was given the time to grieve and even be ill over it. I finally stopped the denial of my life and was given the chance to really see. See things the way they are. Reality and all its bites, and all its pure joys too." She sits next to him to hug his neck.

He is bewildered and yet somehow comprehending her delivery and now this affection.

She then leans in to kiss him square on the lips and knows for the second time in her life, her sureness about living life. She knows this is BT O'Reilly. She knows Michael is helping her, guiding her in some nutty way to love again. She knows they are different men and completely understands this concept. The movie 'Heaven Can Wait' comes to mind.

Her kiss is direct and sweet.   Her mouth, warm and deliberate. He is caught up in her excitement and returns her passion.   As the passion becomes more intense, he realizes he does know her.   *Really knows her and recognizes her.* This scares him and he pulls back.

"I'm sorry. I'm really taken aback. Lauren, you have to give me some time to digest this.   You are everything I have always wanted and hoped for.   I even, I can't believe I'm saying this, I recognize you and your kiss.   Which, to be honest, scares me. How can this be? I'm sorry, I, I'm a little thrown off here. No, I am a lot off balance." He is spinning his wheels, he doesn't know what to say. He is reeling from the kiss and all she has told him. He pushes to get up. He walks to the window.

She sits still.   She knows what he's going through, it's her turn to be still in the knowing. She waits a few minutes then walks over to the bar.   She pours him a neat whiskey. Lauren takes her time getting to him.   Quietly she insists. "Here, drink this bit o'Irish. It's my turn to steady you."

He swallows it all at once. He looks at her in dismay.

"I know this is a lot to take in, BT."

He is trying desperately to understand all that has transpired when the phone rings.

Lauren answers it. She turns to hand him the receiver with pain in her face.

"Yes?" He asks.

He is silently listening for what seems an eternity to Lauren. *Damn, I know he said she is only a friend, but why do I let her affect me so? Why can't she just leave me alone? He says she's my sister, that certainly wouldn't keep her away from BT. And she's so happy, to talk to him. Just like that other time she called Michael. How can my mother not have said anything? What is all this? Damn, just when I've been making such progress, why am I letting her take control of me?* Lauren berates herself internally and tries not to look at him. When she does, he is expressionless. His face is blanched, more than it's been this night.

BT quietly returns the receiver. He looks at her and says, "We've got to get over there. They have more information. But first, we have got to get some rest. Then there's something we have to do."

Chapter 36

Lauren Ashlynn stands in front of a door she never wanted to enter again. It's an incredible door really. Big and beautiful of rich mahogany. But where it leads is a horrible place and who is there is even worse.

They are ushered in by a young servant girl and shown to the study. The woman sits there staring at them as if they are aliens. She is old and shrunken, but still can weld the power of intimidation. The old saying, 'if looks could kill' fits well.

"Well child, you certainly are not looking your best. Tell me why you are here."

"Hello grandmother, it's nice to see you too. This is my friend, BT O'Reilly." Lauren says formally standing in the doorway. She stands her ground, not wanting to explain or acknowledge why she doesn't look her best, giving the woman any more ammunition against her.

Milicent dismisses her with the wave of her hand, "Don't you be indignant with me. I deserve respect from you. Oh, I know who he is. You may both enter." She demands.

"Thank you for seeing us, Madame." BT includes.

"What do you want of me, girl?" She ignores him.

"As you know grandmother, the Charity Ball is in a few days. I would like to borrow some of your beautiful things from that era. There will be a contest for authenticity. Would you mind?" Lauren asks hiding her fear.

"Don't patronize me girl. I know that. What are you looking for, Mr. O'Reilly? Just what type of evidence do you hope to find here?" Milicent asks with reproach.

"Madame?"

"I am fully aware of who you are, young man. Now tell me. What do you want to find in my home?"

"Madame, I have fallen in love with your granddaughter and have come here to ask for her hand in marriage."

Lauren is stunned. *Marriage? Whoa, I didn't see that coming.* Yet, she holds her resolve steady, doesn't look at him and awaits the woman's next attack.

"I see. I should thank you for helping her, I understand you were resourceful in finding her during her terrible incarceration."

"Yes, Madame. Her father and I were very worried."

"Lauren, you seem to have managed things well without my help. What is it you want of me?" Milicent turns her bitter attention back to her granddaughter. Holding the complete adherence, she always commands.

"The clothing, grandmother."

"Yes, I see. Clothing and marriage. I do not see you for years, then you come here demanding from me." She waves her hand in a belittling manner, as Lauren tries to interrupt. "On the other hand, you have done well for yourself. You made a name on your own and have found a man that has also done well. Consider the clothing my wedding gift. I believe you still remember where they are kept. You have one hour to decide your choice. One hour only."

Expelling her, she turns to BT. "Young man, you are to remain here. Goodbye." With that, a nurse is at her side and pushes her wheelchair away through another passage.

He turns to see Lauren go, but she is already out of sight. *What a contentious old bat! She does wear her bitterness well though, I'll give her that!* He remarks under his breath. When he considers the elaborate, monitoring system he noticed when they entered, he sheepishly sits down. He knows he is being watched and it feels creepy.

Lauren finds her way up the marbled, cantilevered staircase. Not one thing had changed since she was a little girl. Incredible art work and sculptures adorn the old and imposing walls.

It could be a perfect museum of the twenties. Ironic that in that time it was full of life but in this old place, so cold and dead. Like that dreadful woman down there. Lauren shakes off a chill and eerie shiver with her silent thoughts.

"Get to your business and get out of here." She whispers and races right to the old wing. She was not allowed in as a girl, but did manage to sneak in. Lauren loved it so because it's like in a movie, an old haunted room outfitted with cobwebs and squeaky door. The old bureaus, trunks and boxes of dress-up in a large array. However, this is not play-time she reminds herself. She needs to find something. Anything that will provide a small clue or bit of evidence.

The decrepit, formidable woman would not leave documentation, she would be sure that all was gone. Wouldn't she? All of this is too horrible to think that she arranged Michael's death and would try to kill her *other* granddaughter. This haunted story has turned into a real gothic horror.

Lauren looks through scrap books, old papers, anything that can help. Nothing. The attic area is huge, making it difficult to search thoroughly. Old carpets rolled up and everything, heavy laden in dust. Any movement of them, would cause suspicion from the grime tracks and her foot prints.

She checks her watch again, "Better just get that dress and get out. Time is a'runnin'." She proclaims, trying to remain calm, she opens the armoire and sees it. It is even more beautiful than she remembered, even enclosed in it's clear wrapping. The fine cream silk, touched with a delicate lace. There are other dresses too, but this one was always her favorite. She was caught so many times as a child looking at it, making her almost afraid to touch it now.

Despite the old fears, she pulls it out. The shoes are wrapped in plastic on top of a box, she hadn't seen as a

child. Her hands shaking, she takes the box and opens it. There, lie the most perfect pearls. They are absolutely incredible, many strands of different lengths, probably worth a fortune. She is delighted at the matching earrings.

She puts on the necklaces, but they tangle and one brakes. Spilling beads everywhere. Nervously, she starts collecting them back into its box. Trying to reach under the armoire, she gets timid, due to the thickened cobwebs and unknown small area. Lauren finds a cane and uses it to pull the loose articles toward her.

Panic sets in as she checks her watch again. Corralling the beads, she hears a rustle of paper. She draws the stick back and forth under the cabinet and jars it loose. Yellow and sticky with age, she tucks it in her shoe. She continues to pick up as many rolling pearls as she can.

Lauren changes course and advances on a huge trunk, looking for men's clothing. After finding several articles that would work for BT's costume, she grabs an empty box for her belongings. Takes one last look around to be sure nothing is a miss. For good measure, she takes up the cane and leaves.

She scurries down the stairs. BT is standing next to old Miss Peddle in the grand, formal entry waiting for her. "Lauren. What is your hurry?" She bellows.

"Miss Peddle, how nice to see you again. As you know I was on a time schedule, I was concerned I had run over it a bit." Lauren replying, curtly. Assuming she would be searched and of course how appropriate it is to be by her,

258

the grizzled, wicked nanny.   The woman became her grandmother's lead-assistant after Cloresent died.

"And just what do you have in that box?"

"The items I picked for the ball. It's grandmother's gift to us. Isn't that nice of her Miss Peddle?"

"Humph," is her contemptuous reply.   Hurriedly, she searches the large box, when she finds the little one, she looks at Lauren with distrust.   Deliberately and in slow motion, she opens the box.   It is painfully obvious the necklaces are broken.

"What have you done, you ungrateful child?" Provoking the old terrors that she did to her years ago.

"Miss Peddle, they are beautiful aren't they? But very old and I imagine the strings are quite brittle by now. I will have them properly repaired and returned to grandmother. You can count on it." Lauren surprises herself at the way she is able to stand up to her versed fears and intimidations. Although trembling inwardly, she stands straight with a firm resolve.

The old woman closes the box with an indignant slam and continues her search on Lauren. Then directs them toward the door. BT takes the box for Lauren as she leads their way out. Nothing is said until they are safely miles away.

"You sure managed those old women well. How did you live with that kind of tyranny?" BT breaks the ice, asking Lauren in amazement.

She looks at him dazed. It was all hitting her now, and with the adrenaline wearing off, physically shaking. "I could use some water."

"Sure, baby," he says getting worried as her face turns a milky-white. Fortunately, already in the city, he is able to pull into a convenient store. He returns to her with a cold bottled water at her side of the car.

"Thank you. Oh God, BT I can't believe I went there. I can't believe I spoke to them like that. My God, I have never, ever done that.   Standing up to that old bitch, peddle-ass! WOW!"   Lauren exclaims in her shaking excitement. She downs the water, spilling it down her front, still rattled.

BT sputters into laughter. She looks silly, which endears her to him. She begins to giggle until they laugh off the nervous anxiety. Their sides ache and faces are wet from tears, it's a moment in time when all stands still. Breaking the intense stress they have been sharing for so long, a new awareness develops in commitment, trust and understanding.

She gets out of the car and puts her arms around his neck. He picks her up and spins her around, both in subsided laughter. When he stops, he puts her down and becomes suddenly serious, "Will you marry me Lauren?"

"BT I thought that was a great ruse. You're not serious, are you?" She searches his eyes, she sees he is quite serious indeed. And she is too. "I want to. I really do. I am falling in love with you. I think. I know. But we still need time. We've got a lot of things to work out. Remember, you're the

one that was confused last night! Or was that this morning?" She laughs.

"I know. But after I said what I said to your grandmother, it felt right. Sitting in that musty room, waiting for you, it gave me a chance to think it over. What you said last night, it's too unbelievable, but too right. I can't explain it, Lauren. But I do believe Michael is fighting for you through me. And there are times when I don't know if it's him or me.

"I do know that I love you. And if he has helped me get that, then I am grateful. I am concerned about something, though?" He gives her the unmistakable, mischievous grin.

"What?"

"Well, you seem to be the expert in these soul matters."

"No, I'm not. What?"

"Will he always be here or am I not here? Am I him now. Or is he me? Hmmm..." He nuzzles her neck in delicate tickles.

"I don't know!" She smiles with pleasure. "I believe we will have to go see someone," partially teasing him.

"A preacher?"

"No, silly. I meant a psychic. BT, I am serious, well sort of. I don't know. But that's what I mean, we have to understand what is happening. We need to do research on this too,

besides all these other details." Her expression changes to surprise.

"What?" he exclaims.

Lauren wiggles her toes and pulls off a shoe to pick at the old paper. Carefully she peels it open and looks up at BT. "I found it when the pearls broke. I'd almost forgotten it. Here you read it, I'm shaking too much."

"Not here. We better get out of here. I have a feeling we're being watched. And we're not out of the woods yet." With that, he puts her back in the car and drives them to Deirdre's. It's time they share what information they have with the others.

They make introductions. Deirdre and Lauren gape at each other. BT takes Lauren's hand and sits her next to him on the bold yellow fainting couch. He takes out the letter leaning his elbows on his knees and explains. "Lauren found this stuck under the armoire, where she found the dress she collected for the party.

"She was running out of time because she was looking for clues. A box of pearls, they broke, she scrambled to pick them up, of course they rolled under the closet, you found the cane then, right?" Looking at her to confirm his telling.

She would not look at the other men or Deirdre, only him. She nods and he continues. "So, the cane helps her wrangle them toward her but she heard paper. Taking the cane, she jiggled it loose, stuck it in her shoe because she knew she would be frisked afterwards and ran down."

He addresses their questioning eyes. "Yes, the old nurse indeed pulled out her pockets and searched her! OK, here goes." He reads aloud.

Chapter 37

My Dear Friend and Mistress,

I am so sorry for all your troubles. I am not sure what will happen to you or me. Especially if this note is found. I will be long gone from here at any rate. If you ever do find this, I hope it finds you well and will help you.

I loved you so much and tried to take good care of you the best I could while you were in that horrible place. We shared so many nice talks and you were so loving to me and to your baby inside of you. It was so good to have some tiny moments of pleasure while living in this awful mansion.

Please forgive me if you do not want to hear this truth. But you loved your baby so much, I can't imagine you not knowing her. When you awoke that morning, the day before you were to go off to school, you were so confused. It was because they drugged you for weeks, until your belly went down. They wanted you to forget what happened.

You slept and slept. You ate little even though I tried to feed you soup and water. They made sure that only Cloresent and I were with you. They thought I was too close to you, so they

BEAT ME MANY TIMES TO KEEP MY MOUTH SHUT. THAT'S WHY I COULDN'T HELP YOU UNDERSTAND YOUR "FUNNY DREAM". THEY ALWAYS WATCHED ME, SO I COULDN'T SNEAK TO YOU ANYMORE LIKE I DID BEFORE.

MY FRIEND, LILY, TOLD ME HER SISTER SAID THAT HE WAS A NICE MAN. SHE WORKED AT THE HOSPITAL AND KNEW HIM. THAT HE DELIVERED THE BABY AND TOOK YOU TO THE HOSPITAL AFTERWARD. HE WAS PROUD YOU NAMED HER DEIRDRE. THERE WASN'T ANYTHING IN THE PAPER ABOUT WHY.....

"Oh GOD." BT drops the letter mid-sentence and begins to sob in his hands.

The women look at him in alarm and then back at each other. The men stand, exchange a knowing glance at each other and wonder if they should have told him. Deirdre gets to him first, puts a hand on his shoulder, as Lauren picks up the note. She studies where he left off and reads:

THERE WASN'T ANYTHING IN THE PAPER ABOUT WHY THE POLICEMAN GOT SHOT THAT NIGHT.

"Oh, God, no. Ohhh...BT. Oh no." She turns to hug his back.

"That policeman was my father, Lauren. *She* had my Da shot..." BT cries in her arms.

Louie takes the letter and continues reading:

THE NURSE, HER NAME WAS MADGE, SAID SHE WAS WASHING THE BABY WHEN SHE HEARD THE GUN SHOT. IT SCARED HER AND SHE WAS SO WORRIED ABOUT THE

BABY, SHE COVERED HER AND RAN DOWN THE OPPOSITE HALL TOWARDS THE BACK DOOR. WHEN SHE PEEKED AROUND THE CORNER, FROM HER HIDING SPOT, MADGE SAW STRANGE PEOPLE GO INTO YOUR HOSPITAL ROOM. ONE WAS DRESSED AS A NURSE, SHE NEVER SAW BEFORE. IT FRIGHTENED HER EVEN MORE, BECAUSE THEY WEREN'T PAYING ATTENTION TO THE FRONT OF THE HOSPITAL WHERE THE COMMOTION WAS AS THE OTHER DOCTORS AND NURSES WERE. SHE SAID SHE HAD A BAD FEELING, SO SHE SNUCK OUT OF THE HOSPITAL AND WENT TO LILY'S PLACE.

WHEN MADGE FOUND OUT HER FRIEND WAS THE POLICEMAN THAT WAS SHOT, THEY BOTH PANICKED AND LILY HELPED MADGE TAKE THE BABY AWAY. LILY LATER WHISPERED TO ME WHAT HAPPENED WHEN I WAS FINALLY ALLOWED TO GO OUT TO DO ERRANDS. SHE WAS AN EXCELLENT BAKER THAT YOUR GRANDMOTHER APPROVED.

LILY WAS VERY SAD THAT SHE NEVER HEARD FROM MADGE AFTERWARDS BUT KNEW SHE HAD TO KEEP SECRETS. THEY BOTH WANTED A CHILD, THEY KNEW IT WAS WRONG TO TAKE HER BUT DID IT ANYWAY. I NEVER HEARD WHAT HAPPENED TO YOUR BABY BECAUSE I WAS FINALLY ABLE TO ESCAPE. LILY HELPED ME TOO. BUT THE TRUTH IS, YOUR BABY WAS SAVED BY MADGE AND LILY AND THEY WERE BOTH LOVING WOMEN.

Now it's Louie's turn to stop reading, with hand at his mouth. Joe takes the letter and continues:

REMEMBER, I HAD OVERHEARD THAT THE BABY WAS TO BE TAKEN FROM YOU TO BE DROWNED. THAT'S WHEN YOU CAME UP WITH THE PLAN TO ESCAPE. WHEN YOU ASKED ME TO HELP YOU ESCAPE, I WAS TERRIFIED. I WENT TO MY FRIEND, FEDRICO, YOU REMEMBER THE GARDENER, HE WAS LIKE A POPPA TO ME. I CRIED AND

CRIED FOR YOU, I DIDN'T KNOW HOW TO HELP YOU. HE HUGGED ME HARD AND SAID HE'D MAKE A PLAN.

I WENT IN, LIKE I ALWAYS DID AND CLOSED THE DOOR. WE RUBBED DOWN YOUR BELLY WITH THE LARD THAT I SNUCK IN. I HELPED PUSH YOU UP AND OUT OF THE TINY WINDOW. BUT I LOST MY FOOTING AND FELL WHEN YOU GOT STUCK. I GOT UP AS HE PULLED YOU TO SAFETY BUT I WAS HURT AND COULDN'T GET OUT THE WINDOW TO ESCAPE WITH YOU BOTH.

SO, I GOT AS CLOSE AS I COULD SO FEDRICO COULD HEAR ME, I BEGGED HIM TO TAKE YOU AND CLOSED THE WINDOW AT HIS NOSE WITH MY STICK. I LIMPED BACK, HID MY DIRTY CLOTHES AND MADE MYSELF SICK.

LATER, WHEN THEY FOUND YOU WERE GONE THEY CAME TO ME AND SAW I HAD THROWN UP ALL OVER MYSELF. THEY DIDN'T BELIEVE ME THAT I WAS SICK. SO, THEY BEAT ME OVER AND OVER AGAIN. I NEVER SAID ANYTHING. I NEVER KNEW WHAT HAPPENED TO MY FRIEND, EXCEPT WE WERE GOING TO RUN AWAY FROM HERE. HE WANTED TO HELP ME FIND A NEW PLACE THAT WAS GOOD. I DON'T HAVE FAMILY, YOU SEE.

THEY LOOKED FOR CLUES AND SAW THE TIRE TRACKS FROM HIS TRUCK AT THE WINDOW. THEY WENT LOOKING FOR HIM. THEY BEAT ME MORE. I WAS GLAD HE GOT AWAY TOO, THEY WEREN'T NICE TO HIM. I DO KNOW THERE WAS A LOT OF MONEY PAID TO FIND HIM AND SHUT PEOPLE UP.

YOU WERE TAKEN AWAY FROM THE HOSPITAL ASLEEP AND CAME HOME THAT WAY, TILL YOU LEFT FOR SCHOOL. THEY KEPT YOUR MEMORIES FROM YOU. THEY ROBBED YOU OF YOUR BABY. I AM SO SORRY THAT I COULD NOT HELP YOU. I PRAY EVERY DAY TO GOD THAT YOU AND HE FORGIVE ME.

"Louie? What is it?" Joe asks him. They all look at him.

"My Dad," he mumbles, eyes watering.

"Damn it, this is horrible for all of you. Deirdre?" She is stunned, pale and wavering. Kenny goes to her and helps her to a chair.

He starts to pace and continues quickly. "There's no date. OK, this must have been for Joseanne. It proves you two are sisters. That your grandmother was behind all of it, back then. There's no proof she is behind what's been happening of late though, but, damn, she has to be. I still have some leads, some new ones to follow up."

Deirdre gets her color back. Her concern is for Louie, she moves to and bends down in front of him, "What about your Dad?"

"He didn't commit suicide, at least I don't think so. He must have finally escaped that place. I thought he was weak. He was always afraid, I didn't know how bad it really was there. Damn, I was so mean to him. Did he make a new life for himself to stay protected from them? My nonna, eh Gran never questioned what they told her. And I was hurt, angry and...young. I got out as soon as I could, left after school finished that year and started anew. In L.A." He says bewildered and shaking his head in his hands.

Joe quietly remarks. "Maybe I can find out. This Marie, she escaped, how? Lily, a baker. It sure would be interesting if

we can get them to this party." Now he has all of their attention, mouths agape. "Good look on you all! I did say that out loud, didn't I?" He chagrins.

"Well, there's more. D, it's noted in the letter that you were taken from the hospital from what sounds like caring people. That's new. We assumed somehow, someone had to have taken you and figured they were not nice. Hence, the foster homes. We checked years of records to find out who your mother is." He looks over to Lauren sheepishly and stumbles, "Excuse me, both of yours, ah, your mother too."

Then he turns in a fan fare movement and formally announces. "Deirdre, would you like to reveal more of your family? Get these two up to speed?" He motions to BT and Lauren.

Chapter 38

Joseanne's mirrored reflection is blinding. Dress of stark white, reminds her when she was set up for marriage. Her mother, consistently, made things turn. As proclaimed years ago, upon her return from school, everything was arranged. She was to join matrimony for prosperity and status as if it were the Medieval times.

Fortunately, Stefen Ashlynn was a nice man to her. Although that quality, she knew, was not a chosen prerequisite by Milicent. He passed muster for appearance sake. And that was her life: appearance. She moved through it as if it were celluloid. No feelings and no fulfilled desires. Just a robot doing what she was told, what was necessary.

He has always been funny and caring, despite her coldness. Lord knows how he had tried to win her over, actually wanted her to be in love with him. He certainly fell in love with her, why, she has never been able to understand. The life he provided her was so opposite of what she ever knew, that gave her some happiness.

Always haunted from the things she had seen and experienced were better swept under the many rugs. Her husband certainly was not to know. Secrets demanded

respect, thereby made no room for closeness, let alone intimacy.

She is still a beautiful woman. But the coldness in her own eyes stop any wonder. She had never known her father. Joseanne never could find out anything about him. There was only the enigma of him, that he lived well and left the mansion for them. All Milicent would say was that *she* made things happen and that it was the power of *her* empire.

Men had only a few purposes, according to her. They were used to protect them and to carry out *her* work. Surveillance was done with guns; the mansion was under constant guard. The Grand Dame explained that as: "Because of their extensive wealth, others did not like that. The world was evil outside those doors; therefore, it took a lot to protect them."

Joseanne was not allowed to date. The boarding school never allowed boys or men around and kept the severe strictness she was used to. She was only allowed to come home once and that was to marry a man and join a new family she did not know. All because of more money and power. But it didn't matter anyway, she had surrendered her life, caring, and to asking questions years ago.

And so, her life went on. She had a baby girl in the designated nine-month time. She was a good wife and did what was expected. But when it came to the child, nannies were hired. Stefen loved their child, played with and tended to her as much as possible.

However, a prominent business man had more important things to do. Social events, most nights and weekends took

up their time. Vacations were for the fashionable socialites, so they kept up with the well-defined pattern of the highest social echelon. The Ashlynn's climbed the ladder properly.

As a result, Joseanne was able to obtain some recognition from her mother. She was the quintessence social butterfly, with a high-profile husband and she produced an heir. Because they lived in Los Angeles, it made life easier, she did not have to see her mother. Except for the occasional, important, social event of the year.

Through the years, as far as Joseanne knew, Milicent's life became more secluded than ever, due to her aging. Not that Joseanne knew about the businesses, or cared, she understood all was as usual.

The superstar, Deirdre Kennsington, was having the biggest social affair of the decade. Politicians, foreign dignitaries, and other famous people all meeting under one roof for a big charity ball. It didn't matter to Joseanne what it was for, just the chance to be there was good enough. Even if it meant seeing her mother.

Deirdre, of course, was gorgeous and a fine actress. She was young and had the world on a string. To be independent, a star and in control of her life, is quite a feat she really admired. But then, wasn't that her mother?

After flying to Chicago, the Ashlynn's checked into one of their favorite suites at The Drake. The glamour event was only in a few hours here and Joseanne could again sparkle at what she did best: shallow and surface mingling.

Chapter 39

"Do you know who my wife is totally immersed in conversation?" Stefen asks BT after he walks up to him in the grand ballroom of The Drake Hotel. "I've seen her socialize with perfection. But I've never seen her to be so... real. Who is that man that is bringing out this rawness in her? She is being so, genuine."

O'Reilly looks at Stefen to check his reaction, Stefen doesn't break his attention. "That is Louie d'Langino. He is Deirdre's agent." BT is embarrassed that he knows what they are probably talking about.

Stefen doesn't look at BT, but stares at his wife many yards away. "I've never seen her so animated, engaged in a communication. What can they be talking about? And how does she know *him*? I feel jealousy coming on."

Lauren walks up to them and is also interested in her mother's demeanor, not taking her eyes off her. "Dad, I've never seen Mother so..."

"Energetic? Vitalized?" He responds snapping at her question.

Lauren bolts in question at her father, he's never reacted or snarled like that to her. BT brushes her arm to interrupt her thoughts. "I was just telling your Dad who Louie is. That he has helped us through our investigations and how we have been able to piece many things together." They exchange a fleeting look at each other.

Several more moments pass, it's as if they are watching a movie set in the twenties. The art deco set is glorious of black and white faux marble floors. The richly appointed polished walls with their intricate engrained designs make for a delight to behold. Ornate carvings of the crown moldings frame the hundreds of potted palms and greenery. Gardenias are everywhere. Real plants blooming as well as floating flowers in glass jars and vases of all sizes fill the expansive ball room. Containers filled with blue tinted water adorn the floors and tables.

Hundreds of candles and twinkling lights of cream and cobalt blue emit a lovely and romantic ambience. All set under a multitude of elaborate chandeliers. The sculptured, rod-iron balustrade of a staircase circles itself up to the ceiling. This eye-catching center point of the bar, is decked out with twinkling lights of blue that glisten hundreds of liquor bottles.

Joseanne obviously is shaken and takes Louie's arm to steady herself. He escorts her to the three of them. Jos lights up with a big smile at her daughter, and Lauren looks over her shoulder to see where her attention is. She turns back in time for her mother's open arms to embrace her warmly. Lauren is stunned stiff, her arms still at her side. Louie stands next to BT.

Jos whispers in her ear, "My darling, Lauren. Will you ever forgive me? I am so very sorry for not being good to you. I love you."

Lauren pulls in her arms to hug her mother, questioning, yet receiving the gesture with tears welling.

Milicent is wheeled in by her nurse, with Miss Peddle and two scruffy bodyguards. She's flailing her arms, demanding to be where Jos is and yells. "What is the meaning of this public display?"

Lauren immediately tenses in her mother's arms at her grandmother's voice. Joseanne holds her tighter in protection. Lauren has never experienced this behavior from her, so relishes it, relaxes and continues the embrace. Joseanne completely ignores the old woman's berating and takes extra minutes to hold her daughter. She then pulls them apart, puts her hands on her shoulders, smiles a misty smile and nudges her toward BT.

She turns to her husband and takes his hand, despite the continuous rantings. She smiles broadly at him and leans into his ear to whisper, "I love you. I hope you will forgive me for our past." She shakes his hand to emphasize her words before letting go. Then, Joseanne faces her mother's tirade.

"Hello Mother!" Holding out her open palmed hand at her. This flabbergasts the ancient woman for but only a minute before she continues her barking. Joseanne, still holds her hand out in addressing her and speaks over her very calmly. "I am so happy you are here. Yes, things have changed and

there is and will be a great deal of public attention from now on."

Milicent, opens and shuts her mouth, begins to slam down her hands on the wheelchair's armrests in defiance. The nurse pats her shoulders to calm her, but Milicent bats them away between yelling and beating the armrests. One for always in control, she is quickly and shockingly unmanageable. Her stern authority and domination is eroding right before all of their eyes. People that once were spread about the huge hall mingling, begin to take a quiet assembly behind Stefen, Lauren, BT and Louie.

Joseanne, continues her steady resolve in holding court, but this time drips with a sickening sweetness. She explains as if Milicent is a child. "Mother, it's so rare for you to be losing it like you are! Why this just isn't like you! Especially Mother when it turns out this party is in your honor! A reunion of sorts! So many people have come to see you, isn't that remarkable?" She continues on through despite the rantings.

"As a matter of fact, even our brightest star has come to see you! Look Mother, it's Deirdre Kennsington! Oh Mother, isn't she beautiful? Didn't you try to kill her several times after taking her away from me at her birth? Oh Mother, and the incredible and kind policeman that helped me, did you have him killed?

"Mother, your own daughter. You had imprisoned me. I had to escape the prison you held me in during my first pregnancy. But oh wait, Mother. I know you want to explain

yourself and apologize. But wait!" Joseanne demands as Millicent reddens and shrieks at her to stop.

Pummeling the chair, her words become hoarse. "Stop this at once. You can't prove anything."

"Proof? Proof you ask? Oh Mother, that isn't going to be necessary! Showing off your sense of humor! Oh Mother, that's really a good one!" She mockingly laughs.

"Look Mother, here are two old friends that have come to share their stories with us. Fedrico and Marie!" Joseanne invites them over with her open arm. Joe escorts them over and stands as a sentinel. He is accompanied by a striking gentleman that BT recognizes.

Milicent screeches out. "They are nothing, they know nothing. No one can touch me."

Joseanne disregards this and heightens her conclusion. "It is so wonderful to see their lovely faces again after all these years. Such a fine reunion indeed, Mother. Isn't this thrilling? I sure do think so! And I'm sure all of our guests do too!" Waving her hands to all that have gathered behind her.

"Oh dear." Dripping in sarcasm, "You know Mother, you are beginning to turn a bit purple, you may want to calm yourself. Miss Peddle won't you try and help contain my Mother? She is not looking very well."

At that she turns to her husband and embraces him. They hold each other like they will never let go. She trembles,

weeps and buries her face in his shoulder. Lauren steps to them, taking her mother's hand.

BT joins Joe, along with an old friend of his, Paddy Patterson, together they stare down Milicent. Her very old and frail body doesn't stop her aggression and combativeness. Her bodyguards are agitated as Joe feigns a salute to Milicent and proclaims. "The FBI are here to investigate all of you." At that, several agents surround her and her gang, the woman continues her diatribe as they are all taken away.

Louie steps over to his father and declares. "I thought you were dead. Oh my God, Dad. Poppa, I love you!" They embrace and cry together. "What happened to you? I want to know everything." Louie takes him to a small table in a secluded corner to talk.

"Oh Son, my beautiful Son." Fedrico can't stop touching his hands and shoulders, he pats his cheeks many times in delight. "Let's see, how do, where do I begin? Miss Joseanne." They sit and he commences. "Marie came to me awfully frightened. She was more scared even for her mistress. She asked me to help them escape because she heard the baby was to be killed after the birth.

"I have played this scene in my head so many times. I told her I would help. I wanted away from that place so bad. I wanted to take sweet Marie away too. She was so young. It was such a very bad place. The time came, I drove my little truck up under the window.

"Marie helped the Miss up and through but she got stuck. Marie kept pushing to get her out. I went back to fetch her after getting the Miss in the truck. Marie let me know she had fallen and hurt herself, then slammed the window shut in my face. I felt awful leaving little Marie there. She was a stubborn one. But we were in such a hurry, I didn't know what to do. I went with the plan.

"So, I drove the Miss to where Mac, he was a fine man, would be on his patrol. I felt awful leaving the Miss there, but I had to go. It was my chance too and I knew she was safe. I knew you were safe. I drove and drove. I stopped for gas several times and drove. I got to New York, I had a cousin there. He helped me get rid of the truck and find jobs. I started a new life with a new name. I always looked over my shoulder. But I was able to forget that miserable place after some time.

"I wrote you so many letters my boy. I couldn't give you my address, but I always wrote you."

"I never got them," Louie feeling defeated with tears.

"No? Ah, your grandmother she didn't like me much. She probably threw them away. I followed you. I saw in the papers your life. You changed your name like I asked you to do in my first letters. If you didn't get the letters, what made you change it?"

"Oh Dad, Poppa, I thought you abandoned me. Nonna demanded it. She said you left me. That I was better off without you. She was always angry that no more money

had come. I thought you were dead. She changed her story many times, said 'they' had you killed and that you left me."

"Yes, I was made to be dead. I sent money in those letters. Oh son, il maschio, I am sorry." They reach over to hug each other, crying again in the sheer joy of their reunion at last.

Deirdre envelops Marie and brings her over to Lauren. In a shaken voice, Deirdre says, "Marie, you are our hero! I think this all calls for a hug! I know, I know, so not my reputation! But what the hell? Let's all have champagne!" She pulls the two women toward her with an imitation patting-type hug. But then something entirely out of character happens and she begins to weep, Lauren holds her fast. Then the three of them begin to chuckle through their misty eyes.

"Actually," Deirdre continues. "Before that drink, how about we get Joseanne and we all go to the powder room? I'm sure we all can use a freshening up!" Joseanne and Stefen turn and Deirdre asks, "How about you come with us to the powder room?" Lauren takes Joseanne's arm and the four women stroll together in unison, laughing.

They have much fun giggling and helping each other with their make-up. After all, Deirdre has her hostess duties to prepare for. Leaving the room, a man stands some feet away, pacing. His hat in hand, he approaches the women cautiously. "Miss Joseanne? Would you mind speaking with me for a moment?"

The women encircle her as in protection. "It's alright ladies, I know this man. I will be along shortly. Shar...Sharky? It is you! It's been such a long time. How are you?" She asks.

"Uhhh, I'm alright. I am sorry to disturb your party. It's just that, well, I want to apologize to you in person. After what you did to your mother, standing up to her like that. Well, it got me thinking, I have a lot to say and be sorry about." He shuffles his feet and is embarrassed, but cannot take no for an answer. So stays and sheepishly looks at her. He is not one to be so skittish, after all he was the Grand Dame's top man. He put out the nasty orders, he had people killed. But this, this is different. Much more than anything he has ever done, let alone express.

"Yes, of course. I remember you were always very nice to me. And if I am not mistaken, you over-saw and protected me? Especially when I went to my favorite tree. You never let her know, did you?"

"Ahhh, well, yes madame. She was always so mean to you, I just couldn't stand it. I was able to get the men off your trail. Actually, I need to tell you...well, I actually held them off so Fedrico could help you escape that day. And later, much later, I'm sorry to say it took too long, I did help Marie finally get away. They beat her badly, you know." Nervously, looking around and over his shoulder, he continues. "I would like to turn myself in to your G-Man over there. They are all watching, I don't want you to be afraid of me."

Joseanne takes his arm and kisses his cheek. "No one is going to hurt you Sharky. Thank you for coming to me, telling me. Things are making more and more sense. I

didn't know for such a long time, until just some minutes ago. It's been an incredible shock as you can imagine. What has made you want to come forward?"

He pats her hand on his arm and starts to usher her to Stefen. "I am not well, actually, I don't have much more time. The damn cigarettes, you know! And after I witnessed your dressing-down to *her*, well I have never seen anyone tear her down like that before. I have seen and been involved with so many bad things, well, I...I, well, I feel it's time I come forward to help them with their investigations."

Joseanne stops and faces him, smiles and hugs him. "Thank you! Thank you ever so much for being here and telling me all of this. And watching over me when I was a child. Ohhh and helping Marie!" They continue walking and she asks. "By the way, what made you come and how did you do so without my mother knowing?"

"Hey now, well, I am pretty good at getting around her! I've been under her for too many years to count. She did trust me somewhat, if she ever trusted anyone. Anyway, I heard her talking about this event. I suggested she take a couple of the other men with that horrible shrew. She agreed. I let them leave, then got dressed up a bit and came in and hid in corners as to not be seen. I guess it worked out!" Sharky sheepishly chuckles.

"Well you did good my friend. Thank you again!" Joseanne squeezes his arm as they walk up to BT, Joe and Paddy. "Gentlemen, this is Sharky!" She announces. "He watched over me, protected me the best he could when I was a child there. He has many things to tell you, please be very good

to him as he wants to help you with the investigations." She kisses his cheek and hugs him warmly, smiles at him and leaves to go to Stefen.

The three men are bewildered to meet and hear this news. They shake his hand in gratitude because as Joseanne and Sharky talked, they were having their own conversation.

After the old woman was taken away, BT and Joe face Paddy and shake each other's hands with excitement.

O'Reilly questions, "Paddy, you've been helping Joe? I should have known you'd be in on all this! By the way, do either of you know Joseanne is speaking to? He looks quite shady, but she isn't afraid of him?"

Joe interjects. "No. But I'm sure we will find out. Back to Paddy here, we've known each other for years. I know you two go back too, I understand you grew up together. Anyway, this whole case has been nothing but concurrence after concurrence. The sync's leading all of these people together is an orchestration to behold!"

"Damn, no kidding. Our Da's would be so proud, O'Reilly," Paddy bear hugging BT. Just as quickly steps back knuckling his wet eye and ahems, "As you know, my Da did everything he could to track down Mac's killer. It was an obsession that nearly drove him mad. You probably remember that's what made me join the FBI, BT. I wanted to make him proud by solving this damned case. That horrid ambush, the crash and Joe's work, well, we've tracked down a lot, haven't we old man?" He slaps Joe Kenny on the shoulder.

283

BT turns to Joe and throws in, "Yeah, we grew up together. His folks took us in, watched over us. Paddy here, is older, about my brother's age." He changes his expression and asks Paddy. "Just what did you find out about Michael's crash?"

"Yeah, I talked with the mechanics at the hanger where D kept the plane. One of the men, man, he was really upset because he really liked him. He said Desport was always friendly to him and the others. But that day, he kept his distance, which was strange. He didn't think much of it until after he heard about the crash.

"He's still kicking himself, wished he had approached the man. You see, it turns out there was a stranger in the hanger, that looked like Desport. At any rate, the mechanic is the one that helped give us more evidence of sabotage."

"I knew it! See I told you so, Joe!" Deirdre exclaims jumping into their conversation and grabbing his arm. All the while smiling broadly and boldly flirting with Paddy Patterson. "We haven't had the pleasure of meeting, Mr. G-Man, or weren't you considered a Bull back then? Ohhh, and quite a fine one at that!"

Blushing as red as his hair, makes BT and Joe laugh emphatically, knowing exactly what he is in for. Being a tall man, his broad barrel of a chest and muscles bulging from the sharp, pin-striped suit, he is rarely befuddled. But this one Paddy Patterson, is besotted.

Chapter 40

"WELCOME TO THE ROARING TWENTIES!" Deirdre exclaims in the microphone on stage book-ended by her bodyguards costumed as Keystone Cops. The excited crowd encircles the stage transfixing on her.

Her perfect, auburn bob glimmers of gold highlights and twinkles off the Flapper Great Gatsby headband from the stage lights. Deirdre's signature full and voluminous head of bouncing curls is stuffed under the radiant wig. Adorning it is a lustrous, antique golden tiara with pearlized feathers that sparkle in her sway.

As she continues to speak, she makes dedicated small movements to show off the dancing sequins and dangling, pearl baubles that drip off her lemon, chiffon dress. "Thank you all for being here and wasn't that an incredible historic event we all witnessed?" She beams at the applause.

"With the drama and business taken care of, please know that this Charitable Trust of mine is a bona fide, on the level and close to my heart organization. We are celebrating how the hungry get fed and clothed, while educating young people in our fine city.

"So, don't be pikers out there and give! For your gambling pleasures, we have rubes and clams you can buy to give even more while you play! We also created little juice joints or as we like to call them, speakeasies for you to converse.

"Now, it's time for Giggle Water and Champagne! And as our Dear Friend Michael, would always call out, ICE CREAM!!! So please everyone enjoy! By the way, there's plenty of real food too! You all are the cat's meow out there with your glad rags, so get those marbles swaying and show off your Oliver Twist moves! Let's get this party started!"

With that, the hall is boisterous. Deirdre laughs and plays it up as the 'cops' escort her off the stage toward the awaiting Paddy to take her arm.   The guests love it and laugh. Immediately, the mingling begins as people line up for food and drink.   In keeping with the theme, the band strikes up with songs of the era and some people start to dance. They show off their costumes that sparkle and shimmy with long pearl necklaces flying with the Charleston.

Deirdre and Paddy stride over to her new family. She is genuinely happy and this new man in her life intrigues her. She continues to run her hands up and down his large biceps and can't help herself from glancing at his broad, coppery, shadowed chin and bristly hair.

Standing in a circle, they smile in welcoming them. Joseanne is first to embrace her. "Thank you for everything you have done, the expense in putting these pieces together. I hope you will forgive me for not being in your life."

"Stop, you're going to make me cry again! And I just fixed my makeup! Besides, there's nothing to forgive, we have all been through so much. I have parents! Who knew! I say it's time to thrive and enjoy life starting right now!"

Waitresses and waiters appear with glasses of Champagne and hors d'oeuvres. Deirdre asks for them to keep coming and escorts the small group to an alcove area.

She and Ro~Lond Valentino designed the hall in keeping with the roaring twenties and made several vestibules, of different sizes, as miniature speakeasies for people to break off for privacy. These are adorned with heavy flocked wallpaper and Tiffany lamps glimmering with an array of colors, making for gaiety. Floor lamps in the corners, along with beautiful mahogany end-tables bookended lavishly appointed high back chairs. Table Tiffanies alight the cozy areas with sculpted, patina naked women lounging in crescent moons.

Joseanne glues herself to Stefen. She keeps looking at him as if for the first time. She cannot stop smiling. Fedrico and Louie join them. Louie remarks, "This is all incredible. You Jos, you were incredible. We tried to figure how we could get her to come to terms once she was here. But you. You were amazing. You brought the house down!"

"Well, I, I'm not sure what to say. Thank you for filling me in. And so quickly! It all flooded out of me and I am thrilled it did. Look at how there are so many lives here. Freed. We are all free at last."

Fedrico, Joseanne, Marie and Deirdre chat amicably of how they have come together. Louie and Stefen find they have a lot in common. With Joseanne at his side, Stefen is happy and at ease to get to know this man. Joe approaches after dealing with the FBI.

"Awe, the man of the hour!" Louie pats Joe on the back.

"What, no. It's all of you, this reunion is what it's all about!"

They all look at him and stare in elation. Louie responds in a heartbeat. "Hey man, if it hadn't been for you...just how did you pull off this last surprise of my Poppa and Marie?"

Joe Kenny is put on the rug and with all eyes on him, he backs up a step. Chagrinned, he tips his hat and explains. "Ehhh, that became easy once I knew your real name. Even though Fedrico changed his name too, I was able to do some tracing. Marie, a little more difficult!" He smiles at her. "But your letter was brilliant. I found Lily, she gave me some clues to chase you down. She says hello to you all. She is not able to get out and about very well but asks you all get by to see her."

They all exclaim and chat incessantly with each other at this new news. This gives Joe a moment to get out of the spotlight and observe, which is what he is best at. He gets a kick out of Deirdre letting go and actually being delighted conversing with women. Correction, family. He figures they will find out what happened to D as a baby and how she got into foster care. But that's for another time.

For now, Joe Kenny is proud of what he has done here. Seeing all these people together. He helped make this happen. He, who always didn't think much of genealogy! Yet he marvels at how all this came about so unexpectedly. Better than they could have planned. Sure, he scoured and pounded the pavement for the keys and proofs, but still and all.

Louie, Deirdre, BT and Lauren had spent hours planning the party while he was off doing what he does best. Deirdre had instructed through Ro~Lond Valentino, that the decor would be arranged with the hotel crew in the massive hall. In line with the historic hotel's decor, Ro~Lond added the exquisite details of design and excitement. He created the menu of feasts and drinks that recalled the twenties.

Joe also helped Louie take charge of security, arranging and coordinating the different security and FBI teams. They all were confounded however, as to how they were going to bring Milicent to justice. Let alone unsure if she would even show up.

As it turns out, Deirdre went public to personally invite her to her charity ball to honor *her*. News sources all over the country picked up the story that was proclaimed to preserve what she, Milicent deTournay, built and to celebrate her as a long-standing citizen: the 'go-getter' of the twenties in Chicago and her non-profit charities. Hoping this would coax her to come out of hiding, canonizing her would be the enticement that even *she* could not refuse. Still, no one fathomed what ended up happening.

When Joseanne saw Louie across the room, their eyes met and she knew exactly who he was. She had seen him in the tabloids, but it never occurred to her he was 'her' Louie. Until she saw him in person. After all he looked quite different, he changed his name and grew up to be an entirely contrastive man than the boy she knew.

Joseanne had become surface minded since she was sent away to school. Never really thought about much except keeping up fronts. She did this with perfection. After all, she was taught by the best. Yet, when she saw him, she looked directly into his eyes, and she *knew*.

A veil of blackness began to drop. She recognized memories that were obliterated. Louie said hello as he approached her, trying to take her hands, "Josie!"

She responded with a nod and indignantly spat. "I don't go by that name." She immediately stiffened, folded her arms in front of her and took a step back. Her defensive measure backed him off a step, but he kept the closeness enough to speak to her privately.

"There's so much I need to say to you. We don't have much time. Josie, I mean, excuse me, Joseanne you have grown to be a beauty," he said confounded with what to say next.

She stood straighter at this, yet something stirred further in side, "I am not. Appearances are deceiving." Despite her defensive stature, Joseanne is blown away as Louie approached her. It wasn't a veil but a foot thick, steel-vaulted door that just flew open. In that instant, it blasted her with light and insight all at the same time.

She began to see and remember things. Like what happened to Dorothy's world in the Wizard of Oz. Color became bright instead of the black and white dull world she had lived in for too much of her life.

Then Joseanne startled herself as she blurted out, "What happened to you? Why didn't you save me?"

"Jos, I am sorry. I didn't know. I was sent away the next day after your party. My father, he, I thought he was killed. I have only just recently learned what happened back then. Joe, Deirdre hired the PI, O'Reilly and I have come into information only, well, now. Lately. Sorry, I'm rambling."

Defenses brought her arms down, she stepped to him and insisted. "Tell me what you know. Please. I am beginning to remember things, episodes, but unsure of what they mean. You're Deirdre's agent. Who is she? Why is she familiar? Please tell me what you know."

"We don't have much time, people are coming in. May I blurt out aspects that I know?"

"Yes. As I look at you, this is so odd. I am feeling things, knowing things. So, forgotten. Please. Yes. Go on."

"Deirdre hired a PI to do research on herself. She had been threatened numerous times. Especially since she started to find out, well, about where she came from. I warned her not to do it, but she is stubborn. Actually, she went behind my back and hired Joe, her PI. He's a fine man.

"He's done more than we ever imaged. Found out more than we thought we could handle. Putting the pieces together, like your Lauren, kidnapped. And BT, his father. Then, because I changed my name after Dad disappeared, we thought he was dead..."

"He rescued me. He and Marie." Jos cut him off remembering. "She couldn't go with me. He laid me somewhere, a park, I think. He said his favorite cop patrolled the area. He knew I'd be safe, so he left me there. Oh my God, Mac. He said his name was Mac. He delivered the baby in his car. There was so much pain, but he kept talking, soothing me. Then I heard him say, 'She is a beautiful, Deirdre!'

"Oh Louie, she is our child. How did she find that name?"

"That's a story. Look, Lauren is there. Looking at us with someone. He's your husband?"

"Yes. He is a good man. I haven't been a good wife or mother. I'm a wreak. Shaking so. Oh Louie, please tell me what I need to know."

"Your mother, has tried to kill Deirdre many times. We think she had BT's father killed because of her." Joseanne looks bewildered at him. "Yes, he was Mac."

"Oh my God." She is struck by how cold and bitter she had become as he hurriedly explained more details.

"I didn't know you were pregnant with our child. I am so sorry. I didn't know. I got to know Deirdre without knowing,

became her agent. We made good and successful lives. I protected her without knowing...I didn't know that she is my daughter until just a bit ago. Oh Jos, this is so much, so fast. I'm sorry. We don't have much time. We're counting on your mother, hopefully expected to come to this event."

"Louie. Oh Louie, my God. I have not been a good woman. I have never stood up to her. The second child, I haven't given her anything. My husband. Oh my God, what have I done?"

"You did the best you could do with what you had to work with. Joseanne, Jos. Listen to me. You did the best you could do."

"Take me to them. Please. I can't stop shaking. What feels familiar from way back when. I haven't felt, let alone all of this much emotion for years, Louie. Please take me there." Louie put out his arm for her and guided her to her family.

He watched how she enveloped her daughter. It pained him as she went to her husband. He had never experienced love like that. He always wondered what that would be like.

And then she addressed her mother. As a child, she was a tortured soul and cowered when it came to her. But today, she stood. Perfect posture, palm out to command the old bat to stop. Not that she did. Yet Jos held her own. And what she said. It was as if she was a part of all the discoveries that they dug up.

She was articulate in a smart, sarcastic way and got her snipes in. Patronized to perfection. It was an incredible

sight to behold. They didn't know how they were going to get the old women to reveal anything. But Jos did it. All on her own and no proof necessary because Joseanne was the clincher. They thought they'd need proof for the FBI, but with how Jos stated the information and how the old women reacted, well, now they could all be free and safe.

Joe Kenny knew people at the bureau. One particular man, Paddy Patterson, that had been following the case for years. He doggedly never gave up. His father before him, by the same name, had started the drive. Even when leads would run dry, he would inevitably turn up some information. Bits and pieces led him to victims and staff of Milicent's abuse. As they got older, they became willing to talk. They weren't as afraid as they used to be, especially with so many others coming forth. Evidence began to be more and more viable.

Now in light of Joseanne's confrontation, search warrants would be produced so that the mansion could be seized. For she was the best witness they had. She stood her ground as all the veils of forgotten truths flooded her fast and furiously. Ultimately, she would work with Joe and the FBI to put the numerous cases together against her mother that happened throughout the years. Despite the charity work Milicent had been known for in her later years, it turns out these too are fronts for non-profits.

Then the old man, Sharky. Showing up like he did and his stories, coming forth with more evidence to tie up even more loose ends, has been more than they could have imagined. Damn, he loves it when a case comes together!

After Joseanne introduced Sharky to them, Joe and Paddy take him to one of the smaller private rooms. BT joins Lauren. Sharky immediately gets to what happened when Joseanne escaped. He couldn't talk fast enough to give them the details. He reiterated what he told Joseanne, how he allowed Fedrico and her to get away. He then provided all the proof they would need.

Sharky went on to explain how business was conducted at the mansion. At the end of each day, the men would report to Milicent. One particular night was sensational because a soldier of hers, Archie, was so proud to tell her his story. He *just knew* she would finally recognize him for the leader he wanted to be in her eyes.

To keep her control and standing, she considered him as her second in name only after his uncle was killed years ago. But in reality, her men knew who to report to and besides, he was nothing to her. A lowly peon.

He had always wanted Milicent in the worst way. He wanted to be the man in her bed and to make her happy. However, she always made it clear to him she needed him to prove to her his worthiness. Because he could never measure up, he took his aggressions and violence out on many women in retaliation.

It was always serious in their reporting to her those nights, but Archie was too exuberant in his telling of what turned out to be his demise. He was across the hospital in a park with his latest floozy. But this day, he touted his chance had finally arrived when he saw the police car racing in, lights

and siren blazing. He saw a cop help put Joseanne on the stretcher, then it was pushed into the hospital.

As Archie told the story, he immediately demanded his dame to get in there and put on a nurses uniform. She was to get Joseanne and the baby, as he rounded up his men to sneak in to help her. They were to drug Joseanne and get back to the mansion.

Meanwhile, he hid in bushes and waited close to the police car for the cop to come back. His proudest moment, he shouted out to Milicent. "I shot that cop for YOU! I AM Archibald deTournay and I KNOW this will make you proud of ME! Even though the only little mix-up was that the baby went missing. But you see, the gunshot made a diversion so my men got your daughter out! Just like I know you would have wanted. So, I did good! I did this all for you!"

She stared at him, not giving any thing away as was her normal fashion. She allowed the cheers to go on from the men for a bit. Then she whispered to Sharky. "Have him shot later but only after he is tortured." She seethed, it was unlike he had seen her in a very long time. Her lips were so pierced in a line, they disappeared, he recollected. With Archie stating the old man's name like that, it must have quickened some old temper. She wanted him gone, bad. And she wanted him tortured even more. Besides she was infuriated with him for making a huge mess in killing a cop, let alone loosing the baby.

After this testimony, Joe decides to hold off giving BT the news on how his father was killed. Yet, he still wonders about the ambush, he needs to get more details on that. But

for now he reasons, there is so much happiness here, it can all surely wait for another time.

Paddy couldn't help ask Sharky if *she* was responsible for Michael Desport's death, especially after he just told of his findings.   He is elated with having this treasure trove of information, knowing he will be able to put to rest cases and offer closure to so many victimized people.

"Ahhh, I thought you might ask." Sharky says.   "I know there is much more for me to report to you and I know we will get to it. But yes. She had me hire an elite, which we often did not do for most jobs. She was getting so exasperated with the actress making headlines, she wanted her gone.   At least that was the plan.

"She became even more infuriated after that attempt failed. In Hawaii, I hired thugs that really screwed things up. Well, let's just say she blames me and everyone else when she doesn't get her way.   I'm old and tired of her, this is my chance to get out."

Stiffness leaves Joseanne to hold her husband. She didn't know that Stefen's greatest desire was for her to love herself. After all, she didn't know how until this new and very bright day. But here she is, alive, well and discovering what happiness truly is.

Stefen nuzzles her neck and says. "You know, earlier I was jealous as can be seeing you become, well, emotional with Louie.   Then I experienced your transformation with our daughter and your mother.   But as I watched you with Sharky, I have to say my beautiful, I really like this woman

standing next to me. That shares passion with others, even if it is another man! I always knew you'd come home to me. And now we have two beautiful daughters. What a life, my love!"

"Oh my dear, thank you! Yes, it is a fine life indeed. Now!" She confesses with tears.

The world has become open, alive and free to express herself. All of this happening within minutes of seeing her very old friend and father of a child she did not know she had. Joseanne is very clear and thrilled to hold on to Stefen all the more, her new life and world.

Whispering to Stefen with glittering eyes, "I love you so much. I am sorry. I am sorry for being cold, angry and bitter to you and Lauren. I love you Stefen. I have always loved you. I am sorry I could not express it."

Stefen pulls out his hanker-chief for her, she wraps her face in it and buries in his shoulder and weeps. "Shhh, it's alright. It's all right my love. I love you too. I always knew you were in there. You're here now, we're together. Shhh, all is well!"

With this new and healthy fortification, she moves to Lauren and BT. Since she was one of the last to speak and be with Mac, Joseanne offers comfort to him.

She hugs Marie and Fedrico many times, thanking them for their courage. She continues to remember other scenes and things as they play out before her wet eyes.

Louie turns to his Poppa with so much pride. Letting out pent-up breaths he hadn't realized he held for so long. He feels a freedom that is new. He smiles as he puts his arm around his old man and realizes finally what the old Italian saying means: fortune favors the bold.

Deirdre puts her arms around them and cracks, "I'm becoming such a sucker for all this hugging! Me crying for real, it's obscene Louie! I mean, no, I don't think I can call you that! But you," turning to Fedrico, "may I call you Poppa?"

The old man shifts to her with twinkling, wet eyes and takes her hands, "Oh yes Nipotina! Oh yes!"

Lauren and BT savor all that is happening with the people before them. They marvel at all that has transpired, their new family to behold. They hold hands and take in the emotions of joy among the little groups.

BT shifts to look in Lauren's eyes. "I haven't told you yet how stunning you are tonight, Lauren. That beaded headpiece plays with your incredible eyes! Your dress suits you beautifully, not to mention it shows off those cute knobby knees of yours!"

"Thank you, I think?" Smiling up at him, she says, "You are quite handsome yourself. I like you in suspenders! And my new found lucky cane! It's been quite a show, we've had a lot going on this evening.

"It's nice to catch our breaths, relax and get to know the new people in our lives. Oh, as a matter of fact, will you excuse

me?" Lauren shakes her hand loose from BT and steps to Deirdre.

After her embrace with Fedrico, Lauren taps her on the shoulder, "May I also get a hug from you two?"

"Of course!" They chime in together. And hug they do, with happy tears.

"No dry eyes here!" Deirdre exclaims. "Poppa, will you excuse me for a moment?"

He nods, Deirdre takes Lauren's arm and they step a few feet away. "I wanted to talk to you…" they both say together, laughing and hugging again.

"Seriously, Deirdre, I want to apologize for, well…not taking you in before now. I, well I, I was so jealous of you for so long. And that dedication to Michael…"

"It's alright, please no need. I understand. I know I come off as a threat, huh, that just might be changing!" She winks. "It's just that both of your men, happen, er, happened to be really good friends. I love them both, we go back you know. But it was never what you have. I never knew Michael to be as happy as he was with you. And BT, just look at him, he can't keep his eyes off you. Besides, I look forward to being your sister and getting to know one certain FBI, G-Man!"

Lauren beams at her as Deirdre reaches out to hug her again. They embrace, rejoicing in their private alcove of the great hall. They join the rest of their family gathered in a circle.s

Lauren picks up a glass of champagne, clinks her glass with the inside of her many rings and declares to them all: "Here is to loving to live and living to love!"

Beyond their little bubble, the party is going strong in the great hall, people are dancing and laughing as all parties and life ought to be: fun.

here & there

Epilogue

"You know, Lauren, all the talk of reincarnation isn't really valid." BT leans into Lauren's ear sitting next to her in first class. Flying back to Los Angeles, he is finally feeling relaxed and free enough, even eager, to discuss his component of Michael. With his signature mischievous smile, he continues. "Don't you need to have your own body for that to happen?"

"Funny! Haha." She turns from flipping her magazine to face that grin. "Oh, I see what you're doing!"

"Whaaat?" Feigning. "OK, you got me! Seriously, though, I've been doing some thinking on all we've been through, what you said. And the truth is, well," he lowers his voice close to her ear, "I really do believe he has been here to change, make things come about, even help solve all that's transpired."

Lauren pushes his chin so she can speak into his ear. "Yes, look at all that has happened. We have all flown too close to the sun. We all needed help, answers, and solutions."

She reaches for his hand. "It all became dire as it seemed like we were all falling apart and yet, we've fallen together.

Look how he has helped you and me be, errr, find our souls together, to be at peace and even in love."

She lets that linger a few heartbeats. "He's leaving, isn't he?"

The man's soul was with BT much more than he let Lauren in on. It was as if Michael kept pushing for things to happen and to bring about Lauren to be with him. And justice. Not only for his own death but for BT, the need for revenge he held on for so long was done. Answers. Relief and peace.

At times, BT found he would purposely hood his eyes. He came to find that if it was just enough, as in a contemplative introspection, he could see a shadow of Michael. Maybe it was more of a very strong feeling of him.

Nevertheless, the man was with him most of the time. What he thought of as his plight in being crazy, was turning out to be his healing. And ever so grateful indeed.

Interestingly enough, the more he let Michael in and after telling Lauren the truths of it, he found the nightmares had stopped. "Yes." He says honestly.

"His time is finishing." They announce together. With this, they squeeze each other's hands tightly and smile through moist eyes. The rest of the flight, they rest in anticipation of what's next.

The limo takes them to BT O'Reilly's home. Putting their suitcases down, they kick off their shoes and make their way to the beach. Together they release Michael Desport.

Lauren had snapped many flowers along the path building a loose bouquet. She steps into the ocean and tosses them out in a fan. The gentle waves collect them, they shimmer and glitter from the sunset as if winking at her.

She proclaims. "Thank you, Michael, my love of goodness. Thank you for helping us find the truths, to be free. May you be free. Here's to you being there, until we meet again, My Love."

BT can feel Michael leave him. A swishing glide of movement it is. He salutes the sea, standing there on the beach watching Lauren, her feet in the Pacific Ocean. He vows he will take good care of their Lauren.

ABOUT THE AUTHOR

A story in the making for almost the last 30 years finally comes alive!   Dawn began writing this book in 1993.   It started with "lines" that would come here and there. Written on scraps of paper when finally hundreds needed to be placed. She literally cut and pasted, then a friend typed the words on paper.

From California to South Carolina, she helped build a saloon, lived, grew and loved. Writing the story blossomed and characters were created on an old word processor into pages and chapters. But an ending to the story would not come to be.

Then back in California, it stopped...the words and lines simply stopped, with still no ending. Years went by, she picked it up here and there, but nothing happened, except for the dust.

Then one sleepless night, on the 24th of March 2021, in the wee hours of the morning, the ending was revealed! It was as if on a movie screen that played out in front of her. She wrote and wrote and edited too.   Her creation finally manifested!

So never give up, because you never know what miracles may come from magic and mystery!

Made in the USA
Columbia, SC
13 July 2022

63427734R00190